DANUBE STREET

a novel by

Linda Tweedie and
Kate McGregor

Published by Fledgling Press 2018
www.fledglingpress.co.uk
ISBN 9781912280131
Printed and bound by:
Martins the Printers, Berwick-Upon-Tweed

Prologue

The overpowering stench as he smashed open the front door stopped him dead in his tracks. It was the rank odour of decaying flesh and body fluids, coupled with the sweet cloying reek of poverty that hit him like a truck. The flat was freezing cold and almost derelict. The only furnishings were an ancient, stained sofa and a coffee table littered with the evidence of the tenant's pastime. He was having great difficulty retaining the contents of his stomach. God knows how long the poor soul had lain there decomposing with the needle still in her arm.

Christ, it was true; the faint mewing of a child confirmed the rumours. She'd been pregnant right enough. It was a blessed miracle that something so tiny, so neglected, could still be alive. Only just though, its pulse was so faint, it seemed impossible the wee mite could survive much longer. Time really was of the essence. Wrapping the baby in a foul-smelling blanket he dashed for the door. There was nothing more he could do here and the smell was unbearable.

His instructions had been crystal clear. Find the girl and return immediately to Danube Street. There was to be no involvement from any authority, no matter the circumstances. Looking at this tiny scrap of humanity, could he take the risk? It was almost the same distance from this shithole to either destination, the Western General Hospital being slightly closer. He was no doctor but even he knew this child wouldn't survive without immediate medical treatment. However, he wouldn't survive without the payment for this job. It was no contest; he'd have to take his chances on the child surviving.

He turned out of Caledonia Street just as the first police car screeched to a halt, followed by several others and a couple of ambulances. He heaved a huge sigh of relief, he'd made it just in time. It was a pity no-one had gone to her aid when she needed it. They were quick to respond now, when it was too late.

God knows what the kid's future would be, if it had one. What fate lay in store for the wee soul? The product of a junkie, a crackhead mother, father unknown and delivered to the richest, most notorious Madame in the country.

CHAPTER ONE

How it all began

Five hundred quid and a magnificent pair of diamond stud earrings. Not bad for a few hours work, Stella Gold smiled to herself. It was a far cry from the early days when the most she could command for her services was the price of a bag of toffees or perhaps one of those trashy magazines she had devoured back then. My God, how her world had changed.

Catching sight of herself in the antique Venetian mirror, her reflection still took her by surprise. Even after all these years, Stella found it hard to associate the exotic creature staring back at her with the naive country girl she'd once been.

Nowadays she dressed in the latest haute couture, decked out with fabulous jewellery, courtesy of grateful clients. She was an incredibly beautiful woman. Unlike the short and stocky build of her native Scotswomen, Stella was unusually tall. She stood five foot ten, with a figure to die for and a mane of lustrous auburn hair, but it was her eyes that fascinated those who met her. Rivalling the famous actress, Liz Taylor, Stella's eyes were the deepest shade of violet and mesmerised even the hardest of men.

Stella Gold was a legend. The Madame ruled over the most infamous bordello in Edinburgh; a magnet for red-blooded males, single or otherwise. Always the first port of call when merchant or naval ships docked. Danube Street was the attraction, never to be missed by visiting clergymen of every denomination. It was considered a rite of passage for the city's most eligible bachelors and feted by Arab princes, debauched German counts and several high-ranking government officials.

Stella personally entertained only a few, very special clients;

the elite, who were either immensely rich or unbelievably powerful, usually both. These captains of industry and political leaders deemed it an honour to be allowed to shower their favourite courtesan with fabulous gifts. In turn, they had no fear that Danube Street would divulge their secrets. No scandal, such as the Profumo Affair, would ever emanate from these portals.

Over the years, she and her girls had had countless numbers of movie stars and members of the aristocracy on their client list, and more than one politician had been caught with his pants down. Danube Street was not only the sacred haunt of the tartan criminal fraternity, it was always first on the agenda for the notorious Kray Twins when they visited the capital. Rumour had it the two had offered their favourite Madame a fortune to open up in The Smoke. But London was not for her. Although few people would have had the courage to refuse such a request from the brothers, it hadn't fazed Stella. She was intimidated by no man. She reckoned as long as she held his precious family jewels in the palm of her hand and knew all his dirty little secrets, she had nothing to fear from anyone, including the Krays.

Danube Street's ladies made the Kama Sutra look like Good Housekeeping, and for a price, they would provide whatever entertainment a client requested, no matter how bizarre. It was more than a brothel, it was an elite gentlemen's club.

Despite the trappings of wealth and her cultured voice and appearance, Stella Gold had begun life under very different circumstances. She was from extremely humble origins, far from the bright lights of the city. Stella, born Agnes McLeod, had been reared in the wilds of Ayrshire. The only daughter of a tenant farmer, she had endured a harsh, rugged life.

Agnes hated her dull, dreary existence. She was always cold, always hungry, abhorring the muck and the reek of the farm; she yearned for excitement, glamour and wealth. She coveted everything she saw portrayed in glossy magazines; a far cry from her life as it was.

She had always been popular with the many itinerant workers who passed through. As a cute toddler, she would sing, dance and blow kisses to the delight of her captive audience. Year after year Agnes developed into a delicious piece of jailbait, her skirts just too short and tops just too low. Well aware of the covert glances, she flagrantly displayed what was on offer, but that was a lifetime away. Circumstances had most definitely improved since then, Stella mused.

"Boss, boss, you need to come downstairs quickly," an urgent plea accompanied loud hammering.

"Lord, can I never get five minutes peace?" the Madame grumbled to herself.

Pulling on a silk wrap, she called back, "What is it, Kitty, what's all the commotion?"

"It's one of the Williams brothers, he's about to kick off."

A cold fury gripped Stella at the mere mention of the name Williams. She and the brothers went way back and their vendetta had not lessened over the years.

"Okay, I'll be right there."

As she walked across the luxurious room Stella dialled a familiar number. "It's me. Your brother is causing problems. If you don't want to arrange a funeral, you'd better come and get him."

"I'm on my way," said the person at the other end of the line.

CHAPTER TWO

The Early Days

"Oi! Fuck off, Mam," the young lad yelled as he was woken out of a dreamless sleep and landed with a thud on the bare floor.

"Shut up, gerrup and shift yourself. Go in with Granny. Go on, give me peace," the woman said as she ushered the still half-asleep boy towards the other room.

"No, Mam, she stinks," the youngster whined.

Jack loved his gran and would do anything for her, but he didn't love sharing a bed with the old woman. The fact that she hadn't left it since they moved into this rat-infested dump was the main reason. That and the 'accidents' that frequently occurred didn't make for sweet wet dreams.

"You've got a fucking nerve," his mother countered. "You don't exactly smell of roses. Now get up! We've got company."

"Company?" the lad snorted.

He hated it when she brought work home, but the weather was so bad tonight he supposed she had no choice. Mind you, it was damned near as cold in the tenement flat as it was out in the dank wet night.

Rubbing his eyes, he recognised the punter his mam had brought home. He was one of her regulars, the Sleazebag. Jack didn't know his name, his mother probably didn't either, they just referred to him by the nickname they had bestowed on him. Jack referred to him as such because of his penchant for touching the young lad and wanting Jack to be in the room when his mum was working. No chance.

Jeannie, his mother, also despised the man. He always wanted extras and never wanted to pay the full amount, even after they'd set the price. He was a fucking creep and even though she didn't give a shit about Jack, she wouldn't trust this pervert as far as she could throw him. Well, not unless the price was right.

Sleazebag was chatting to Jack when the boy suddenly jumped up and headed for the door.

"What the fuck happened there?" she yelled at her customer. "Where has he buggered off to? He's got school in the morning."

"I gave him money to get me cigarettes."

"How much did you give him?"

"A ten-bob note. I had no change."

"You gave him what? Well, you can say goodbye to that. We won't see him again tonight, not if he has money in his tail. He'll be off and running, and don't think for a minute I'm stumping up for it. C'mon, let's get this over and done with, big boy."

Twenty minutes later, fully dressed but still fuming at being conned, Sleazebag had Jeannie pinned to the wall demanding the money he'd been done out of.

"Why the fuck should I give you it?"

Jeannie had been around the block too many times to be caught out, anyway why should she give it back? The stupid bugger ought to have known better. Imagine, giving a ten-year-old money. Erse!

Grabbing hold of the only vase she possessed and tipping out the contents (half a dozen daffodils the boy had given her last week for Mother's Day), she crashed it down on the punter's skull.

Staggering all over the flat, crashing and bumping into the few sticks of furniture, Jeannie guided him towards the door. Once he was out in the close she slammed the door shut.

It took a few minutes for him to realise he wasn't getting back in. His money was old news and a couple of the neighbours looked quite handy. Time to go, but he wouldn't forget either of these two thieving bastards. No, he'd bide his time.

Meanwhile, young Jack thought all his birthdays had come at once. His first stop was the chippie.

"Give me a large fish supper, Toni, with five pickled onions."

"Letta me see the money first," the small Italian demanded. "Hey, your mama's ship has come in then. She winna the pools?"

"Aye, something like that," the lad answered.

He was so used to being treated like a third-class citizen, the insults simply bounced off him. The ten-bob note in his pocket was like winning the pools.

"A bottle of Red Kola and a Mars Bar."

"You no say please, you little shit?"

"Aye, when you say thanks," Jack retorted as he handed over the note and carefully counted the change back into his pocket.

Making himself comfortable on the wall outside the chip shop, he settled down to enjoy his feast. It had been a long time since he'd had such luxury. The crisp fish smothered in sauce amid the piles of hot chips was actually making him drool. On the other side of the road he caught sight of his benefactor staggering along, cursing to himself, Jack couldn't resist the taunt.

"Hey mister, spare me a fag?" the impudent little bugger called out.

It certainly wouldn't be the last time he crossed Constable Hamish Ross.

6

CHAPTER THREE

Luxury Items

At a tender age, Agnes McLeod realised how easy it was to manipulate the opposite sex. On countless occasions, she was caught frolicking in the barn or out in the fields, and despite frequent thrashings, nothing deterred the girl. More than a few workers had been run off the farm by her irate father, wielding his shotgun.

Where Agnes went there was sure to be a bevy of predatory males following. With her mane of tousled hair, those striking eyes, and a swagger perfected by hours of practice, she spelt trouble.

The mothers of the village boys had, almost without exception, warned Mrs McLeod to keep her daughter away from their sons. An order Agnes found hilarious.

"Tell them to keep their sons away from me," she laughed. She had no qualms about letting the old farm hands cop a feel, but for a price: threepence. Threepence would buy her the latest comic, or a bag of sweets, luxuries seldom seen in the McLeod household. For the more demanding customer, sixpence would have her toss them off, although she hated the mess this entailed. Sex held no intrigue for the young Agnes, she'd been around farm animals all her life. It was simply an act of nature as far as she was concerned. These dirty old men all wanted something, but she wasn't giving it away for free.

"I'll give you five bob," the Irishman offered. "Five bob, if you'll go all the way."

"No chance." Agnes pushed the smelly old man away. He'd been chasing her around the farm all afternoon.

"Ten bob, then. I'll make it ten bob and I'll be careful, you'll be quite safe," he tempted the greedy young madam.

Despite her behaviour, Agnes was still a virgin. This transaction would take her to a whole new level, but ten bob was a lot to turn down.

"Let me see the money first," Agnes demanded.

Sure enough, he pulled a crisp ten-shilling note from his inside pocket and the deal was struck. She didn't enjoy her participation in the 'game' and wanted it over and done with as quickly as possible. What she did enjoy was the money and the things it could buy. It was easy money.

By the end of the summer she'd amassed nearly twenty pounds, an incredible amount. Not once did her mother question where all the magazines, sweets and other luxuries came from. Of course, she had her suspicions, but she didn't want to know.

As she had grown up, Agnes had no real friends. She was shunned by her classmates, jealous of her popularity with the boys. She was always the one chased in the kiss and catch games but despite this, she was a solitary figure.

Life for Agnes changed when her mother's youngest sister arrived at the farm, pregnant and in disgrace. Mary, technically Agnes's aunt, was the only person the young farmgirl had ever encountered who had the same attitude to life as she. Despite the older girl's predicament, each found in the other a kindred spirit.

Mary was what was termed a 'late baby' who'd arrived unexpectedly in the final stages of her poor, washed-out mother's 'change'. The woman, who was way beyond child rearing, let the youngster run free. She got up to all sorts of mischief, having no boundaries or discipline, and quickly gained a reputation for being a 'bad girl'. When she ran away from home aged fifteen, with someone else's husband, she proved the gossips right.

It was not long before Mary was dumped by the errant husband and on her own in the city. The runaway was soon brought down to earth with a bump. Promises of high living and dancing the night away in one of the city's many discothèques vanished with her lover. The honeymoon was well and truly over. With no money and soon to have no roof over her head, she was on her hands and knees scrubbing steps. Frozen to the core, her once soft hands chapped and bleeding, she suffered the worst of the Scottish winter weather. There had to be more to life than this, lamented Mary.

"Hey, watch what you're doing," a smartly dressed young woman shouted at her as she dodged the dirty water.

"Sorry, miss," replied Mary, keeping her head down. She wanted to smack her but she couldn't afford to lose this job.

"You will be," said the nasty piece of work, kicking the bucket over deliberately, drenching Mary and undoing her last half hour's work.

Seething, Mary watched as the woman was greeted by a middle-aged man, old enough to be her father, and ushered into the waiting limousine. What did that toe-rag have that she didn't?

"Fuck off, bitch, this is our patch," shouted one regular. "Go on, beat it, or else."

Mary walked away quickly, only to be met with a bruiser of a woman at the next corner who resembled an Irish navvy in a frock. This was proving more difficult than she'd anticipated.

"How much?" asked a creepy bloke sidling up to her. "I asked you how much?"

She wasn't going to be able to do this. Christ, she couldn't talk, she was so nervous.

"A fiver, I'll give you a fiver," the would-be punter continued.

Mary shook her head.

"A tenner then. That's all you'll get down this neck of the woods. Take it or leave it."

Mary nodded to the queer-looking man. "Where?" she croaked.

"I take it you're new to the game," he laughed. "For fuck's sake, come this way." He walked off between the huge tenement buildings.

What am I doing? she asked herself, scared witless. He could be a serial killer or an axe murderer, you heard of such stories. Relieved he wasn't, she had, however, made one vital error. She'd failed to get her money up front and as she was 'sorting' herself, the bastard took off, leaving her high and dry. She'd never make that mistake again.

Over the next few months she earned just enough to keep a roof over her head. She was no match for the streetwise working girls, nowt but a babe-in-arms compared to them. They at least got reasonably paid for what Mary gave away for almost nothing. Chased off all the good patches, attacked by the established girls, and to make matters worse, the inevitable happened, the stupid fool fell pregnant. What the hell was she going to do? She had no money for an abortion and returning home was not an option. Her only hope was her sister. Surely she'd take her in, and allow her to stay on the farm for the remainder of her confinement?

CHAPTER FOUR

Jack of all Trades

Most folk would find it hard to be cheerful in Jack's circumstances, but he was a sunny-natured lad and the fact that he had not known any other existence helped. He lived with his mother Jeannie and his old granny in one of the many dark and dank flats in a tenement in the Port of Leith, right across from the dock gates. Jack's playground and his mother's workplace. Jeannie, hard though it was to believe, had once been a respectable wife and mother, and a good-looking young woman to boot. But the war changed all that. Her husband, Jack's father, Able Bodied Seaman Hunter, had gone down with his ship in the last month of the conflict, leaving mother and son destitute.

Responsible for her old mother and her baby son, Jeannie had tried her hand at everything. Sewing, cleaning, factory work, anything to keep her family afloat, but it seemed she had only one real talent and, left with no alternative, she turned to the oldest profession in the world.

She was taught her trade from the best: Stella Gold, the most infamous Madame in the city. To begin with, life was reasonably good. Stella looked after her girls. They were all well accommodated, safer than walking the streets and they made good money. But the house rules were strict and those who disobeyed were not tolerated.

Jeannie Hunter, one of the most popular and highest earners, unfortunately developed a taste for mothers' ruin and worse, a dependence on the brown stuff, which was absolutely forbidden in Danube Street. Despite giving Jeannie chance after chance, Stella came to the end of her patience and Jeannie was turfed out on her ear. With that came the end of her decent earnings.

Over the years Jeanie drifted from House to House on a downward spiral and due to her drug habit, legendary temper and not being the looker she had once been, she ended up at the very bottom of the pile, resorting to working the docks.

There was seldom enough money to keep their heads above water and with his mother's expensive habits, it fell to Jack to supplement the household income in any way he could. Fortunately, Stella had a soft spot for him, despite his mother having been one of her worst employees. Over the years the Madame found jobs to help him out, making Jack feel indispensable. He was liked by all the girls and staff; there was always a few coppers or a pie to take home to his old gran. Stella Gold was the family's saviour and Jack would do anything for her.

CHAPTER FIVE

Early Nights

"**P**lease let me come. Please. C'mon, it's my birthday. You wouldn't leave me here on my own, surely. I'll tell Dad if you don't. I will. I'll tell him where you're off to," pleaded Rosie, the youngest of the Royce girls. "I'll behave this time, please. I won't make a show of myself," she begged.

There was no way she was being left behind while her older sisters were out having fun and she was stuck at home. No, Rosie definitely wasn't being left behind and she meant it, she would tell.

"For god's sake let her come," Iris snapped at her middle sister, Violet. "The longer we argue with her, the less chance we have of bagging a good one." Turning to the culprit, she grabbed hold of her hair, pulling her face down level with her own. "You pull any stunts tonight, lady, and you won't be fit to go anywhere again. Understand?"

"I won't. Honest I promise," the youngster smirked. She'd known she'd get her own way, she always did.

Retrieving an outfit she'd already prepared in anticipation, Rosie set about transforming herself from an everyday schoolgirl to a jaw-dropping, sixties chick, looking at least three or four years older – mini skirt, boob tube and white knee-length boots, all courtesy of her sisters.

Ten minutes later the three girls, made up to the nines, headed for the American military base just outside the village. Every Saturday night Uncle Sam played host to the neighbours, attracting virtually every single female, and a few not-so-single, all desperate for the opportunity to snare one of the scores of handsome GIs, there for the taking. These guys made the locals look like a bunch of hicks.

Rosie was all psyched up, beside herself with excitement. She knew now what to expect, it had been a shock the last time. How could she possibly have known that the fat, bald sergeant, who looked older than her father, would go sticking his tongue halfway down her throat? She'd nearly passed out. Gagging, frightened half to death and having created such a commotion, she and her sisters had been thrown off the base, much to their annoyance. That wouldn't happen this time. She wouldn't mind the fat old sergeant buying her drinks, but that was all. No way was he getting near her She already had her eye on someone and he was too dishy for words. He could stick his tongue wherever he wanted, she wouldn't complain.

The three Royce girls were infamous in the neighbourhood: wild, up for anything, a law unto themselves, daughters of the local baker and his fancy foreign wife. All three were stunners with that sultry, Mediterranean look, so different from the local girls with their plain, bovine features, all hewn from good farming stock. Rosie and her sisters had an innate confidence, a swagger and the arrogance of those who knew just how good they looked. And tonight they had excelled themselves.

The two older girls had often visited the base, hellbent on becoming GI brides by securing a husband who would whisk them off to the land of TV dinners and drive-in movies. They never missed an opportunity to fraternise with 'those dammed Yanks', as their father called them.

"You behave yourself. Don't be taken in by any of these buggers, they'll promise you the earth just to get into your knickers." Violet prodded Rosie sharply to emphasis her words.

"So, for God's sake be careful and be back here by ten. Remember. Ten, not a minute later, we have to be home before the pubs empty out."

"Okay, okay," agreed the young one, anxious to get away from them.

A moving sea of bodies, gyrating to the sounds of the band in the semi-darkness, mesmerised the youngster. Rosie spied him as soon as she entered. Up there on the stage, the singer looked like he had just walked off the set of the latest box office movie. He was gorgeous, a dead ringer for her heartthrob, Elvis. And that voice, she'd never heard anything like it. Her legs turned to jelly and she could hardly breathe. Play it cool, she kept telling herself, don't look too eager. No way was she going to join the bunch of moonstruck idiots already flocking around him. No, not her. She swept past the group without a glance in his direction, looking disdainfully at his admirers.

As she crossed the dance floor heading for the bar, she was accosted several times by eager GIs. She sure was cute, but not his type, thought Private 2nd Class, Toni Francitti. Hailing from Hoboken, New Jersey, birthplace of Frank Sinatra, he preferred his women to be like the girls back home: voluptuous and sexy, not skinny kids. But wow, she had a look about her.

"Hi honey," said Toni, walking towards Rosie, abandoning the disappointed creatures who followed him relentlessly. Taking her hand and gently kissing it, he crooned. The accent never failed.

At this point she almost swooned. *Keep calm, keep calm, and don't let him think for a minute you're interested.* The words were swirling around in her head. She'd listened to her sisters talk about boys for years, but this was no boy.

*

It was past ten o'clock and there was no sign of her. The sisters searched the obvious places with no results; she was nowhere to be found. They had to go. The pubs would be emptying soon and if they were not home there would be hell to pay. The baker was a strict father and ruled by the belt. No way would he tolerate his daughters hanging around these horny Yanks. As far as he was concerned they were good girls who stayed quietly at home with their mother. She, on the other hand, knew fine well what the she-devils got up to. The apples hadn't fallen far from the tree where they were concerned. She had no interest whatsoever in their comings and goings, just so long as they were there to fetch and carry for her and attend to her continuous demands. This lady had other fish to fry. Unknown to her daughters, she too, spent much time at the base, but in far more salubrious surroundings.

Iris and Violet had no choice but to leave and get home as quickly as they could. They were worried sick; she was only a kid, after all. Despite her threats they shouldn't have taken her. They both knew that, but in their own desperation to go, had let themselves be persuaded. Let's face it, she could be a manipulative little beggar at times, they consoled themselves.

"Where the devil can she have gotten to?"

"More to the point, who is she with? I would have thought after the last time she would have been a bit less likely to hook up with someone."

"I hope she's okay and has just lost track of time."

"We need to get back, we can cover for her till she turns up, but if we're all out there will be murders."

Arriving home with minutes to spare, they ran upstairs to change, just as their father arrived demanding his supper. Fortunately, he was not a man given to the art of conversation and the two elder girls successfully fooled him, but not so the matriarch of the house, who for reasons known only to herself, did not disclose the fact that there were only two daughters on duty. They would no doubt pay for this, but thankfully, not tonight.

It was well after midnight when the sisters heard the rattle of stones on the glass. The little monkey, she could bloody well stay out there in the cold for a bit longer, having worried them half to death.

This was to be the pattern for the following weeks. Despite dire warnings, threats and beatings from both her sisters, Rosie stayed out every night, returning home just before dawn, when the baker, finished for the night, would find his youngest, now his favourite, up, dressed and with his breakfast on the table. Unlike the other lazy good-for-nothings he housed.

CHAPTER SIX

Confinement

Even in her present condition, Mary was not downhearted. This was merely an inconvenience, she assured Agnes. Despite her predicament she was determined to recoup the situation. She had grand ideas for her return to the capital. Mary had a 'Plan' which Agnes was delighted to hear, included her.

For a start, there would be no walking the streets touting for business. No, she'd learned from her brief sojourn, that wasn't where the real money was made. Also, to avoid being caught with another unwanted pregnancy, they would visit the new family planning clinic recently opened in Stockbridge, not too far away.

The two spent hours huddled on Agnes's lumpy bed, under the rough horse blankets, planning their future.

Agnes was enthralled by Mary's tales and ambitions and, ludicrous though it might seem, neither considered their plans unusual or unattainable. After all, Agnes had been indulging in these practices for as long as she could remember; only the price tag was different. She drank in every detail of Mary's 'sexploits' and tricks.

There was only one drawback. For their scheme to work, they needed money!

"What are you planning to do with the child?" her sister asked Mary over supper one night.

"I haven't really thought about it," Mary lied glibly. "Probably put it up for adoption. I'm sure some poor, childless couple will be willing to pay good money for a healthy newborn. I'm back off to town as soon as I have a bit of cash in my pocket."

Her sister, aghast at Mary's callousness, approached her husband with a solution to the 'mother-to-be' problem and her own desire for another child.

"Only if it's a boy, mind," he decreed. "I'm not shelling out for another useless female."

"I'm sure it will be a boy. Even the midwife agrees, she's carrying so far down," his wife assured him.

"Well, we'll see. As I said, I'll decide when it's born. Christ, it could be black the way that mongrel carries on and I'm not getting tucked up by her."

The answer came in the form of a lusty, seven pound baby boy, four weeks later. Roderick McLeod was a chubby, red-headed cherub, who captivated both the farmer and his wife. Negotiations began in earnest. Mary soon figured out that the child, instead of being her nemesis, was in fact her passport to freedom.

"Once you've been paid, there's no coming back for more," the farmer insisted.

"I know, but you have to make it worth my while," Mary demanded. "I want three hundred pounds." She was equally as determined as the potential parents.

"Don't be ridiculous, lassie. Where the hell would I get that kind of money?"

"I don't care. But remember, this is probably your only chance of having the son you're both desperate for."

So, for the princely sum of two hundred pounds, Mary furnished the farmer and her sister with a son-and-heir. Gathering her belongings and relieving them of their first-born child, she and Agnes headed for fame and fortune.

Agnes McLeod never forgot her first glimpse of Edinburgh. Princes Street on a Saturday afternoon was amazing, she had never seen such crowds. Store after store had fantastic window displays, attracting thousands of shoppers. On the opposite side of the street, workers could be seen eating lunch in the spectacular gardens with the world-famous castle perched high on the rock. Music blared from the bandstand and pipers busked for the tourists. For a girl straight from the farm, this was exciting, exhilarating and she wanted it all.

Thanks to Mary's negotiating skills, the two were able to secure a lease on a smart apartment in the west end of the city, which would double up as home and work. By trawling around the numerous secondhand stores, and with a bit of bargaining, the girls lavishly furnished their new place. Mary was determined to attract only the higher end of the market but how exactly that was to be accomplished was beyond her for the moment. After only a month in town, however, they were quickly running out of money.

"What are we going to do, Mary?" Agnes asked. "The rent's due next week and we're down to our last fiver. I thought you said customers would be queuing around the block?"

"They will, once word gets out," the older girl tried her best to convince her partner.

"And how's that going to happen?" a disappointed Agnes asked.

"I don't know, but what I do know is we're not going to get anywhere sitting on our behinds waiting for punters to knock on the door. Get yourself dressed. We're going out on the town."

"But we're skint."

"You have to speculate to accumulate," Mary quipped. "Now get a move on."

CHAPTER SEVEN

All Gone

The world was possibly at its blackest. President Kennedy had been assassinated and with the war in Vietnam escalating, one of the first duties of the new president had been to deploy a huge number of troops to the war zone. This news was barely reported in the UK, but in a small village in rural Scotland, it changed the lives of two young people forever.

Rumours were circulating daily, not if the troops would be sent overseas, but when, much to the consternation of Private 2nd Class Francitti and his girl, Rosie.

"We could get married before I ship out," Toni proposed. "I know it's sooner than we'd planned, but I want you to be my wife."

They had spoken about getting married since the first night they'd met. Toni had told her all about his family back home in New Jersey, where his Italian parents ran a bakery, just like Rosie's.

"Let's go see the chaplain tomorrow," Toni urged. "I might not be here this time next week."

"Don't you think it's a bit soon?" Rosie asked. "I can't imagine my father will give permission."

"You don't need his permission. Don't you want to get married?" the puzzled GI asked.

"Of course I do, but it's all a bit of a rush." Rosie was dreading having to tell him the real reason for her reluctance.

"You knew I wouldn't be here much longer and I've no doubts, I want us to get hitched before I leave."

Much as Rosie wanted to marry her beau, there was one major problem. One she couldn't overcome, with or without her father's permission. Her age. She was only fourteen.

"What! Are you kidding me? Jesus, Rosie, I could be court marshalled, probably thrown in the brig. Why didn't you tell me? This changes everything. Christ! Fourteen?" he shook his head in disbelief.

"It doesn't have to. We can wait. Please, Toni," she pleaded.

"Wait? I've no idea how long I'm going to be in 'Nam for, and let's face it, I've no idea if I'll even come back. Sorry, kid, we're over," he said and stony-faced, he walked away from a weeping Rosie.

There had been an unusually high amount of traffic flowing through the village since early morning for a street which saw, on average, a couple of cars, maybe two or three horse and carts and the odd tractor. Truck after truck trundled along the cobbled High Street. The war had begun in earnest.

As the trucks passed the baker's shop, there, on the pavement, in full view of the entire village, a case at her side and dressed in her Sunday best, stood Maria Royce. The villagers were agog, but none more so than her three daughters when a gleaming black staff car drew up. The driver jumped out, ushered Mrs Royce into the vehicle, stored her case in the boot and drove off. It was impossible to tell who was more flabbergasted, her daughters or their neighbours. The news spread like wildfire and before the car had disappeared from sight almost everyone had been apprised of the scandal, except for the poor, cuckolded husband.

Since her arrival as a young bride, Maria Royce had been studiously ignored by every woman in the village. She was the enemy. No-one addressed or acknowledged her in the street or even in church. Many would decline to be served in the shop by her. She'd had the nerve to capture, ensnare and join in holy matrimony with the village's most eligible bachelor. To compound her wickedness further, she had produced three deliciously good-looking, arrogant young girls who had in turn enraptured every male, married or otherwise, with their mother's beguiling ways.

The baker, having completed his usual twelve-hour shift, had gobbled his breakfast and gone for a few hours sleep, oblivious to the comings and goings – mainly the goings – of his errant wife.

"What the hell will we tell him?" uttered Iris.

"God knows. Do you think she's coming back?" questioned Violet.

"I don't know. Maybe someone's ill and she's had to dash off to help."

"What about the shop?" ventured Rosie.

"What about the bloody shop?" answered Violet.

"Look at it."

All three girls turned.

"Jesus wept," said Iris.

The shop was packed to capacity, there was hardly room for them to push their way in. There was no way they could break this development gently to their father now. The noise from the crowd had roused him from his bed.

"What's going on downstairs?" he asked as he poked his head round the door jamb, rubbing his eyes in disbelief. Seeing the downcast faces of his three girls he knew immediately he wasn't going to like it, whatever it was.

CHAPTER EIGHT

Good Advice

The head concierge in the North British Hotel, Robert Conrad, had worked in most of the top hotels for years and could spot a brass a mile off, but these two were a joke. With skirts up to their arses and tops down to their navels, their wares were on display for all to see. Unlike the girls who regularly worked the hotel, who were smart, well-presented and discreet. These two stuck out like sore thumbs and would be more suited to touting for business along Rose Street, where girls like them were ten a penny.

He couldn't have riff-raff offending his patrons. Discretion was essential in any situation front-of-house and the last thing Robert wanted was a scene. Nothing should upset the equilibrium of his hotel.

"Shit," he muttered under his breath. They had already attracted the attention of Sir Malcolm. This was going to be tricky.

"Evening, sir," Conrad addressed his guest. "I wonder if I might have a word with the young ladies," and turning to the two girls he said, "Would you come with me please?"

"What's the problem, old man?" Sir Malcolm interrupted. "I was just about to buy these pretty young things a drink."

"I'm sorry sir, but I believe one of them to be under age and that is against the law."

"It's not against the law for me to buy her a soft drink, is it?" the old man challenged Conrad.

"Of course not, sir," he replied, glaring at the two interlopers.

"These ladies are my guests. I take it you have no objections?"

"No sir, no objections at all." Conrad backed off, seething. He'd catch up with these buggers later.

Sir Malcolm Dunlop, the seventh Earl of Wemyss, had been married to Lady Edith for forty-two years. The two had last slept together on the night their son and heir had been conceived, thirty-nine years ago. His wife considered his sexual demands intolerable, leaving him to seek his pleasures elsewhere.

Agnes and Mary spent the remainder of the weekend in Sir Malcolm's suite, a most satisfying arrangement for all parties. The old roué introduced the girls to his most decadent pleasures. These tricks would serve them well, entertaining debauched old toffs.

Having made enough money to pay the rent for the next three months, they'd gained their first regular client.

Their real achievement that weekend was being befriended by Robert Conrad. They had the savvy to know that if they didn't take care of the concierge, this would be their one and only time outwitting him. So, with a more than generous tip, they gained an invaluable friend and mentor.

"Your first mistake," Robert advised them, "is the way you dress. It shouts cheap hooker. You look like you'd be more at home working the docks."

Both girls were indignant, their attire was the latest fashion.

"I'm sure it is," agreed Conrad, "but look around you. Can you spot any working girls?"

"No," they both acknowledged.

"That's because they blend in. Be discreet. Make that your motto and you'll get into any top hotel without arousing suspicion. Always look after the staff and they'll look after you. Good luck."

Having realised how out of place they looked and how right the concierge was, the twosome made another round of the secondhand stores, producing a fashionable, chic and ever so slightly older wardrobe for Edinburgh's latest 'working girls'. If nothing else, these two were fast learners.

When she looked at herself in the mirror, Agnes was astounded at the exotic being staring back. Determined to leave all vestiges of her past behind her, Agnes McLeod disappeared and Stella Gold was born.

Stella and Mary were amazed at how many Sir Malcolms there were in the city, each with their own peculiar peccadillos and word quickly spread amongst his many school chums. In a matter of months, they found themselves catering to the more depraved members of Edinburgh society who were unable to fulfil their cravings elsewhere. Money was rolling in and soon their purchases from the secondhand emporiums were replaced with items from the exquisite department stores for which Edinburgh was renowned. Stella Gold took to the profession like a duck to water. The future looked bright. That was, until the night they met the Williams brothers.

CHAPTER NINE

Ghost Town

Rosie still couldn't believe her eyes. The base was almost deserted, a huge empty graveyard with only a few civilian workers preparing for the next influx of troops. As for the love of her life, he'd been bundled into the back of a lorry along with the rest of his platoon. No backward glance, no promises, nothing. The two people in the world she loved and who were supposed to love her had gone. At least he had an excuse, he hadn't gone through choice, but her?

Rosie had gone up to the base every day in the hope they were on manoeuvres or some temporary exercise. She childishly clung to the hope that they'd all return and things would go back to normal. But no, they were gone and now she had another problem and was seriously beginning to panic. She had no idea what would happen when news of her condition came out. It was Violet who got suspicious first. Rosie looked fuller in the face and her blouses were straining across her chest. Then there was the sickness. She hadn't paid too much attention to begin with. None of them had been particularly observant, since their mother had gone off with her fancy man. A bloody Major, no less, and nobody had had an inkling. She hadn't given her a family a second thought when the offer of a better life came her way.

No better than she should be, was the general consensus of the village women, who were already making a play for the poor deserted husband. The only saving grace out of the scandal was that the shop had never been so busy.

*

Violet had been eager to speak to her sister since the shop opened that morning, but the continual stream of customers had prevented her from doing so. Lord above, she hoped she was wrong. It was bad enough being the talk of the village since their mother had skipped off, but an illegitimate child, and one to a Yank, didn't bear thinking about. She couldn't keep her suspicions to herself any longer.

"Have you noticed anything different about her ladyship lately?" Violet nervously quizzed her older sister.

"Good God, Violet, I haven't had time to look at my own face in the mirror never mind anyone else's. Why, what's wrong with her?"

"I'm worried about her. She's put on a bit of weight and she's been sick the past three mornings."

"No, she's not that stupid, surely? She wouldn't. It'll be a bug or something, she's only fourteen," Iris blustered.

"Jesus, what do you think they were doing all those nights, her and GI Joe? Playing feckin' tiddlywinks?"

"Dear God, we'll be run out of the village. They won't stand for it. Mum's disappearance is one thing, but a pregnancy?"

"This will put paid to any chance we might have with anyone decent. Let's face it, we'll all be tarred with the same brush. Like mother like daughter, only in our case daughters."

"She has to get rid of it, and quick."

"How do you propose to accomplish that little feat? I can hear the jungle drums beating already."

"She'll have to go to old Ma Higgins, there's no alternative."

"But that costs money, and he's not likely to cough up. Can you imagine it? Excuse me, Dad, could you lend us a hundred quid so Rosie can get rid of her bambino? Sure, he'll give us double to be on the safe side."

"Shit," exclaimed Iris, turning to face her dad, and by the

look on his face he had heard everything.

Rosie was on the twelve o'clock bus with her suitcase, twenty pounds in her hand and instructions never to darken his door again.

CHAPTER TEN

Sticky Fingers

Ronnie and Freddie Williams were two rising stars in the city's underworld. Good-looking, well-heeled and no door closed to them. They had so many fingers in so many pies it was joked that they each needed another hand.

Darlings of Edinburgh's glitterati were enthralled by the brothers' dangerous and sinister reputations. It was an open secret that they had disposed of their predecessors, but nothing, of course, could be proved.

They were the sons of the infamous bare-knuckle champion, Johnny Williams, and had been brought up in the bosom of a large, Irish travelling family. The brothers learned from an early age how to take care of themselves and by the time they were in their teens they'd become a major force to be reckoned with.

Their father, a hard-living, hard-drinking fighter, known the length and breadth of the country, ended up a punch-drunk, penniless waster, reduced to challenging anyone to a fight for the price of a drink.

The brothers, shamed by their father's downfall, and although they had fought their way through the ranks, had no intention of following him into the ring.

"We're far too pretty to let someone spoil this for a few quid," remarked Ronnie, stroking his brother's handsome face.

"There are much easier and quicker ways of making a buck," Freddie grinned.

With the backup of their travelling kin, the Williams brothers swept through the capital taking no prisoners.

Since they had become more prominent there had been

no challenges from any other pretenders to the throne. The brothers were firmly in charge and nothing, no matter how trivial, happened without their say so.

Stella and Mary first encountered the two one evening in Denzlers, the smart Swiss restaurant across from their apartment.

"Did it hurt?" Freddie asked Mary.

"Sorry, did what hurt?" She answered coyly.

"When you fell from heaven?"

Stella almost choked at the cheesy pick-up line. "You're not falling for that, surely?"

But Mary was already smitten.

Years later Stella could recall that exact moment in time as if it were yesterday and she would regret it till the day she died.

From day one the foursome went everywhere together. Invitations to the most exclusive parties, mixing with minor celebrities and sporting stars, were now the norm for the girls from the sticks. Entry to the owner's enclosure on race days and tips straight from the horse's mouth meant champagne all the way. On frequent visits to the casino, the girls would be handed a fistful of cash and told to go play the tables while the brothers attended to business. Neither questioned where the money came from. Whatever the brothers were engaged in was extremely lucrative because they were generous to a fault.

If ever there was a case of love at first sight it was Freddie and Mary. However, one issue marred Mary's happiness: Stella's constant reminders of Freddie's insanely jealous streak.

Both girls oozed sex-appeal and attracted attention wherever they went and boy, did Freddie love it. However, if another man even glanced in Mary's direction there was hell to pay, and someone was guaranteed a visit to the hospital.

This behaviour terrified Stella and she frequently

challenged Mary about his violent temper. The older of the two girls was so besotted with her man she wouldn't hear a word against him, despite arriving home after most dates in blood-stained clothing.

From the day they arrived in the city Mary and Stella had agreed it would be safer to keep work and social life separate. To clients they were sisters from abroad, and to avoid awkward questions in their social life they masqueraded as nurses, living in the nurses' home where, of course, everyone knew the rules concerning male visitors.

For once the evening had gone off without a hitch and Stella had just begun to relax when she heard the commotion. How could she have believed they could get through a whole night without incident?

The four had enjoyed a fabulous meal at the opening of a new Italian restaurant. The food and wine were outstanding and they'd been treated like VIPs. These boys certainly got first class treatment wherever they went. It was Ronnie who had suggested finishing off the night with a visit to the casino.

As usual, Mary and Stella were given a bundle of cash and sent off to amuse themselves, while the brothers joined a group of their associates at the bar.

The tables were quieter than usual and the girls were chatting, quite innocently, to a couple of guys who weren't having much luck. Freddie, catching sight of some lowlife punter chatting up his woman, crossed the room in seconds. Picking up a glass, he strode purposely towards his target and, without warning, viciously smashed it into the guy's face.

Stella was desperately trying to calm a hysterical Mary as Ronnie grabbed his brother, hauling him off before he could do any more damage.

"Get out of here," Ronnie snapped at the girls.

As he propelled Freddie out of the building, he stuffed

some notes into the manager's hand and instructed him to get the injured guy to hospital.

"Christ! When are you going to wake up and see him for what he is? A vicious control freak who will turn on you one day," Stella exploded.

"He just gets a bit jealous."

"Gets a bit jealous? Fuck, Mary, that's another one hospitalised, and for what? What were you doing that was so bad that the poor guy deserved being glassed and scarred for life?"

"I was only blowing on his dice for luck," Mary sobbed.

Mary saw Freddie as her knight in shining armour and if the truth be known, she was secretly thrilled her man would fight for her. She couldn't understand that what she saw as romantic, Stella saw as dangerous.

Nursing a drink into the small hours, Stella fretted about Freddie's actions. Although this was nothing new, it seemed as if there was more malice in his actions.

Another normal night out with the Williams brothers, she thought as she climbed into bed.

CHAPTER ELEVEN

Pick Up

Jack Hunter had no idea how long the girl had been sitting there, but it had to have been at least a couple of hours. She'd been there all the while he'd been back and forth delivering punters to Danube Street.

Business had been quite slow today. He'd managed to waylay a couple of farmers on their way home from the cattle sales. There'd be little profit for them to share by the time Stella and the girls had finished with them, he chuckled to himself. A brace of young bucks with more hair than wit had been his second capture and he was now eyeing up a corpulent clergyman, who looked ripe for the plucking.

Jack earned his money by directing, or redirecting gentlemen to the infamous bordello in Danube Street, run by the even more infamous Stella Gold. He worked mainly between the bus depot and the railway station, snaring unsuspecting out-of-towners with promises that, by following him, they'd have the time of their lives. How could anyone doubt this charming, likeable rogue? And before the punter knew it, he'd arrived at one of the most famous addresses in the capital.

Having delivered the clergyman, he had returned to the bus depot, curious to see if the girl had gone. No. There she was, still sitting, still waiting, and she was quite a looker too. The bus depot was a dangerous place at any time, but especially after dark. A hangout for pimps, dealers, druggies and all nefarious walks of life, certainly not a safe place for a fledgling like her.

"You okay, miss?" Jack approached her. She was even more startlingly good looking close up. She would be absolute mincemeat left here on her own, he thought.

The girl looked straight at him. A single crystal tear ran down her cheek, captivating Jack. If only he knew that Rosie could cry to order; she had mastered the art as a toddler. This little trick had seen her get away with murder over the years. Who could deny such an innocent?

Truth be told, she was a spoiled little hussy, who from an early age could twist most people around her little finger. She had only to turn on the waterworks or that beguiling smile and even the iciest of hearts would melt.

This had worked perfectly until this morning and she was still shocked to the core. Her father had turned on her with a viciousness which astounded all three sisters, roaring that he would have nothing more to do with her. Before she knew it, her bags were packed, a twenty-pound-note stuffed in her hand and she was on the bus, heading for the city. It had all happened so fast.

Her sisters, who in the past had always stuck up for her, and on many occasions taken the blame for whatever the little minx had done, were way out of their depth. She was on her own this time. They sure as hell had no intentions of following her out of the door. Anyway, knowing Rosie, she'd fall on her feet. She always did.

With her lips quivering and more tears, she looked up at her rescuer. "No," Rosie answered him.

"Who are you waiting for?" Jack enquired. She was probably the best-looking girl he'd seen in a long while, if ever, and from a connoisseur of female flesh that was saying something. She had a look about her. She could make fortunes this one but, unfortunately, she was a bit young and definitely too innocent.

"No-one," the girl replied. "I don't know anyone, I don't know what to do," she cried, turning on the full works.

Jack was hooked, Rosie had notched up another sucker.

"What the devil are you doing in this den of iniquity, and

why are you on your own?"

Rosie had concocted a tale during the time she had been waiting for a saviour to appear. She'd known all along that someone would come to her rescue, they always did. She supposed she would have to make up a story, a believable one, as to why a young innocent like her was homeless, penniless (nobody needed to know about the twenty-pound note stuffed in her bra) and alone in the city. She decided to be an orphan. One who had been thrown to the wolves by a wicked stepmother on the death of her beloved father, only a few days ago. She also had to pretend to be older in order not to be carted off to an orphanage, so she'd be seventeen, she'd certainly pass for that.

By God, she was good. This halfwit had swallowed it hook, line and sinker. It looked like she was okay for a bed tonight. Thank the lord, she hadn't been looking forward to spending the night in the toilets.

"I can't take you back to my place," the young lad was explaining. "But I'll take you to my boss, Stella, she'll help you out and we can sort something more permanent tomorrow."

"Thank you, oh, thank you. I'll never forget your kindness, sir."

That was a bit smarmy, she thought, but she needed to keep this one on side for a few days. At least until she got settled somewhere. Surprisingly, she hadn't really been worried about her situation; she had known something would turn up.

They pulled up outside a magnificent house ablaze with lights, and there seemed to be a party or reception taking place. Damn, Rosie thought to herself, she wasn't dressed for company. In fact, she didn't have anything with her that would pass for good and she knew first impressions counted.

"Not the front door," Jack pulled her back. "This way." He led his charge down the area steps into the basement. "Sorry, luv, tradesman's entrance for us. Believe me, you don't want to go in through *that* door."

"Yes, I do," the young girl muttered to herself. "I most certainly do."

CHAPTER TWELVE

Get out of Jail Card

Rosie's introduction to Danube Street was memorable, to say the least. Driven along George Street, into Hanover Street and down over the Dean Bridge, the lad had brought her to Danube Street. It was obvious from the row of Georgian town houses that this was a wealthy part of the city. Rosie was smitten immediately by the gracious, elegant façade. Looking through the large sash windows, she could see that there was a party or some-such taking place, which made the house look even more glamorous to the young country girl. Having to make her entrance through the basement rankled her and she vowed that one day she would not only enter by the huge front door, with its shining brass knocker and nameplate, but that she would be someone of consequence. The sound of dozens of police whistles and the clump of heavy boots interrupted any further conjecture.

"It's a raid," yelled Jack at the top of his voice and, bundling Rosie and the other two occupants of the room into the coal cellar, he flew back up the outside steps to find out what was happening.

The meat wagons were filling up fast. The police were arresting punters as well as workers. From the other side of the road Jack spotted 'the missus', as Stella was known to her nearest and dearest.

"Don't worry, I'll lock this place up tight and get it back to order," Jack called to her. He'd had to take care of things after the previous raids and was an old hand at the job.

"Come to the court in the morning," Stella replied. "You'll have to bail us out. You know the procedure."

"Okay, boss."

*

It was almost an hour later before Jack considered it safe enough to let the three women out of the cellar, by which time they were covered in coal dust and quite indignant that he had left them in such conditions. Especially Rosie.

"You should have left me to the mercy of the inhabitants of the bus station, rather than run the risk of being arrested for prostitution," she snapped at Jack.

"Have you been carted off?" he bellowed back. "No, you haven't, so belt up and let's get things put right."

The other two occupants of the cellar were Kitty and Dora. Kitty, the cook-cum-housekeeper who'd given Stella and Marcus the guided tour the day they took over, was originally a working girl. Way past her best, she'd arrived back at Danube Street one day, battered and bruised. Stella had, without question, taken Kitty under her wing and when healed she'd simply taken up residence, assuming her new role. The other occupant, Dora, was a deaf mute who'd wandered into the kitchen one winter's morning. Cold, dishevelled and terrified, she never left. Kitty treated Dora like the daughter she'd never had.

"Don't argue with him, lass, he's right. We have to get this place ready for business. These feckers make some mess, and I'm sure most of them do it just for the hell of it."

"Is this a regular occurrence?" asked a bemused Rosie.

"Not really," replied Kitty. "But a new Chief Inspector has taken over. The last one was never out of here, a great pal of the missus, but this one's a queer kettle of fish altogether. He's determined to make his mark and of course, we're easy meat. This is the third time we've been raided this month. Once the missus gets him sorted out it should all settle down."

"Stop blethering and get to work," Jack insisted, hurrying the three of them upstairs.

"Hey, who died and made you the boss?" Kitty snapped at Jack. She turned to Rosie and said, "You have to work for your supper in this house, dearie. There's no such thing as a free lunch."

Free lunch, she had to be kidding. There was no chance Rosie would be hanging about till then.

Rosie Royce was dumbstruck at the elegance and opulence of the working rooms. She had never seen anything like them, not even in the cinema. Despite the disarray they were breathtaking, each room surpassing the previous one. Huge four poster beds covered in Egyptian cotton sheets, silk throws, and plump cushions, all in beautifully decorated surroundings. Even the Terror Rooms had an air of darkly malevolent beauty.

Rosie shuddered to think what went on in there, but knew instinctively that here was where the real money was made and the real power wielded. Surprisingly for such a youngster, in fact, one so naive, the instruments and apparatus did not intimidate her in the slightest.

The three women worked tirelessly and by 10pm things were pretty much back to normal. The time had flown past, listening to the tales and exploits told by Kitty, who was not in the least ashamed or embarrassed to admit her previous employment and only sorry that she was of an age when, as she put it, even with the lights out, no bugger would take her on.

Throughout the evening there had been a constant stream of visitors hammering on the front door, demanding, or in some cases pleading for admission.

"This is bad for business," Jack moaned. "We have to do something about this fucker, he must have a weak point."

"His Achilles heel," said Rosie.

"His what?" Kitty and Jack spoke in unison.

"His Achilles heel," Rosie repeated. "In olden days, I think it was Greek or Roman times, there's a story about some soldier who, no matter who tried to defeat him, succeeded. Hundreds of challengers tried to beat him, but couldn't. Till one day this guy called Paris came along and spotted that the only part of his body not protected was his heel. So, Paris dipped an arrow in poison and fired it into his heel, killing Achilles."

"Eh?"

"Paris found his weak spot."

The two listeners looked blankly at Rosie.

"Are you trying to say we should finish this geezer off with a bow and arrow?"

"No! You have to find his weak spot, like Paris found Achilles' heel. Forget it, just ignore me," said an exasperated Rosie.

"Never mind fairytales, if we don't get this sorted soon, we could be out of business. He wants us closed down and Stella put away for the foreseeable."

"Oh my God, what will we do, where will we go?" asked Kitty, wringing her grubby hands.

"Shut up, Kitty, it's not going to come to that. We'll find a way."

"I've made up a bed in the alcove for you,' Kitty turned to Rosie. "By the way, you never said what you're doing with Jack, and why you're here?"

"She's my cousin from out of town," Jack hurriedly answered, staving off any further questions. "You know what it's like. Family problems."

"I didn't know you had family outside your ma and granny." Kitty wasn't letting him off that easily. She smelt a rat, but it would keep. There was a story here and she'd find out what, or her name wasn't Kitty Murphy.

CHAPTER THIRTEEN

Trouble Maker

It was three days before Rosie came face to face with the infamous Stella Gold. The activity in the house astounded her. Business had resumed immediately after the girls had been up in front of the bench. This was a regular occurrence: all pleaded guilty, were fined twenty pounds and case dismissed. All except Stella that is; she was charged with a more serious offence – 'Living off Immoral Earnings' and warned, should she appear before the bench again, she would receive a custodial sentence. Stella would worry about that if, and when, it happened.

"So you're Jack's latest squeeze?" stated the intimidating older woman. "I have to say you're certainly a cut above his usual vagabonds. He's a real pushover is our Jack and he's fallen for every sob story in the book."

"I'm not his squeeze," retorted Rosie. "I'm not his anything. He just offered to help me."

"He did, did he? So how far gone are you?" Stella asked bluntly.

Rosie blanched and instinctively clutching her slightly swollen abdomen, asked, "What do you mean, how far gone am I?" *Was she bloody psychic, she thought to herself.*

"Listen, dearie, I've housed many runaways over the years and probably ninety percent of them were pregnant, chasing a man because they were pregnant, disowned by their family because they were pregnant, didn't know who the father was, but still pregnant. It doesn't take a genius to work out why so many land on my doorstep, so I'll ask you again, how far gone are you?"

"I'm not any 'far gone', my stepmother threw me out after my father died," said the indignant girl.

"Have it your own way, but listen to me, lovey, I'd keep the fairy stories till bedtime and if you want my help, then you'll cut out the nonsense and let's see what's to be done."

"Thanks very much, but I'm fine."

"Well, if you don't need help would you tell me why you've been sleeping on a makeshift bed in my kitchen?"

"I was helping Kitty and Dora after the raid, but everything seems to be in order now, so I'll be on my way."

"You're a stubborn young bugger, I'll give you that. Look, girl, help is here if you want it, but I'm not going to plead with you to take it. I've far more pressing things to deal with."

"Six months, I think," Rosie muttered.

"Too far along for a visit to Ma Higgins," Stella mused. "We'll have to look at other options, but not at the moment. If you want to stay, you're welcome, but let me tell you, if you thieve or upset any of my girls, you'll get the hiding of your life."

"I'm not a thief or a troublemaker," Rosie answered, her eyes blazing.

"By heavens, you've got plenty to say for yourself and with looks like yours, you were born to cause trouble. Now, away back and lend Kitty a hand till I work out what's to be done with you. She spoke highly of you, by the way, that's why I'm willing to give you a chance. There's not much that can get past old Kitty."

"So, she's taken you on," smiled Kitty. "I thought she would. It's a shame about your wee problem, but you're not the first and you certainly won't be the last. Is it a visit to Ma Higgins?"

"No, I'm too far on. I wouldn't have anyway, it's a mortal sin."

"I'm glad, she's an old butcher. But as far as mortal sins go, it's a far worse sin to bring an unwanted bairn into this world," Kitty pronounced, "than stopping one from entering."

Watching Rosie's reactions to her words, Kitty was struck, not for the first time, at the similarities between the pair. Stella and Rosie could be sisters, not necessarily in their appearance, but in their mannerisms and speech. Each displayed the stubborn confidence that theirs and only theirs was the right way to do things. Kitty could see many a spat between the two while they were under the same roof. The old woman hoped the pair would become allies, but she sure as hell wouldn't bet on it.

CHAPTER FOURTEEN

Play Time

"How much?" Ronnie Williams spluttered.

"Fifty quid," repeated his brother as the two made their way to the first floor apartment. "They charge fifty quid," he paused slightly and added, "an hour."

"An hour? Fifty quid an hour? You're off your fucking nut, mate. No brass is worth that kind of money."

"According to the gossip, they are."

"Listen, I don't care if their snatches are lined with mink and they piss pure vodka, I'm not paying that amount of dosh for a shag."

"Don't be such a miserable bastard," cajoled Freddie. "If you're that skint, I'll pay."

"Don't you be a smartarse. Of course I'm not skint. It's the principle."

"Time to make your mind up," his brother rang the bell.

"This had better be good," muttered Ronnie. "In fact, it had better be fucking outstanding."

The door was opened by a tall figure dressed entirely in black PVC with six-inch spike heels, wearing a mask.

Wow! All thoughts of fifty quid vanished.

For some time, Freddie had been hearing through the grapevine about these two foreign, possibly Russian sisters, who, for an exorbitant fee, would blow your mind. With a bit of persuasion he had talked Ronnie into paying this notorious duo a visit. So here they were, standing like a couple of schoolboys playing truant.

"Come in, gentlemen," said the hostess in a strong Eastern European accent as she led them across the hall to a pitch dark room.

"Undress," commanded a second, disembodied foreign voice, accompanied by the crack of a whip.

Stella had almost fainted when she opened the door to find Ronnie and Freddie standing there expectantly.

How the fuck were they going to get out of this mess? Almost hysterical, she pulled an unsuspecting Mary out of the room.

"Christ, Mary, have you seen who our next clients are? For fuck's sake, what are we going to do?"

"Grab our clothes and run," came the answer. "I'm not joking, we need to get out of here before they realise who we are."

"Don't be stupid. We have to go through with this."

"How? There's no way we can pull it off."

"We carry on as normal, but for the love of God, say as little as possible. If you concentrate on your accent we might just get away with this."

"I can't, there's no way I'll be able to keep up the pretence."

"You've no choice if you want to get out of here alive. Christ, if he batters someone for saying hello, what the hell will he do if he finds out we're not bloody nurses?"

Fearfully returning to the room, the dominatrices began their work. It was imperative they gave these clients the experience of their life, and they almost pulled it off.

Just as Freddie was about to come for the third time, he called out Mary's name. She, to her cost, instinctively answered. Could their downfall have been any simpler?

A loud gasp, silence, then all hell broke loose. Freddie, despite the complete darkness battered and beat the poor girl senseless. He slammed her head repeatedly against the wall; the screams, the feral grunting and the crunch of bone would live with Stella forever. There was nothing the elder brother or she could do to stop him. It seemed to be never ending and was the most terrifying experience Stella had ever endured.

Finally the room fell silent. The only sound in the dark

was Freddie's heavy breathing. The evil, sadistic thug was exhausted.

During the whole sickening incident Ronnie Williams stood stock still, not saying a word or moving a muscle. With his hand clamped tightly over Stella's mouth to ensure her silence, he probably saved her life. His brother was psychotic and during one of his episodes he would turn on anyone: mother, father, brother or stranger.

Snarling into Stella's face, Freddie growled his sinister warning, "If you grass, you're dead, just like your mate," and grabbing their belongings, they left.

She had no idea who called the police, possibly one of the neighbours. While Mary was rushed to hospital, fighting for her life, Stella was taken into custody. She was questioned relentlessly for almost twenty-four hours, but maintained Mary had been alone with a client and she had returned home to find her battered, bleeding and near to death.

For weeks Stella was so traumatised she could barely function. She left the apartment only to visit Mary in hospital and returned home to sleep. What was she going to do without her? Mary was the brains behind their set up. Stella knew nothing about life or money. She did know, however, that she was in serious danger. It was only a matter of time before those evil bastards would come back and finish her off.

What was she to do to protect herself, or Mary, if she ever recovered?

Edinburgh Evening News

A young woman was admitted to the Royal Infirmary yesterday with serious head injuries. The police are treating this attack as attempted murder and are appealing for witnesses. The woman's identity will not be released until relatives have been notified.

CHAPTER FIFTEEN

Terms and conditions

"I'm not sure what I'm going to do with her, Jack. You do know she's pregnant?" Stella informed her young friend.

"I guessed," he replied.

"It's going to be at least four months before she can work, and let's face it, she could have the kid, leave, and I get nothing back on my investment. On the other hand, she's a real looker and by God she's got a way with her. She could make a fortune."

"I don't think she's cut out for this life, Stella, but she has nowhere else to go."

"You hope she's not cut out for this life, you mean. And as for having nowhere else to go, that's not really our problem, lad."

"I'm making it mine."

"Jesus, you've not gone soft on this one, have you? Jack, she might look like the Virgin Mary but believe me, she's not. Don't forget she's carrying another man's child. She might not even know who the father is. Forget her, son. You of all people should know better."

"I know, but I can't see her stuck."

"I'll agree to house her on one condition. You stay away from her until she's had the child. If you do, she can bide her time here. But, if I see you hanging around or making a play for her, I'll ship her out. It's for your own good, lad. So do we have a deal?"

As he nodded his head in agreement, Jack knew Stella was just looking out for him, but what she didn't know was how completely infatuated he was with Rosie. He had fallen hook, line and sinker, couldn't get her out of his head. God knows how he was going to keep away, but he would have to.

Rosie was so relieved to know she could stay on in Danube Street until the baby was born. Despite all her bravado, the thought of being on her own as her pregnancy progressed terrified the young girl. She was obliged to help Kitty and Dora with the running of the house in exchange for her board and lodgings, and occasionally she would be expected to work in the salon in a meet and greet capacity. On those few occasions, it amused her at the number of requests for her company she received. This didn't go unnoticed by a few of the old hands.

"You do understand I'm making an exception for you, Rosie? Anyone else in your condition would be asked to leave the minute they began to show." Stella told her.

The Madame had a strict policy on pregnant girls working in the house. It was a definite no-no. As soon as any mother-to-be started to show, she was retired immediately. This was not for any philanthropic reason: a brothel was no place for squalling brats. That's not what her clients came to hear.

"I expect you to carry on assisting Kitty and Dora, helping out as before. However, after the child is born, things will change. You'll be obliged to work out front and I want it understood now that this is a condition of your stay. If you don't fulfil your half of the bargain, believe me, you'll have to leave the city. I'll find you and you will regret it, do you understand?"

Stella's grave expression left Rosie in no doubt that the Missus meant every word.

"I understand. I'll keep my side of the deal," promised the young girl.

CHAPTER SIXTEEN

A child is born

Rosie loved the atmosphere in the house, the continual hustle and bustle, the endless ringing of the doorbell, punters coming and going. Arguments amongst the girls were a regular occurrence; there was never a dull or quiet moment. She was popular with most of the inhabitants, a wizard with hair and make-up, having watched her sisters for years.

"Lend me a hand, Rosie," was a frequent call.

"Do my hair for me," was another.

"Fetch me a drink."

She was never off the go.

There were a few females though, a clique, who had no time for the pregnant interloper, especially Margaret, or Big Mags as she was known. Mags considered herself to be Head Girl, although there was no such position. She was a nasty, vindictive bitch, who preyed on the weaknesses of others; most of the girls were terrified of her. She was a bully who struck out for no reason. Mags had taken an instant dislike to Rosie and, pregnant or not, she became the big woman's current target, never missing an opportunity to belittle or torment her.

Until Rosie's arrival, Mags had thought of Jack as her man. She wouldn't tolerate any of the other women going near him. Anyone caught chatting with Jack would face her wrath. As soon as she met Rosie Big Mags knew instinctively that she had competition. Jack was now lusting after the new girl and she needed to get shot of her, no-one would come between her and handsome Jack.

"A fucking kitchenmaid, if she goes near him again, I'll fucking stab her," the woman threatened. "Hey, Cinderella," she shouted across the kitchen to Rosie. "Here, I've found your glass slipper." She held up a dirty sodden old shoe which had been kicking around the yard since Rosie had arrived. One of the dogs had likely brought it in.

Pushing the young girl down on a chair, Mags, with two of her cohorts held Rosie down, trying to jam her foot into the soaking wet, disgusting footwear, all the while sneering and sniggering at Rosie's predicament.

"Leave her alone, you vicious bugger." Kitty came charging out of the pantry waving a heavy metal pan. "Let her go or I'll break your head. I'm warning you."

The two holding Rosie immediately let her go and backed away from Kitty, but Big Mags held her ground.

"Get away from her. I won't tell you again." Kitty swung the heavy pan catching Mags on the side of her head.

"That was just a warning," the angry little cook shouted at them. "One step closer, madam, just one step and I'll be up those stairs to the missus and you know who she'll believe," Kitty threatened.

"We were only having a laugh," the big woman answered sullenly. "Just a bit of fun."

Mags bent down, nose to nose with Rosie, and whispered her warning, "This isn't finished yet, bitch. She won't always be here to save you."

"Are you alright, dearie?" Kitty helped Rosie up.

"I'm fine, forget it. She's just a bully, and I won't always be pregnant."

"Maybe so, but you are now, so keep away from her. She's a nasty piece of work, that one."

"Why does she hate me so much? I've never done anything to upset her," the young girl questioned her rescuer.

"Look in the mirror, lassie, she's terrified of you."

"Terrified of me?" laughed Rosie. "I don't think so."

"Oh, she's terrified alright. She knows you can take Jack from her, that's why she goes for you every time she sees you."

"Me? Take Jack? Heavens, I've only seen him a couple of times since I got here," Rosie answered.

"That's because he's been warned off you, but don't you go blabbing or you'll get us all in bother," Kitty informed her.

"Who warned him off and why?" asked a baffled Rosie.

"Look, I've said more than I should have so drop it. Just keep away from her."

"You *have* to tell me now, Kitty."

"Hey, I don't have to tell you anything. Just get on with your work and watch your back."

Just as Kitty predicted, it was Mags who made a point of ferreting Rosie out at every opportunity. She made complaint after complaint and there would always be some mishap or drama, which of course, the younger girl was blamed for. Stella was furious with the constant bickering between the two and began to regret her decision to let Rosie stay. The final straw was an accusation from Mags that money had been stolen from her room and the blame landed squarely on Rosie's shoulders. It was only with Kitty's intervention, once again, that she was saved from being turned out. Difficult though it was for Rosie to avoid her enemy, she knew she must till the baby was born. Thankfully Mags had not got off scot-free. She was on a final warning too, so she also had a lot to lose if she continued the vendetta.

Despite Mags' fears, Rosie had barely set eyes on Jack since she'd arrived in Danube Street. He was always on the go, ferrying customers to and fro, or tending the bar in the salon. She was kept equally busy by Kitty, 'idle hands', the older woman would chant any time she caught Rosie having a breather. She missed Handsome Jack, as he was known to the girls. Could he be avoiding her like Kitty implied? Maybe it was the baby. Most men would find it an intolerable situation, but that shouldn't stop them from being friends.

For once, the house was relatively quiet, only a few girls were indoors. Kitty and Dora had gone off down the coast to visit with Kitty's old mother and wouldn't be back till the following day.

Rosie, who was only weeks from her due date, was laboriously changing the bed linen for the evening session. As she made her way downstairs with a large bundle of laundry, she came face to face with her number one enemy.

"Shift, Cinderella," the woman snarled at Rosie, as she squeezed past her, muttering obscenities.

Rosie stood still to let her antagonist past before making her way down the remaining stairs. Suddenly she was propelled forward and, catching her foot on the jumbled sheets, she crashed to the bottom, landing in an awkward heap. Bedroom doors flew open, the inhabitants curious to see what the commotion was.

Big Mags was laughing uproariously and shouted, "Think you can fly, Cinderella? Well, fuck me, you can do everything else in this house." She turned to the girls assembled outside their rooms, "What the fuck are you lot gawking at? She tripped on the sheet but she's fine now. Fuck off and let her be."

"Are you sure she's okay?" asked Izzy, one of the old hands.

"I've said she is. Now fuck off, unless you want to meet with a similar accident."

Aiming a final devastating kick at the immobile Rosie, Mags herded the remaining spectators back to their rooms.

Left on her own, Rosie couldn't move. The racking pains left her breathless and despite her screams, no-one was coming to her assistance. Oh my God, the baby was coming and she knew instinctively there was something wrong.

"Please God, help me," Rosie pleaded. "Help..." she screamed.

Jack had just arrived back, having taken the missus to the station where she was off on one of her mysterious trips. No-one, including him, knew where Stella went, but it wasn't for the want of speculation. As he waited for the kettle to come to the boil, he heard screams. His first thought was that a punter was roughing up one of the girls. He flew upstairs to find Rosie lying in a heap of bloodstained bedding, screaming in pain. He dashed for the phone and called for an ambulance but things were progressing quickly. The baby was coming and Jack had no idea what to do. He knew there were other girls around. Surely one of them must have heard Rosie's yells? Why had no-one come to help? By God, if anything happened to either her or the baby, he'd fucking bray the lot of them. He shouted at the top of his voice, threatening all sorts of retribution, and eventually a door opened and one of the girls, Eleanor, ventured out and wandered along the corridor to see what all the noise was about. Seeing Rosie and the blood, she flew into action.

"Jack, get towels and hot water, we have to deliver this kid now or they're both goners."

The ambulance arrived to the squalls of baby Royce. Jack Hunter was doubly smitten but mother and child weren't out of the woods yet.

CHAPTER SEVENTEEN

Past Times

Stella sat by Mary's bedside day after day, arriving early morning and leaving as the night shift came on. Talking to her, stroking her hair and wiping her face. She often lost track of time and the only people she came in contact with were the medical staff, and the man in the next cubicle, sitting patiently at his mother's bedside. He had been there since the day Mary was admitted and he was still holding vigil.

"How is she this morning, any change?"

"No, just the same, thanks for asking. And your mother?"

"Like Mary, just the same, but I don't think she'll last much longer."

"Oh dear," Stella didn't know what else to say to the dutiful son.

"Can I get you a drink?"

"If it's not too much trouble," Stella smiled.

"I'll bring you some tea and you never know, it might just be drinkable."

Half an hour later the man, who had introduced himself as Marcus Kramer, returned with two steaming cups of hospital tea and some gingernuts. When he handed the packet to Stella she collapsed in a flood of tears. Who would have guessed this small act of kindness would have her blurt out their tragic story, opening floodgates of pent up emotions she had been bottling up since the incident occurred?

"I shouldn't be telling you any of this," the girl confessed once her sobbing had abated. "I could be putting you in real danger if these two characters discover I've confided in anyone. They'll definitely come after me and more than likely you also."

"Don't worry about me. I'm more than able to stand up to those two."

"You know them?" Stella was aghast.

"Let's just say, I know of them. I'm a lawyer and in my profession you come across a lot of shady characters. Finish your tea, I'll check on Mother, then we'll talk."

Marcus had come across the Williams Brothers in the past and it appeared he despised them almost as much as she did. He wasn't inclined to expand on his reasons but assured Stella he would help.

When Stella arrived at the hospital the following morning, the cubicle which had been occupied by Mrs Elizabeth Kramer was empty. The old lady had passed away during the night, no doubt taking her son's promise to help with her.

Stella realised how comforting Marcus's presence had been to her. It had helped, knowing that through the partition wall was someone sharing her burden. But his vigil was now over, Marcus had gone back to his life to grieve with family and friends.

Stella had never felt so alone; she was in the depths of despair. According to the medical staff, Mary's condition was deteriorating and the prognosis was not good. It seemed unlikely she would regain consciousness and if she did, the doctors were of the opinion she had suffered such severe brain damage that there would be little chance of a full recovery. They spoke of switching off the life-support machine, but Stella could not contemplate such a decision. Back home, armed with a bottle of gin and a supply of pills acquired from the drugs trolley, this appeared to be the only answer.

As Stella drifted in and out of an alcohol-induced sleep she vaguely heard hammering on her front door and someone calling her name. Fortunately, unaccustomed to hard liquor, she had vomited up most of the gin, along with the contents of her stomach.

"What are *you* doing here?" Stella asked, slurring her words.

"It's just as well I am," answered her saviour.

"I thought it was them coming to get me, I was so scared," Stella moaned, flopping down on the sofa.

"They won't be becoming after you, not when I've finished with them."

"How did you know where I lived?" Stella asked, still befuddled.

"I told you. In my profession I come across a lot of shady individuals. That and a decent wedge usually gets me the information I want." Marcus grinned as he filled the young woman full of black coffee. "Thank goodness you're not an efficient thief," he laughed, pointing to the remainder of the pills that Stella had not consumed.

"Antibiotics? What in God's name are they?"

"They're used to treat infections. You're probably healthier now than you've ever been in your life," he smiled. "Seriously though, no matter what happens in the future, I want you to promise me you won't pull a stunt like this ever again."

"I promise," Stella murmured, quite ashamed. Here before her was this man who'd helped his mother desperately fight to stay alive and she, wantonly, had just tried to take hers.

The two worked most evenings for weeks, going over and over the events of the past few months.

"Why do you need to know about other clients, and how we worked?" Stella questioned her new friend. "Surely that's only going to infuriate them even more?"

"I want to know everything about your setup so that when we go face to face there are no nasty surprises."

"Face to face? You have to be kidding! There's no way I'm going anywhere near either of them. I wouldn't get out the room alive. Marcus, you've no idea how sadistic those two are."

"Trust me, I do, but you've nothing to worry about. I'll take care of you."

"No disrespect, but you wouldn't stand a snowball's chance in hell against them."

"You're probably right, but as my poor, deceased mother would say, 'There's more than one way to skin a cat,' and believe me, I've got an exceedingly sharp knife, metaphorically-speaking."

"For a moment I thought you meant you were going to challenge them."

"Oh, I am my dear, we both are. But in their pockets, where it hurts the most."

"I'm not sure I'm up to this."

"If you can have grown men believe you're a Russian dominatrix and pay vast amounts of money for the pleasure, you can face up to the Williams brothers with me as your lawyer beside you."

"I can't." Stella all but stamped her foot.

"You can and you will. Haven't you just told me the doctors are talking about turning off Mary's life-support?"

"I can't let them do that. I have to give her every chance. You hear about people all the time being in comas for years, then sitting up in bed and talking."

"Well, if you want that for Mary you better toughen up, girl, because everything depends on you."

"What does?" Stella asked.

"You have to convince the Williams brothers that they should be more afraid of you, not the other way around."

"Why on earth would they be afraid of me? That's ridiculous."

"The police are still looking for the person or persons who carried out the assault on Mary. So, over the next couple of days, I'm going to stir things up at police headquarters, just to make sure that the case is still being fully investigated."

"Surely that will definitely make them come after me?" she asked fearfully.

"I'm going to drop some names into certain ears, anonymously of course. And yes, it will make them come after you, but we'll be prepared."

"Why can't we just let things lie? Then hopefully they'll leave me alone."

"Listen to me, with the Williams' of this world you have to fight fire with fire. You need to always have the upper hand and the way to do that is to have something on them. Call it blackmail, whatever, but your threat has to be bigger than their threat."

"What have we got to threaten them with?"

"We have your signed statement as to what actually took place that night. A full description of what occurred, and an article of bloodstained clothing which can be traced back to Freddie Williams."

"But I made a statement saying I saw nothing, that I came back to find her lying in a pool of blood."

"You were threatened, they terrorised you. Witnesses change their statements all the time."

"But a bloodstained article of clothing? I don't have anything belonging to either of them."

"They don't know that. On the night in question, believe me, they would be so anxious to get rid of anything incriminating they wouldn't remember what happened to a tie, for instance."

"But they didn't leave anything."

"Again, they don't know that."

"Marcus, they would catch up with me and shoot me."

"True, they would, if that's all we had on them. This is where we box clever. Your statement will be put in a safety deposit box and copies held by two other law firms, one in London and one in Glasgow, with instructions that if anything untoward happens to us, these documents will be forwarded directly to the appropriate authorities."

"Do you really think that would frighten them?"

"Yes, I do. Now what do we want for your silence? First of all, Mary will be moved to a private nursing facility, for which they'll foot the bill."

"They'll never agree to that. Can't we just leave it at the statement?"

"No. The more we demand the more they'll take us seriously. How do you feel about running a gentleman's club?"

"A what?"

"A gentleman's club. The brothers own property all over town, but there is a place in Danube Street I particularly want."

"Why do you want that one?"

"I have my reasons."

"For God's sake, why would they hand over property and pay for Mary's care? It's not credible. I'm telling you, we'd simply vanish without a trace."

"Then we have to convince them that if we did, they would each be looking at a life sentence."

"I still think you're mad to even consider taking them on."

"Maybe so, but as I see it, you have a choice. Either you man up and fight for Mary's future, and your own for that matter, or you sit here just waiting for her to die and them to come knocking."

"But if I can't carry it off, we'll both be in the firing line."

"I'm willing to take that chance. For God's sake lassie, give yourself a shake, get angry. Don't you want to get even with them? Did Mary really deserve to end up like she is?"

"No. So when do you want to do this?"

"Tomorrow. Tomorrow we enter the lion's den."

CHAPTER EIGHTEEN

Last Rites

"We should try to contact her family," said Stella. She and Jack had been at the young mother's bedside for hours.

Rosie had been admitted to hospital, together with her newborn baby girl. The child seemed fine despite her traumatic entry to the world, but Rosie's condition was critical and deteriorating rapidly. Her blood pressure was dangerously low and the doctors had been unable to stem the haemorrhaging.

"I wouldn't know where to begin, Stella. I don't know much about her, and, as you well know, most of the girls invent a new identity. By the time they get to us they don't want to be found. Can we get Marcus on to it? Maybe he could trace her family?" said Jack.

"We had better make it quick. She doesn't look like she's long for this world, son."

"Oh God, Stella, don't say that. I don't know what I'll do if anything happens to her."

"Jesus, Jack, I thought you'd gotten over her months ago," said an exasperated Stella.

"No, I just stayed away from her, which is exactly what you told me to do," Jack replied sheepishly.

"Oh, son, I think you are going to have your heart broken."

"It's that bitch Mags' fault. Izzy told me she deliberately pushed her down the stairs. I'll bloody well swing for her, so I will."

"Forget her for the moment, Mags will keep. Let's concentrate on helping this poor girl. Maybe I should call a priest? I remember her talking about mortal sins when I suggested Ma Higgins."

"I've no idea, but it couldn't do any harm. I really wish we could contact her family, Stella. No matter the reason she left home, I'm sure they'd want to be with her."

"You're right. The best person in a situation like this is Marcus. He has a network of contacts and if anyone can help, it's him."

A distraught Jack left the hospital and headed for Marcus Kramer's office, in the hope the lawyer could obtain the information he and Stella thought would flush out Rosie's family.

Seated in the lawyers' impressive office, Jack told the man everything he knew about Rosie, which was, in essence, very little.

"We need your help, sir. It doesn't look like she's going to make it and her family should be with her at this time. There's also the baby to consider."

"Mmm..." the lawyer pondered. "Royce is an unusual name in these parts, and if I was trying to cover my tracks I would certainly pick something less memorable," he reasoned. "So, I think we can safely assume it's her real name."

"That makes sense," Jack agreed.

"Let's try the obvious, the telephone directory. There are five people by the name of Royce listed. Two in the city, one, a doctor in North Berwick, another in Fife, and the last, a family bakery business in Kirkleven," he said as he began dialling.

"Hello, who am I speaking with?" Marcus asked the voice on the other end of the line.

"Iris Royce, how can I help you?" She had picked up the phone, assuming the call was from a supplier or one of the outlying farms wishing to place an order.

"Good morning, Miss Royce. My name is Marcus Kramer, of Kramer and Bourne WS. I'm trying to trace the family of a

Miss Rosie Royce."

"I have a young sister called Rosie. What's happened? Why are you trying to trace us?"

"I need to speak to one of your parents please."

"There's only my father and he's not available." Iris saw no reason to divulge information concerning their mother. And no matter the reason for the call, she wasn't going to wake her father and face his wrath.

"I have to speak with him, Miss Royce, it's of the utmost urgency. In fact, a matter of life and death. Can you please wake him and get him to call me immediately?" He gave her the firm's telephone number and he and Jack waited for the return call.

"Good morning, Mr Royce, thank you for returning my call promptly. I have to establish I'm speaking to the correct person."

"You are. Now what's this all about?" barked the baker, annoyed at having been wakened out of his sleep.

"All in good time. Your name is James Royce, correct?"

"Yes," replied the baker.

"And you are the father of Rosie Royce?"

"No, I have two daughters, Iris and Violet, no Rosie."

"I'm sorry. Your eldest daughter led me to believe she had a sister, Rosie."

"No, just the two," the baker insisted.

"Surely you have three, Mr Royce? I'm calling about the youngest, Rosie."

"I don't know who you're talking about," the baker insisted.

"Mr Royce, this poor girl is lying critically ill in hospital and I'm sorry to inform you, she is not expected to recover."

"This is of no interest to me. Now, if you'll excuse me, I need to catch up on my sleep."

"I don't think you understand the gravity of the situation."

"Oh, I understand perfectly, but as I have already told you, I have only two daughters so whoever is in hospital is nothing to do with me." The baker slammed down the receiver.

"What was that about, Dad?" Iris asked cautiously. "It sounded serious."

"None of your business," he snapped, marching back upstairs to bed.

The two sisters looked at each other. "Something terrible has happened to Rosie," said Violet.

"For God's sake, leave it be. You know how bad he gets if you cross him," Iris pleaded with her sister.

"It's bad whether we cross him or not, and I for one have had enough. Iris, this is just a bloody existence. If we left, what the hell would he do?   He can't run the shop without us."

"You're right, but what can we do?"

"We can phone that solicitor back for a start, and find out what's wrong."

Jack had already made his way back to the hospital by the time Iris got through to Marcus.

"No joy, Stella. Marcus contacted the father, but he doesn't want to know. So it looks like it's up to us to see her on her way," said Jack with a lump in his throat and tears glistening in his eyes.

Stella's heart went out to the young man. Situations and emotions like these were the reason she kept her guard up, refusing to get too close to people. She was already regretting having got involved in this drama and had she known the extent of how the lad felt, she would certainly have stayed away. But she was here and hard-hearted though she could be, she couldn't leave Jack to face this on his own. It was at times like these Stella appreciated her own situation and the choice she had made, all those years ago.

"I had the hospital priest come and give her the Last Rites while you were away. If she's not Catholic, I don't think St.

Peter will stop her getting in for impersonating one," Stella said, trying her best to lighten his load.

"Should we bring the child in?" Jack asked looking down at the pale, still, sleeping girl. "She may as well spend some time with her mother. She's in God's hands now."

CHAPTER NINETEEN

Revolt

"The shop's closed, Dad, and whether you approve or not, we're going to visit Rosie in hospital," a defiant Violet said as she faced up to her father.

"We've spoken to Mr Kramer, the solicitor. He's explained what's happened and we're going to see her before it's too late," said Iris, clinging to her sister for support. "Won't you please come with us? According to him, she's really bad and might not make it."

"She's no daughter of mine, and if you two leave this house today, don't bother coming back. You'll be as dead to me as she is," roared their furious father.

"Listen, you old goat. I've just about had enough," challenged his eldest daughter, talking back to him for the first time. Looking him straight in the eye she threatened, "Think very carefully before making another grand gesture and disowning what's left of your family. If you kick us out, you'll be the one who suffers. Tell me, who's going to look after the shop and cook and clean for you?" an indignant Iris demanded. "You should be down on your bended knees begging us to stay. You wouldn't last five minutes, left on your own."

The baker was stunned at the nerve of his daughter, but he knew full well she was right, he wouldn't manage without them.

Nevertheless, he was a stubborn man who wouldn't give in gracefully. "Do what the hell you want. You will anyway."

"Please, Dad, come with us. You might not get another chance, *and* you have a granddaughter."

Violet knew the moment she saw the expression on her father's face that she'd said the wrong thing.

The baker had stopped abruptly, halfway up the stairs. "She's no daughter of mine, and as for the child, I want nothing to do with it."

The sisters were extremely quiet on the journey into the capital. They may have won the first battle, but both knew their father would not take this revolt lying down. For the moment, however, they had more to worry about than a cantankerous old devil determined not to lose face. Each prayed they would reach their sister's bedside before it was too late.

"My God, Violet, she's so frail," Iris exclaimed, looking down at the inert form of their young sister.

"Are you sure she's breathing?" Violet asked.

There had been no love lost between Violet and Rosie. Violet had always complained that the youngest was the favourite and didn't do her fair share of chores, but, as she watched Rosie hovering between life and death, all past disagreements were forgotten.

"I think so," replied the other as a tall, striking woman entered the room.

"You must be Rosie's sisters," the woman spoke in an extremely cultured voice.

"Yes, I'm Iris and this is Violet. You must be Stella?"

"I am, and I'm pleased to tell you there's been a slight improvement but she's not out of the woods yet. The doctor will be here shortly. He's anxious to get some background details on Rosie, which of course Jack and I couldn't provide."

"Jack, who's Jack?" asked Violet.

"Jack Hunter, he works for me. It was Jack who helped Rosie when she first arrived in town. He's been a good friend to your sister. Neither she nor the baby would be here if it wasn't for him."

The sisters glanced at one another. Surely she hadn't got involved with someone else? thought Iris. But knowing Rosie they shouldn't be surprised. The youngest Royce girl could twist most males round her little finger and it sounded like she'd ensnared this Jack, whoever he was.

"Speak of the devil," said Stella as a tall, devastatingly handsome, young man entered the hospital room.

Violet felt her stomach flip. Now *he* was something else.

"Well, well, who do we have here?" he asked.

"Rosie's sisters, Jack. They contacted Marcus after you left. She's in good hands now, so we can get back to Danube Street and sort things out." Stella was determined to extricate Jack from the misguided responsibility the lad appeared to have shouldered.

Sisters? Well, no-one could deny the family resemblance, Jack thought to himself. Each was as stunning as the other.

"I've told the girls the doctor is keen to speak with them concerning Rosie's medical background, so we should leave them to get on." Stella tried edging Jack towards the door. This damned girl was nothing to them and the sooner she got him out of there the better. But Rosie's saviour was not to be budged.

"I'll take you to the house," Jack told Stella. "Then I'll come back here for a bit."

"There's no need for that, Jack. The girls might not want you hanging around. No, we'll leave Rosie in their hands. Are you forgetting I have a business to run?" The older woman nodded to the two sisters as she made for the door.

"I'll be back in an hour or so. Here's our number if there's any change. Unless, like Stella says, you'd rather I stayed away?" the young man said, handing a slip of paper to the eldest sister.

"Please do come back, Mr Hunter." Violet couldn't take her eyes off this hunk. There was no denying Rosie could certainly pick them, the middle sister thought with a twinge of jealousy.

"Miss Royce?" enquired the doctor.

"Yes."

"The nurse will take you to see the child, and then bring you both back to speak with me."

They were so shocked at seeing Rosie, they had almost forgotten about the child.

Looking into the cot, Violet gave a sharp intake of breath. There was no denying the father was the handsome GI. Lord above, here was a package of trouble if ever there was one.

CHAPTER TWENTY

Retribution

"Get your belongings and get out of this house before I lose it all together and do something I've never done in my life," Jack Hunter, on the verge of lifting his fist to her, roared at Big Mags.

"I never touched her Jack, she slipped, honest, she slipped. Ask any of the girls. Okay, I didn't go to help her, but neither did anyone else, they all hate her."

"Did you not hear what I said? Get your belongings and get out!"

"What about us?" Mags begged him.

"What us? There never was an 'us'." sneered Jack.

"Is that so?" she retaliated. "Well, you're not the boss of me. There's only one person who can sack me, Jack Hunter, and it's not you."

"Oh, but he can," challenged Stella entering the salon. "And he has my blessing, so do what Jack says, get your stuff and get out. If anyone else has a problem, they can pack up and get out too." She turned to Big Mags, "You're lucky you're not up on a murder charge and believe me, that could still happen."

"Stella, please, it was an accident. Honest, I never touched her." Mags knew her pleading was falling on deaf ears. "Well, you can give Miss Cinderella a message from me, if she *does* recover, and I hope to hell she doesn't, tell her I'll get her for this, mark my words. She better look over her shoulder from now on."

Half an hour later, laden with her possessions, Mags left Danube Street. The front door rattled off its hinges as she slammed it behind her. But this door had seen far worse departures.

"I'm telling you, Freddie, I'll get them back if it's the last fucking thing I ever do. A bloody scullery maid? It's like something out of a Catherine Cookson novel. Me, Head Girl, the biggest earner in the house, and I get dumped for fucking Cinderella."

"Here, have another drink, Mags. Don't worry, their loss is my gain," comforted the biggest psycho in Edinburgh.

It had been the first place Mags headed for, after her ignominious departure from Danube Street: the Williams' gaff. She was well aware it wasn't in the same league as her previous house, but it was a job and she wouldn't have to put up with Stella's stupid fucking rules. The big man seemed pleased enough to see her. Helping herself to another large gin, Mags continued to bemoan her current situation.

"So, can I get a start here Freddie? I'm a good worker and the punters like me. I'm sure when word gets around, most of my regulars will follow me," she bragged.

"No problem, but I've already got a Head Girl who won't take kindly to you poking your snout in."

"Look, I'm not out to stand on anybody's toes. The only thing I'm interested in is earning a decent wedge and getting even with those two – her and that fucking ponce, Jack Hunter. He has the nerve to say the kid's not his. Why the fuck would he be so protective if it wasn't? He doesn't have the guts to own up. The bastard was carrying on with her behind my back."

"Forget about them. I'll take care of everything. We'll sort them out together. Nobody insults my girls and gets away with it."

Mags, far too drunk to appreciate Freddie's assurance, had by now forgotten any part she had played in Rosie's accident. She, Mags, was now the innocent victim.

Truthfully, Freddie Williams couldn't give a shit about Mags or her situation, but he was still eager, even after all these years, to have something over Stella Gold, no matter how trivial. His bagging Stella's Head Girl was one in the eye for her, no matter what the circumstances. He pronounced Mags could start right now by giving him a freebie.

Was this really a good move? Mags asked herself. But what choice did she have? There was definitely no going back to Danube Street, that bitch had certainly queered her pitch. She'd pay her back that's for sure. In fact, there was already a germ of a plan hatching. She'd shop the fucker, get the kid taken off her. But how, exactly? Of course. She'd shop her to the Welfare and better still, she'd get some of her pals to do the same.

Mags was feeling better already, nobody shit on her and got away with it. Cinderella's days were numbered. Woe betide her when Mags caught up with her, and she would, Edinburgh wasn't that big.

CHAPTER TWENTY-ONE

Miss Information

"Good afternoon again, ladies," Dr Thomson greeted Iris and Violet. "As I explained earlier, I'm in charge of your sister's case. I need a few details about Rosie, so if you wouldn't mind…" he said as he ushered them into a small office.

"It's all quite straightforward. First of all, I need the usual background information. Full name, address and date of birth."

Without thinking Iris tripped off the relevant details.

"The address we have on the admission form is different to the one you've just given," stated the doctor.

"That's our home address. The other, I presume, is Rosie's place of work," Iris noticed the expression on the doctor's face and his raised eyebrow.

"Her workplace? What does your sister do for a living?"

"Housekeeping, I think. She wouldn't be fit for much more, why?"

"It's a very well-known address."

This information meant nothing to the two out-of-towners.

"Now, date of birth. Think again. The date you've given makes your sister fourteen not seventeen, as we were led to believe. This certainly complicates things."

Again, the expression on the doctor's face alarmed Iris.

"Can I have the name and address of her G.P.?"

"It's Dr McIntosh, 3 High Street, Kirkleven."

"Is he aware of your sister's condition?"

"No, our father sent her away before anyone found out. It's a small village and he thought it would be for the best."

"What about the child's father, is he in the picture?"

"We don't think so. To be honest, we don't know much about Rosie's situation."

"Mm, do you think your parents will assume responsibility for her and the child?"

"It's only our father at home, he and our mother separated recently. He was extremely angry when he discovered Rosie's condition."

"What about your mother?"

"We've no idea where she is, we haven't heard from her, but surely this can wait? We're more concerned whether our sister will pull through or not," Violet confronted the doctor. "What are Rosie's chances, how serious is it? The people looking after her led us to believe she might not make it through the night, is that still the case?"

"Her condition has improved marginally, but the next twenty-four hours are critical. I certainly wouldn't leave the hospital during this time."

"Can we ask a favour?" Iris asked. "Could you delay reporting this to the authorities until we see how things go and give us a chance to speak to our father?"

"I'll hold off until Monday morning. I can't promise anything more. Sit with your sister and pray, that's the best chance she has for now."

"Are you off your head? Do you really think we can persuade that stubborn old goat to come here?" Violet asked her sister.

"Well, we have to try. Maybe if he thinks the authorities are going to be involved he'll swallow his pride."

"I wouldn't count on it."

"You do know they'll take the child from her and put it into care if we can't persuade him?" Iris said with a catch in her throat. "Surely, he won't let that happen, not once he's seen her?"

"Like I said, don't count on it."

CHAPTER TWENTY-TWO

Face to Face

As Marcus pulled up alongside the Unicorn Bar, the brothers' headquarters, a gut-wrenching fear gripped Stella at the mere thought of facing these two men.

"I can't do this, Marcus. I just can't face them." Stella was rigid with terror and on the point of throwing up.

"Here, have a swig of this," he said as he handed the girl a silver hip flask. "You don't have to say or do anything. I'll do all the talking. Just get through the next half hour and we'll be home and dry."

Stumbling out of the car and clutching on to the lawyer, Stella set foot on enemy territory for the first time in months.

"What the fuck is she doing here?" Freddie Williams bellowed at his brother. "I thought it was just the Nancy-boy who wanted a meet? You never said anything about that fucking slag coming with him."

"I didn't know myself." Ronnie spoke quietly to placate his brother. He was more than a touch surprised to see Stella walk into the pub with Kramer. Dressed to the nines and nose in the air, she was a force to be reckoned with, or so he thought. "This should be interesting. Hear them out, and keep schtum. For Christ's sake, don't go jumping in at the deep end like you usually do."

Freddie snorted in anger at being told to keep quiet. He knew Ronnie was right, but it stuck in his gullet to have this dirty slut in the same room as him, breathing the same air. He could feel the rage building.

"Marcus, Stella, have a seat." Ronnie Williams on the other hand was charm personified. "Can I offer you a drink?"

Both visitors declined.

"So, to what do we owe this pleasure?" He smiled as if they were old friends taking tea together.

"My client, Miss Gold, has requested that I act on both her and Miss Mary Jenkins' behalf in relation to a claim for compensation and criminal damages. This relates to an incident involving yourself and Mr Freddie Williams at an address in St Colme Street, Edinburgh on the 20th of April this year." The lawyer presented their case to the two men without flinching, despite the fact that Freddie was now prowling round the room, toying with a flick knife.

Still smiling, Ronnie faced Stella. "Damages, Miss Gold? I have no recollection of any situation where my brother or myself would be involved in any incident which could possibly result in damages being awarded."

"Please direct your questions through me, Mr Williams. The incident I am referring to remains the subject of an ongoing police enquiry. However, unusual though it might be, I petitioned the court to grant me Power of Attorney on behalf of Miss Mary Jenkins. Who is, I'm sure you are aware, currently a patient in the Royal Infirmary. The woman in question is in a coma and unable to defend herself."

"I was always under the assumption that in this country a man was innocent until proved guilty," counteracted Ronnie.

"You're right, of course, but allegations in the right ear will definitely shift police investigations up a gear and bring you both back under the spotlight."

Stella had not made eye contact or spoken with either man during Marcus and Ronnie's debate.

"Let me put you in the picture, Mr Williams. Miss Gold has admitted to having lied about the events on the evening in question. She has now made a full and frank statement as to how Miss Jenkins sustained her injuries and admitted her previous account was made under duress. In other words, she was threatened that if she told the truth she would receive the same treatment. Corroborating this information was the fact that your fingerprints were found on several pieces of equipment, including a metal bar thought to be the prime weapon. We also have in our possession an article of clothing we believe to belong to Mr Freddie Williams, which has traces of the victim's blood on it."

Ronnie Williams was no longer smiling and his brother looked like he was about to explode.

"Calm down Freddie," Ronnie addressed his younger brother. "Mr Kramer, I think you have been watching too many films. It's her word against ours. Our fingerprints may well be on the premises, neither of us have denied being in the apartment. As for a blood-stained article of clothing, that's absolute nonsense. Do you think either of us would be so stupid?"

"The room was in total darkness. Can you be sure, Mr Williams? Would you be willing to take that chance? What if you overlooked something?"

Turning to Freddie, Marcus asked, "What about you? Are you willing to take that chance? If convicted, as things stand, you are looking at ten to fifteen years. If the victim dies, it will be life."

Freddie Williams could contain himself no longer and he lunged, grabbing the lawyer by the throat and dragging him across the desk, knife poised.

The explosion stopped all three men in their tracks.

Stella Gold stood facing the brothers, holding a smoking gun. "The next time it won't be a warning. Carry on, Marcus, and let's get out of this vermin's nest as quickly as possible."

Marcus Kramer was almost as shocked as the brothers but knew that Stella had only bought them a little more time. "As you can see, my client is not playing games, gentlemen. If any harm befalls us, copies of Stella's statement, which are being held with reputable law firms in both Glasgow and London, will be sent to the appropriate authorities. The date, time and place of our meeting today has also been lodged with the same two firms. If we fail to report back by a specific time, the documents will be released."

"You seem to have this pretty well covered, Mr Kramer. What exactly is it going to cost us?"

"My clients have two conditions which are non-negotiable, and both must be met in full or the deal is null and void."

"Get on with it," Ronnie snarled.

"The cost of maintaining Miss Jenkins' nursing care, in a place of our choosing, will be met by you."

"And?"

"In compensation for the trauma and stress experienced by Miss Gold during and since the incident, a property, namely, 17 Danube Street, owned by you, will be signed over to her. The title deeds of this property will be held by one of the aforementioned law firms for safe keeping."

"And should we decline your offer?" asked Ronnie.

"You won't," snapped Stella, with the gun in full view.

Removing a sheaf of paper from his attaché case, Marcus indicated that both brothers sign the documents.

"I'll finalize the legalities within the next forty-eight hours and as long as the agreement is not broken, you won't hear from us again."

Freddie threw the knife with such force, it lodged firmly in the door panel, narrowly missing Stella.

"I can guarantee we'll come across each other again." he snarled menacingly.

"Where the fuck did you get that gun from?" the lawyer exploded when they were back in the safety of the car.

"Thank God I did have it or you would be meeting your maker," Stella replied shakily.

"I almost passed out."

"I know, I was watching. But more to the point, so did they. C'mon, let's get the hell away from here before they have second thoughts."

"You didn't answer my question, where did you get the gun?"

"You're not the only one with shady connections, or able to dispense a hefty wedge to get what you want."

"Touché. The worst is over, Stella. You don't have to come in contact with either of them again. I'll deal with them from now on," Marcus assured her.

CHAPTER TWENTY-THREE

First Impressions Count

Thinking back over the years, Stella recollected her first impression of Danube Street. To say she was shocked and disappointed at the huge mausoleum was an understatement. Unlike the other properties on the street, number 17 looked as if it was ready to collapse at any minute. She couldn't understand Marcus' interest in the place. The stonework was in need of immediate attention and the general air of decay and neglect were certainly not up to the standards she would have expected from Marcus Kramer.

"What a dump!" she'd exclaimed. "You can't possibly want to be associated with this? I honestly don't know what to make of the place." Marcus' companion was stuck for words.

"What were you expecting, Holyrood Palace?" he joked.

"No, not quite, but not something that looked like it wasn't worth one of Hitler's bombs."

"Oh, ye of little faith. This, my dear Stella, when we are finished, will be the most sought after Gentlemen's Club that Edinburgh has ever seen."

"Marcus you're completely delusional, the place needs pulling down. Look at it."

"True, but you look around, look at the other properties. Trust me, this is class. This place will draw money, real money, not the ten bob whores that service the place just now."

"It'll cost a fortune just to make it wind and watertight." Stella looked up at the roof.

"It will cost a bit, but believe me it'll be worth it."

Just then a face appeared at a grimy window.

"We're closed, mate. You'll have to come back later when the new governor arrives."

"He's here. Open the door please."

The huge door, with chipped paintwork and a brass number plate which had not, like the windows, been cleaned in years, swung open to reveal a tiny, bird-like creature of an indiscriminate age, wearing a grubby kimono. Their first impression of the old brass was less than favourable to say the least.

"Hi mister, I'm Kitty. The rest of the girls took off yesterday when the boss told us the place was closing down. They've all gone to other houses."

"No problem, but what are you doing here?" Marcus asked.

"I fell asleep and when I woke, the place was empty. I'm just going to get my stuff and then I'll be out of your way," the cheery soul quipped.

"Before you go, would you mind showing us round?" Stella asked.

"We're fine, Stella, I know my way round," Marcus interrupted.

"Really?" Kitty cocked an eyebrow at Marcus. "Most husbands wouldn't admit to even knowing the place existed, never mind saying they knew their way about."

"Is that so? Well, I'm not most husbands," Marcus retorted.

"It'll save time and Kitty can point out the things we may overlook."

"Believe me, I know this house like the back of my hand, but it's years since I've been here, so maybe you're right."

"It'll cost you," piped up the woman.

"Of course it will. How about a fiver for your time?"

"Make it a tenner and you've got a deal."

Evidence of the house's former glory was severely lacking. The inside was as dreadful as the exterior and Stella couldn't help thinking he'd lumbered himself with a money pit. However, Marcus seemed not to be fazed in the slightest. The whole house was a shambles; each room seemed filthier and more decrepit than the one before. There were unmade beds, the floors were strewn with dirty clothes and the salon was beyond belief. How anyone would pay to enter these portals was astounding.

"Could do with a run round with a hoover," joked the ex-resident.

"I've seen all I need to," Marcus said as he handed the ten pound note over to Kitty.

"Where will you go?" Stella asked the chirpy wee soul.

"Oh, I'm fine. I've got a place along Rose Street."

"Thanks for your help, Kitty, and good luck."

"Good luck to you to miss. Can I ask what you're going to do with the place? Are you and your husband going to live here?"

"No," laughed Stella. "Marcus isn't my husband, we're business partners. We're going to open a gentleman's club," she answered.

"Sorry, I just thought…" stammered Kitty.

"Nothing to be sorry about, how were you to know? Well, I hope things work out for you."

"You too, miss, and you never know, maybe I'll come and see you when you open." Kitty ran upstairs to collect her few belongings. "Good luck and as I said, I hope it works out for you."

"So do I," answered Stella. "So do I."

Over dinner that evening, in the magnificent Grill Room of the George Hotel, Marcus outlined his extensive plans for Danube Street.

"Take a look around, Stella, I want to create surroundings that will surpass this place. It's of the utmost importance that we don't let anyone get wind of what we are proposing to do with the property. If pushed, we're turning it into a hotel or guest house and you are the proprietor."

"Okay, that seems feasible," agreed Stella.

"And I can have no connection whatsoever with the place. As far as anyone is concerned, I'm just your lawyer. The title deeds are in the name of Stella Gold."

"It's weird, Marcus, I feel as if Agnes McLeod never existed. I don't think of myself as anyone other than Stella Gold, even when I'm with Mary. She seems to have settled into the new place, by the way. I'm going to visit her at the weekend."

"That must be a load off your mind, knowing she is being well cared for."

"Not really. I keep waiting for the bubble to burst. The Williams boys rolled over far too easily. They put up virtually no fight, and trust me, that is so out of character for them."

"Don't go looking for problems, we'll deal with them when they arise," Marcus frowned at the thought. "The main problem we have with the renovations is who we get to oversee the work. Not only do I not want to be seen around the place, I simply don't have the time."

"I'll do it," said Stella.

"You? Don't be ridiculous, what do you know about building work?" Marcus laughed out loud.

"Exactly the same as I knew about the sex trade. Nothing, but the builders don't have to know that." Stella stared defiantly at him across the table.

"That was a bit different."

"How was it different? Hopefully nobody's going to be facing a smoking pistol," Stella replied sarcastically. "Well, not unless some bugger is trying to steal from us. Think about it. It makes sense, Marcus. I can't stay in that apartment a minute longer, so I propose we make some accommodation suitable for me to live in on site and take it from there."

"It's far too risky, a woman on her own."

"But running a brothel is a stroll in the park? You know I can handle myself, and if it gets too risky then I'll hire security. Either way I'm moving into Danube Street."

"I'm not happy about this, and I don't think it will work. Builders won't take orders from a woman, and certainly not one who looks like you."

"The builders will take orders from whoever pays their wages, and if not, then there will be no wages."

"You've got it all worked out, haven't you?" Marcus smiled wryly.

"Not really, it just makes sense to me. And if there are problems, surely it would be the owner who would make the decisions? According to you I'm the owner, so, what's the problem?"

"Okay, point taken."

"How is this business going to work, Marcus? It seems very one-sided. You put up all the cash and I reap the benefits. Let's get this straight now so there is no confusion further down the line."

"You're pretty street-savvy for someone from the sticks," the older man smiled at his companion. "I'll bear the cost of all the renovations in the form of a loan. The capital will be paid back over a fixed period. After the expenses have been met the net profit will be split – a straight fifty-fifty."

"What if I change my mind, or get married? Or it doesn't work out, where do I stand?"

"I'll buy you out."

"That's it?" Stella questioned him. "No ties, no hidden agenda? Marcus, I may be from the sticks, as you put it, but I'm not stupid. Nobody gives away that kind of property to a virtual stranger, no matter how much they want revenge. So, tell me now, what is this is all about? What do you want from me in return? If you don't start talking, I'm off. I'll sort out Mary's care somehow, but I want the truth and I want it now."

Nothing could ever have prepared Stella for Marcus Kramer's reply.

CHAPTER TWENTY-FOUR

Mary's Tale

"I'm just going to give you a shot Mary, you won't feel a thing, dear." A kind voice spoke quietly into her ear.

Of course, I won't feel a thing, you stupid cow! I can't feel anything, do anything, or see anything. In fact, I can do nothing except lie here and remember what life used to be like. I can't even do that half the time. Just when I think I'm getting somewhere, along comes another do-gooder who jabs another needle in me and tells me I won't feel a thing. I know, I know, just fuck off and leave me in peace.

It's the talking that's the worst. There's always somebody talking, telling me what they're doing or what they're going to do. If you want to help, tell me when I'm going to feel the sun on my face or the wind in my hair, not a fucking care plan for the next six months.

The nursing home had a policy that staff should chat with patients, no matter their level of consciousness. As Matron said, maybe they can't hear what we say, but it won't do any harm.

She was wrong, it did do harm, it drove this particular patient almost insane. Mary tried and tried to communicate, she tried so hard to move, tried to blink, tried to speak, but nothing. All she could do was listen to the noise, the relentless noise in her head. It was some time before she realised what it was. It was her, she was making the noise; she was screaming, but no-one heard.

Mary had been transferred to this private nursing home on the coast, where hopefully all her needs would be catered for, at a price of course. Not that she or her nearest and dearest would have to worry about that. As far as her few relatives were concerned, her insurance company were footing the bill. If only they knew.

Mary heard the two discussing her care time after time. It seemed they needed the money to keep her alive. Stupid, stupid fools. Why would anyone want to stay alive in this condition? The only one who seemed to understand and communicate with her was 'the man'. She knew him, knew him well, but she couldn't for the life of her remember his name.

"I hope you appreciate it's me who's paying a fucking fortune to keep you in here," Freddie complained.

Who was he? How did she know him? The name was dancing on the tip of her tongue. Think, Mary, think, she told herself.

"We had a visit from your partner-in-crime, threatening to shop us, but I'll take care of her, and that fucking two-bit lawyer. Do they really think they could take on the Williams Brothers and win?"

It's Freddie. Mary's memory clicked into place. Freddie Williams, the love of her life, the only one who seemed to understand what was going on. The only one who could help her end this living nightmare. Freddie would release her, he was her hero.

CHAPTER TWENTY-FIVE

Prodigal Daughters

"Hello, Dad, it's me. Just to let you know Violet and I are staying here overnight."

"Indeed you are not," bellowed the baker. "No respectable girl stays away from home overnight. You'll catch the last bus from St. Andrews Square at ten fifteen. If you are not off it…"

"I know, I'd better not come home. Don't you think that threat's getting a bit old hat, Dad? As I was saying, we are staying the night in the hospital and depending on how things go, we'll be home sometime tomorrow."

"Humph," her father grunted.

"Don't you want to know how Rosie is?" Iris asked.

The line went dead.

"I'll take that as a no," she spoke into the mouthpiece.

The patient had been restless most of the night and on a few occasions the situation didn't look at all hopeful. Her temperature fluctuated dramatically and her breathing was so shallow at times it was difficult to know if she was still with them. Despite her sisters' ministrations, it didn't look like the poor girl would see the dawn. But their prayers were answered. The terrible fever broke around four in the morning and, although exhausted, Rosie had turned the corner. She wasn't, however, out of danger yet. The copious amounts of blood she'd lost needed to be replenished and Rosie had a long way to go to get her health back.

"What do you think she'll do with the baby? Surely she won't want to keep it?" Iris asked her younger sister.

"God knows. I don't see how she can," replied Violet.

"The longer she stays in here, the more chance the welfare will take them both into care. That doctor will only hold off till Monday."

"What doctor?" a feeble voice asked. "What will he hold off till Monday?"

"Oh, you're awake. How do you feel?" Violet asked.

"You gave us quite a fright," added Iris.

"Never mind how I am, how's my baby?"

"The baby's fine, she's in the nursery. It's you we need to concentrate on. You had a close shave, Rosie, it was touch and go for a bit."

"Well, I'm back in the land of the living now and I want to see my baby," demanded a weak Rosie, struggling to leave her bed.

"Don't be ridiculous," insisted Iris. "You're in no fit state. Violet will fetch her."

With the baby at her side, Rosie was more settled and returned to the conversation she'd overheard earlier. "What were you two discussing? Something about a doctor holding off?"

Her sisters exchanged worried glances.

"It was nothing," replied Violet.

"It didn't seem like nothing. Don't lie to me."

"We're worried the welfare will take you and baby into care," her sister explained.

"Why? What reason would they have to take us into care?"

"You're underage and have nowhere to live. Dad isn't likely to welcome you back with open arms."

"I've got a place to stay. And a job," Rosie protested.

"A job?" sniffed Iris. "You call that a job?"

"Listen to me, when I was destitute these people came to my rescue. I didn't see any of you lot check to see if I was surviving."

"We had no idea where you were, and, c'mon, you know as well as I do, you always land on your feet."

"Land on my feet? You call this landing on my feet? For God's sake, Iris, I almost died. As for the welfare, well they can fuck off. No-one's taking my baby anywhere."

"Don't be so sure. We need to get you and the little one out of here as soon as possible."

"She's right, Rosie. Are you sure you can go back to that place?"

"Don't call it that place. Stella promised I can stay on for a bit until I get things sorted. Where else am I going to go? As you say, I can't see me and the baby being welcomed back to the family home."

Just then, Jack entered the room. "Hello, girls. How are mother and daughter faring today?"

"Mother and daughter are doing just fine." Rosie answered.

"Hey, that's great. Kitty and Dora have been busy fixing up one of the storerooms at the top of the house. It looks brilliant, wait till you see it, a proper nursery. All the girls have been helping out." Jack picked up the baby and passed her to Rosie saying, "Is it not about time this bundle had a proper tag? What about carrying on the family tradition with the name of a flower?"

"No, definitely not," all three sisters agreed.

"Okay, something biblical? Ruth or Esther?"

"No, she doesn't look like a Ruth. Or an Esther, for that matter. What about Hope? Let's face it, that's all we've had for the past while."

"Hope? I like it, it suits her. Hope Royce sounds good."

"It does, but it should be Hope Francitti." Tears trickled down Rosie's cheeks.

"Maybe one day," Iris sympathised with her young sister.

"Don't be stupid, there's no chance of that ever happening," said Rosie sorrowfully. "He didn't even know I was pregnant. No, she'll be Hope Royce."

CHAPTER TWENTY-SIX

The Authorities

On the other side of the city, Miss Susan Bridges grimaced at the pile of case notes lying in her In tray. Where to start? The rookie social worker had certainly been thrown in at the deep end. Having recently finished her training full of hope and determination, Susan Bridges had been ready to change the world as a newly appointed welfare officer for the city of Edinburgh.

That was a mere three months ago and disillusionment had well and truly set in. The young woman had realised all too soon, hers was a thankless and virtually impossible task.

Edinburgh was nothing like it had been portrayed. The city is made up of a string of villages, she'd been told. Really? She had certainly not come across anywhere similar to the place she had spent her childhood; the village where her father was the minster and her mother one of two teachers.

No. These so-called villages were mainly a cluster of rat-infested tenements, not fit for human habitation. Where infant mortality was worse than it had been in the Middle Ages and she, together with Miss Frances McIntosh, a fifty-odd-year-old bitter spinster, were responsible for the welfare of a hundred thousand children, housed within the city limits.

Prioritising was the name of the game. Susan skimmed over the morning's new case notes. Two from the police, a mother incarcerated over the weekend, probably for drunk and disorderly conduct and who had left her children on their own. This was moderately urgent. Three youngsters, victims of sexual abuse by members of their family, required urgent attention, and the last, a newborn baby, mother underage, at present in the Royal Infirmary, low priority.

Just after eleven, Susan Bridges received the first of several calls.

"Hello, I want to report a kid in danger."

"With whom am I speaking?" Susan asked the caller, and was not in the least surprised at the response.

"Never mind who I am. You need to get this baby. Its mother lives on Danube Street. She's a brass and she's going to sell the kid as soon as she gets out of hospital."

"Name?" Susan asked her caller.

"I told you already, I'm not giving you my name."

"The mother's name," said an exasperated Susan.

"Royce, Rosie Royce. The father's name is Jack Hunter. He's her pimp and arranging the deal."

"Did you say the mother and child are in hospital. Which one?"

"The Royal, but if she's not there she'll be back on Danube Street."

The line went dead. Mags was pleased as punch. It was time to get the others on the case.

Susan was pretty sure it had been a hoax call. More than likely a couple of working girls who'd fallen out. This was not unusual. In fact, there were at least a couple of such calls a month, but the name was familiar. Flicking back through her In tray, there it was – Royce, an uncommon name. A bit of a coincidence she pondered, reading through the notes once more. A hospital report from the paediatric consultant; baby less than a week old, mother a fourteen-year-old girl, father unknown.

"Hello. Is that welfare?" Effie, Mags' new best buddy, asked. The older prostitute was making the call simply to put a stop to her continuous harping. Effie didn't really hold with shopping anyone to the welfare. She'd had a few run ins with them over the years, but was sick to death of listening to Mags droning on and on.

"Hi, I want to report a kid being sold, to a baby farm."

"Who's speaking?" Susan asked.

"A concerned friend. The one you want is..." There was a pause and Susan could hear whispering. "Eh. Her name is Rosie Royce and she's in the Royal." Again, the line went dead.

Susan pulled out the file on the Royce girl. It had seemed quite straightforward, but now she felt she should dig a bit deeper.

The last call was taken by Miss McIntosh while Susan was speaking to Dr Thomson.

"That case you're working on, I took another call concerning the mother and child while you were on to the doctor."

"What did they say?" she asked her superior.

"Same as the previous. Anonymous and concerned the baby is going to be sold."

"What do you think?"

"Truthfully? A lot of nonsense, but we can't take that chance. If it should turn out to be true, it will be our heads on the block. So, make a few calls and see what you can dig up. What did the doctor have to say?"

"Not much, he was more concerned that the mother is only fourteen and her address is Danube Street."

"Did you say Danube Street? That puts a whole new slant on the case."

"It does? Why?" Susan asked.

"It's the most notorious brothel in Edinburgh."

"So, I should definitely look into this further?"

"Well, if you want to keep your job I would say yes."

The sound of the telephone ringing broke into James Royce's sleep. Pair of lazy good-for-nothings, the father cursed his two daughters as he climbed out of bed to answer the damned machine. He was oblivious to the fact that one of his daughters was dealing with a delivery and the other had a shop full of customers.

"Hello, is that Mr James Royce?"

"Yes."

"Father and guardian of Rose-Elizabeth Royce?"

"No. I am certainly James Royce, but Rose-Elizabeth is no daughter of mine. Who are you?"

"Mr Royce, I am welfare officer Susan Bridges and I'm investigating a case which involves a Miss Royce, currently a patient in the Royal Infirmary, Edinburgh."

"As I've just said, that young woman is no daughter of mine. I've washed my hands of her and I've nothing more to say on the matter."

"Sorry, Mr Royce, but it's not quite as simple as that. You may have washed your hands of the girl, but in the eyes of the law you are still responsible for her and failing to act as such could result in criminal proceedings."

"Don't you threaten me, young woman. She's nothing to me," the baker shouted down the line. "If I have to go to prison, then so be it."

"Mr Royce, calm down. Let's see if we can sort this matter out."

"There's nothing to sort out as far as I'm concerned," he retorted.

"Would you be prepared to sign guardianship over to the department and allow us to assume responsibility for her and the child?"

"With pleasure. I take it I would then be absolved of any legal or parental responsibilities?"

"You would."

"Excellent. How quickly can this be done?"

"As soon as you come to my office and sign the requisite documents."

"It's my day off tomorrow, I'll drive into town first thing."

"Ten o'clock tomorrow then."

"Sorry, Dad, we were both caught up. Who was it?" Iris called from the stairwell.

"No-one important, I've dealt with it. I'm back off to bed. Try not to disturb me again."

CHAPTER TWENTY-SEVEN

No Going Back

"Good morning, Mr Royce, have a seat." Susan Bridges ushered Rosie's father into one of several interview rooms in the auspicious City Chambers.

James had never visited the building before and was somewhat overawed by his surroundings.

"Can I get you some tea, coffee?" the young woman offered.

"No thanks. Let's get this over and done with as quickly as possible."

"As you wish, but this is a big step, Mr Royce. Are you sure you want to go ahead? It's not too late to change your mind. The department would assist you in dealing with Rose-Elizabeth and the baby, without actually taking over guardianship. The last thing we want to see is the break-up of a family."

"I told you categorically on the phone, the girl is no longer a daughter of mine. I want nothing to do with her. I hope this has not been a waste of my time," the baker barked.

"Not at all, Mr Royce, but we have to make sure you're doing the right thing and that you understand what these measures entail. We wouldn't want to be too hasty."

"There's nothing hasty about my decision, missy. The girl brought shame on my family, I want nothing to do with her, is that clear?"

"Yes, quite clear, but as I said, I do have to make you aware of the situation. Once we apply to the court for custody, there is no going back. Maybe when you have had time to consider the situation, you might feel differently?"

"I have not and will not change my mind about the

'situation' as you call it. Now, please can we get on? I have another appointment this morning."

"Very well, Mr Royce. Once you have signed the requisite documents an application will be presented to the Sheriff and Rose-Elizabeth Royce will be, from then onwards, 'A Ward of Court' and, being under the age of sixteen, her child automatically becomes the responsibility of the city also."

"How long will this all take?" James Royce asked curtly.

"I would hope to have everything in place within the next two to three days. We will remove the child as soon as a suitable foster home is available."

Without a backward glance, James Royce left the City Chambers. He had two more calls to make that day and he was already running late. He made his withdrawal at the bank and headed to his last port of call.

Pacing up and down the small shabby room, Maria Royce waited anxiously for her visitor to arrive. Oh, God, what if he'd changed his mind? What if he didn't come? No, he must be going to forgive her. Why else would he have written and arranged to meet? He'd obviously realized he couldn't live without her.

Maria had spent the morning packing her few belongings and making herself ready for his visit, she wanted to look her best for him. She knew that for a woman approaching forty, she was still a stunner.

A loud knock at the door brought her back to earth and with a final glance in the grubby mirror she opened the door to her husband.

"Hello, Maria," James said, looking round the room. "Not exactly the Ritz, is it, my dear? I was under the impression you'd left us for better things."

"I'm so sorry James, so sorry. I can't tell you how much I miss you. God knows what possessed me to leave. I'll make it up to you, I promise," pleaded his desperate wife.

"Make it up to me? How in the name of God do you think you could ever do that?" he said incredulously. "We're way beyond that, Maria. You humiliated me in front of my family, my friends and my neighbours. There is no going back, that's not why I'm here." At that moment he noticed the suitcase. "Going somewhere?" he smirked.

"Please, please, James, take me back with you. I have nothing. I can't even pay the rent this week."

"Well, you should have thought of that when you skipped off with your Yankee fancy man. No, I'm not taking you back, quite the opposite in fact. I want a divorce. I've met someone else," he bluffed.

"I don't believe you. There's not a woman within miles who can hold a candle to me, or make you feel like I did."

"Is that so? Well, let me tell you, lady, if you were the last female on earth I wouldn't touch you with a barge pole." He pulled a sheaf of documents from inside his jacket and demanded, "Here, sign these."

"What are they?" Maria knew what the documents would be.

"They're divorce papers."

"No way," Maria spat at him. "Not a chance. Anyway, we're Catholic and you'd have to get a dispensation from the Pope."

"It doesn't really matter, I can apply to the court. This way would simply have saved time."

Realising her husband was serious, Maria demanded, "It'll cost you five thousand pounds."

"Are you off your bloody head, woman? Where the hell would I get that kind of money?"

"You forget I did the accounts. I know exactly what money you've got stashed away. I want five thousand or no divorce. And remember, it could take several years without my consent."

"Fair enough, I'll wait," James replied as he headed for the door. "I didn't think you would agree but I was in town on business anyway. By the way, aren't you interested in how your daughters are faring? I'm surprised you haven't asked after them, being such a devoted mother."

"I think of them every hour of the day," Maria replied. "Every day I pray for them."

"Well, whoever you're praying to isn't listening. You might be interested to know I've just come from the welfare department. Our youngest, if she is mine, has just given birth to a daughter and as she's underage, is now a ward of court."

"What does that mean?" his wife asked.

"It means that I've washed my hands of her and her brat. The child will be put into care, and Rosie? Well, she can do as she pleases."

"What about Violet and Iris?"

"I'm surprised you remembered their names. They're fine for the moment, but believe me, their time will come."

"What do you mean, 'their time will come'? You'd better not harm them. I'm warning you," threatened Maria.

"That's rich coming from you. The mother who abandoned them, left them without a thought. I'm sure they'd love to see where you're living now."

"You've just given me an idea, James. You're right. They do need a mother's guidance. I think I should come back to the village," Maria said slyly. "Maybe I need to come back and keep an eye on things. If you don't want me, there are one or two bachelors who would be delighted to have me warm their beds. What do you think of that, James? How would your new bride-to-be feel about me living across the road?"

James had no doubt that this Jezebel would do exactly what she threatened and she was right, there was certainly more than one bachelor who would welcome her into his bed.

He knew he'd only get his freedom for a price, but at

what cost? "I'm telling you now, five thousand is out of the question. Five hundred is all I'm prepared to give you."

"Twenty years of marriage and you offer me a paltry five hundred pounds? You would be laughed out of court."

"So, you're leaving the country? What about the daughters you profess to miss and pray for?"

"They're not kids any more. They don't need me. So, if you want a divorce, you'll have to make me a better offer."

"One thousand and that's final. Take it or leave it."

"I'll leave it and get my own solicitor."

"How exactly do you intend raising the money? By lying on your back, as usual?"

Maria slapped her husband with all her might, causing him to stumble. He caught his foot on the case she'd packed earlier and fell backwards into the marble grate, cracking his head.

"You're nothing but a pathetic excuse for a man. Mean, miserable and absolutely useless in bed. No wonder I looked elsewhere, I hate you!" Maria screamed at the inert form of James Royce.

It was some time before she calmed down sufficiently to realise her husband hadn't moved. Tentatively she turned his head to reveal a gaping wound. "Oh, my God. Oh, my God," she kept repeating to herself. What was she going to do? It had been an accident, but who would believe her? She couldn't stop shaking. She was hysterical and even attempted the kiss of life, but he was gone and she was going to end up in prison.

She couldn't face that, she'd have to leave the country, go back home to Italy, but how, she had no money? What the hell was she going to do? James had come to buy her off. Maybe he had money on him? He wouldn't have wanted to come back here once she'd signed the papers. She emptied her husband's pockets and came across his car keys, a comb and a brown envelope, an envelope stuffed with money. Her payoff. Just how much had he reckoned she was worth?

The envelope contained a measly two thousand pounds.

Not nearly enough in her opinion, but more than enough to get her home to Italy. Maria Royce was nothing if not a survivor and for the moment, all else went out of her head. She needed to book an airline ticket, so slipping on her coat she made for Princes Street and within the hour, she had a one-way ticket to Milan.

Maria Royce had made her escape.

CHAPTER TWENTY-EIGHT

Missing in Action

Arriving home, the sisters were surprised to see the house in darkness, but more importantly, there was no sign of life at the bake house and their father's car was not parked in its usual place.

This had never happened before. The girls didn't know what to think. Business always came first with James Royce, regardless of what may have occurred.

"What do you think has happened?" Violet asked nervously. "It's not like him."

"I've no idea, but the car's probably broken down, or he's run out of petrol. You know what a meanie he is about spending money on that old boneshaker."

Having been around the bakery since they could walk, each knew exactly what had to be done. But with time marching on and still no sign of their father, the daughters were becoming more worried by the minute. It was time to call in help, so Iris set off to fetch old Willie, who worked in the bake house at weekends.

The three of them worked tirelessly through the night to get the shop open at its usual time but there was still no sign of their father.

"Hello, Sergeant Mitchell. It's Iris Royce here."

"Morning, lass, what can I do for you?"

"It's my father, sergeant, he hasn't been home all night. I'm worried something's happened to him."

"When did you last see him?"

"Yesterday morning. He had an appointment in town. He left here about nine o'clock."

"Do you know who he was meeting?" the sergeant asked.

"No, he didn't say, but that wasn't unusual. He hates anyone knowing his business. He keeps everything close to his chest."

"I'll check with headquarters to find out if there have been any accidents. What's the registration number of his car? We'll circulate it, just in case he's broken down. Don't worry, most of these cases turn out to be nothing more than a breakdown or the driver having a bit too much to drink."

It was almost lunchtime before Sergeant Mitchell arrived at the bakery. By this time, the two Royce girls were beside themselves with worry.

"Thankfully there have been no reports of any car accidents. Since your mother left, has he been depressed or not himself?"

"Of course he's been depressed and as you put it 'not himself', but he's not been suicidal if that's what you're hinting at," snapped Iris.

"What about alcohol? Has he been drinking more than normal?"

"Not that we've noticed."

"Could he have been seeing someone else?"

"I wouldn't have thought so. Father is a creature of habit. I'm not sure where a new woman would fit in."

"Right. I'll go back to the station and file a report. Call me if you think of anything more. I'm sure he'll turn up safe and sound."

If only Sergeant Mitchell's predication could have come true. Forty-eight hours later and there was still no word of their father's whereabouts. The daughters were frantic. James Royce was a most fastidious man and nothing would have kept him away from his home and business. Deep down both sisters knew their father was not coming back; he would have got a message to them somehow.

As yet, they had decided not to inform Rosie of their father's disappearance. Although she was on the mend, according to the medical staff, she was still some way from a full recovery. Until they had some definite information, they would keep this to themselves. But as it happened, Rosie was just about to receive news concerning her father.

The new mum had just finished feeding Hope and settled her down for her nap when she became aware of a group of people outside her room. She had a sickening feeling in the pit of her stomach and knew instinctively these people had something to do with her. Picking Hope out of her crib, she held her close to her.

"Rosie, this is Miss Bridges, a welfare officer," Matron spoke kindly to her. "You have to be brave."

"What has a welfare officer got to do with me?"

"Miss Bridges has a court order to take Hope to a place of safety."

"A place of safety? Why? What have I done? You know she's well looked after," Rosie's voice was rising hysterically as she spoke. "She's safe here with me. I don't understand."

"Neither do I, Rosie, but you have to let her go with Miss Bridges for now."

"What do you mean, for now? She's my baby and I'm not giving her to anyone. You can't do this," said Rosie sobbing and clinging onto Hope.

"We have to take her, Rosie. You're underage and it's against the law," answered the welfare officer.

"I'm sixteen," she lied. "Let me keep her. I'll look after her, my family will help. Please, please wait till my sisters come. I'll get them to bring my dad. He'll look after us."

"It was your father who signed the papers, Rosie. He doesn't want any responsibility for you or Hope. I did try to change his mind," the welfare officer explained to the distraught girl.

"Stop this at once," the matron intervened. "You're upsetting the child, and my patient is far too weak to be harassed like this. Come back tomorrow when she is more rested."

"I'm sorry, I can't do that," argued Susan Bridges. "I have to take the child now." Wrestling the baby from Rosie's grip, she left immediately.

The young mum was inconsolable. "I don't believe it. My father wouldn't do that to me. He loves me, he was just a bit angry. He'll come around. They've stolen my baby," the girl wailed.

Matron picked up the document. "I'm sorry, Rosie. This has been signed by James Royce, who I presume to be your father," and she showed Rosie the signature on the court order.

"Iris, it's Rosie. Get Dad on the phone now, I have to speak to him," demanded the youngest sister.

"I'm sorry, darling, but he's not here. Why do you need to speak to him?"

"What do you mean he's not there? Where the hell is he?" shouted Rosie.

"Stop shouting. I don't know where he is but he's not here, what's wrong?"

"What's wrong? I'll tell you what's wrong. He's had Hope taken into care. The welfare has just taken her away." By now Rosie was screaming down the phone at her sister.

"He couldn't have, Rosie. He's been missing for three days. We didn't tell you because we didn't want to upset you, but we're worried sick."

"Worried sick? Well, I hope the old bastard is lying in a ditch somewhere, bleeding to fucking death for what he's done. As God is my witness, if I ever lay eyes on him, I'll fucking swing for him."

"Rosie, it couldn't have been him. Listen to me."

"If it wasn't him, some bastard's forged his signature, because I've seen it, plain as day. As he would say, 'as of now I'm no daughter of his' and if you keep defending him, you're no sisters of mine."

The line went dead.

"What the devil was all that about?" asked Violet.

"It appears our beloved father has taken out some kind of court order to have Hope put into care."

"He couldn't have."

"That's what I said, but he did. I think we'd better call Sergeant Mitchell."

"Something's happened to him, Iris, I can feel it. He would never stay away this long. If he doesn't come back, what's going to happen to us?"

"Do you never think of anyone but yourself, Violet? For God's sake, our father's missing and our niece has just been carted off to heaven knows where, and you want to know what's going to happen to you? You're unbelievable." Her elder sister walked away in disgust.

CHAPTER TWENTY-NINE

History Repeats Itself

"Jack, it's Rosie, I need you to come to the hospital right now and get me."

He could tell from her voice something terrible had occurred. "What's wrong, what's happened?"

"They've taken the baby, Jack. The welfare has taken Hope and it's my father's fault," Rosie broke down sobbing.

"I'll be there as quick as I can." Jack wanted desperately to assure Rosie all would be well, but he knew from past experience it most likely wouldn't be.

"I had to bring her back here, Stella, there was nowhere else. She can't go home, not under these circumstances and I won't abandon her, no matter what you, or anyone else says."

"Take her upstairs. I'll send Kitty up to help," Stella agreed reluctantly. It seemed she still hadn't seen the back of Rosie Royce.

"How could her father have done this?" Jack pondered. "You know he's missing?"

"Maybe he realized what he'd done and felt guilty," offered Stella.

"From what I've heard he doesn't seem the type. What are the chances we can get the baby back?" Jack asked.

"We? Surely not, Jack. Don't tell me you're thinking of taking on this responsibility?"

"There's no-one else. Maybe if I claimed to be the father, she could get Hope back."

"She's got a family, Jack. She's their responsibility, not yours. Don't do anything hasty. We'll speak to Marcus in the morning and find out what her options are."

It was nearly one a.m. before Stella made her way back upstairs. Jack, dozing in a chair by the fire, jumped as she entered the room.

"She's hardly stirred," he reported.

"Good. You go and lock up and I'll sit with her till morning."

Unknown to Jack or the rest or the household, Stella understood exactly what Rosie was going through. Hadn't she felt the same pain and desolation all those years ago?

Stella's anguish was no different to Rosie's. Okay, she hadn't had her son snatched from her bosom by some do-gooder; she had willingly given her baby up in a very civilised and genteel manner, but that had made it no less traumatic.

She understood the despair Rosie felt at losing Hope. A loss that would never leave her; knowing out there, someone else was caring for your child. If anything, the emptiness grew deeper as the years passed. Stella wouldn't wish such desolation on her worst enemy. She would do her utmost to help Rosie, but not at the expense of Jack. Stella knew they weren't meant for each other, not that Jack could see that. Anyway, she had plans for him.

Thinking back, Stella had been naive agreeing to Marcus' proposition. The wily lawyer had taken advantage of her youth and gratitude, playing on her fear of the Williams brothers. Her desperation to give Mary every chance of recovery had blinded her to the reality of his immoral request.

She still felt incredulous at what had actually taken place that fateful day and how deep her resentment towards Marcus grew with each passing year. Sitting with him in the elegant, Palm Court Restaurant, taking afternoon tea, all those years ago, amidst the splendour of the city's most prestigious watering hole, a far cry from the farm she'd grown up on. She had been so thankful to her benefactor that his suggestion had not seemed at all unreasonable. With the terror of the Williams brothers abated, thanks to her sponsor, it had seemed churlish not to consider his request. Especially when it appeared she had everything to gain, and in Marcus's words, nothing to lose, except for a few months' inconvenience.

Marcus Kramer Q.C. was the last of his line. Being an only child and given his predilections, his circumstances seemed to be a lost cause. However, he was desperate to have a son and heir and would exploit any opportunity to rectify the situation. It seemed the fates had presented him with a solution in the form of Stella Gold. The young girl was so beholden to him, so eager to repay her saviour, he was positive he could convince her to fall in with his scheme, no matter how outrageous or improbable it seemed.

Being unwilling to leave conception to chance, Marcus had a plan. A doctor, who, thanks to the lawyer's best efforts, had recently escaped being struck off, would artificially impregnate the young woman. A clinical procedure which was, assuming all was well with the pair, guaranteed success.

Marriage and children were way off the radar for Stella. She had no desire for either and it was Marcus' assurance that from day one she would have no responsibility for the care and upbringing of a child that had led her to consider his proposition. She was a young woman with the world at her feet and no intention of being tied down by motherhood. Years later that decision still coloured her life.

They were married in secret at Gretna Green with two passers-by as witness to their nuptials. Everything had to be done by the book, Marcus insisted. All the legalities observed to avoid any complications in the future.

No celebration, no marking of the auspicious occasion, the ceremony was over in twenty minutes.

The newlyweds had returned immediately to the city; Marcus to his magnificent townhouse and she to the small bedsit which had been created for her while the renovations to Danube Street were being carried out. And there she was, a married woman, a rich married woman to boot, and if all went to plan, a soon-to-be pregnant, married woman.

Not quite the wedding dreams were made of. No beautiful white meringue dress, no bridesmaids all in pink, no father walking her down the aisle to the sounds of the Wedding March, and no handsome bridegroom sharing her bed.

Here she was, a bit tipsy, having drunk the best part of a bottle of cheap wine and all alone. But, perhaps not. She jumped. What was that noise? Someone was moving about upstairs.

Jesus, where was all her bravado now? She wasn't so brave on her own with an intruder on the premises. What the devil should she do? Hide and hope they might just go away? There was nothing of value for anyone to steal. The building was stripped back to its shell. The gun. Where had she hidden the small pistol she'd used to scare off the Williams brothers? If she was going down, she'd take someone with her.

Stealthily she made her way up the back stairs to the ground floor. She could hear footsteps above. Should she stay where she was or make a run for it? she wondered.

"Hello, Stella, looking good as usual." Ronnie Williams smirked as he descended the wide stair case.

Without thinking Stella pointed the gun and fired. The exquisite chandelier the architect had been at such pains to save was no more.

"Give me that thing, you stupid mare, before you do some real damage." Ronnie grabbed the pistol from her grasp. "That's twice you've missed. One day I might teach you how to fire the thing properly."

"What are you doing here?" her voice shook with fear.

"I was just passing and saw the lights on. Calm down, I'm not going to hurt you."

"Well, if you've seen all you want, don't let me keep you. Marcus will be here any minute; he's parking the car."

"Don't tell porkies, Stella. I saw him leaving half an hour ago. I'm interested to see what the place is going to look like when it's finished, when I take it back from you. You do know I'm going to take it back?"

Stella was determined he wouldn't see how terrified she was, no matter how unbelievable the scenario.

Giving him the grand tour she described how each room would be fitted and how the club would operate. Her articulate account confirmed to Ronnie Williams just how astute and clever this young woman actually was. Despite what had happened, he liked her, she had guts, real guts. The fact that she had the audacity to take him on was more than many of the hard men of the city would attempt. If only she could overcome her terror and hatred of him. He wasn't a psycho like his brother. Oh, he could handle himself; there was no doubt about that. He was no angel and he would take any man down who got lairy but he didn't enjoy violence, not like Freddie.

"I don't suppose you have anything to drink?" he asked his hostess.

"Only some cheap wine and it's awful," she replied.

What the fuck am I doing? she thought. *I'll be asking him to tea next.*

"I've got a bottle or two in the car, shall I fetch them?" he asked, like a boy on his first date.

"Have I got a choice?" Stella asked coldly.

"Not really," he replied smiling.

"Then why bother asking?"

She really did have guts, there was no denying it.

It was the builders crashing about that woke her just after eight, alone and naked. My God, what a dream, she smiled to herself. Until she saw the empty bottle and two glasses.

CHAPTER THIRTY

It's a Knockout

"You'll only make matters worse, lad. You would automatically be charged with statutory rape and jailed," Marcus explained. "Rosie was under the age of consent when the child was conceived and trust me, you would never be allowed near Hope with a charge like that hanging over you."

"I just want my child back," cried Rosie.

"That's not going to happen. You're only fourteen, and in the eyes of the law you have no say in the matter."

"She's what?" bellowed Stella. "Only fourteen! Dear God, I could get the jail for harbouring a runaway and no-one would ever believe I didn't know."

"I only found out myself when I picked her up from the hospital," Jack admitted.

"I'll be fifteen in a couple of weeks," Rosie replied sullenly.

"I was going to ask if you would trace the foster family," Stella asked Marcus. "But quite frankly, there's no point. Rosie, you have to be prepared to accept that your baby will most likely be put up for adoption and there's not a thing you can do, am I right, Marcus?"

"Yes. I'm sorry to say, Stella, but that's exactly what will happen. She's already been placed with a foster family, however, this is only temporary. She'll be placed in a permanent home soon."

Marcus, watching Rosie out of the corner of his eye, warned, "Don't think for one moment you'll get away with what you're considering, girl. Every police force in the country would be on the lookout and you'd definitely never see your daughter again, for sure."

"It doesn't look like I'm going to see her anyway." Rosie turned away looking defiant.

"I'm sorry I'm not the bearer of good news," Marcus continued. "The only possibility, and it is a long shot, is if one of your sisters applies to the court for guardianship,"

"Please, Marcus, please. It's worth a try. There has to be something you can do?"

"I'll petition the court, but don't get your hopes up," warned Marcus.

A foster home? The thought filled Jack with contempt. He'd been in three such homes during his childhood. He'd been beaten, half-starved and had run away from one to avoid being abused by the man who was supposed to be his mentor, who should have shielded him from harm and kept him safe. Jack hated anything to do with social workers and as far as he was concerned, the whole care system was a farce. The only qualification needed to become a foster parent seemed to be a spare bedroom.

Jack Hunter was a street-smart kid; with a mother like his he'd had to be. He had learned to fend for himself from an early age. On a number of occasions, throughout his young life, he had been a victim of the care system. After several forced spells away from Jeannie and his gran, he learned to stay out of the spotlight, not to cause problems at school and generally play the game by not drawing attention to himself. He managed, for the most part, to avoid interference in his life.

Although his mother allowed him to run wild, Jack had two benefactors who were not willing to let his life go the same way as most of his contemporaries. Stella kept him in work and out of mischief. Under her sharp eye he was kept away from the usual temptations. Jack's other patron was Norrie Buchanan, a retired world champion boxer, who ran the local boxing club.

Norrie was a tough, savvy, fearless guy who'd begun life in circumstances not too dissimilar to Jack's. He, too, had been written off as a lost cause, told repeatedly he would amount to nothing. Norrie had been determined to prove all his doubters wrong. Reared in the same slums, he couldn't have had a worse start in life, but Norrie was a street fighter destined for great things. His career might have raised him out of the dire poverty of his youth but he had never forgotten his roots.

Jack idolised the champ and it was Norrie's belief in him that kept him out of the clutches of the many temptations that polluted the already dangerous streets.

At fifteen Jack was, by far, the star of the club – he was out-boxing lads much older than himself. He had only ever lost one fight and that was way back in the early days.

At last it seemed that things were looking up for Jack. With Norrie's help he had a future, and a bright one at that. The pinnacle of his career came when he was selected to represent his country at the Commonwealth Games. Even his mother was impressed, but not enough to encourage this fantastic opportunity. Jeanie had been on one of her infamous benders for the past month, earning virtually nothing but spending like there was no tomorrow. With the threat of eviction looming again, it was up to Jack to sort things out.

Jack, like most street kids had indulged in his fair share of petty thieving; the odd bit of stuff from Woolies or nicking a couple of bottles of beer from the local 'offie'. This was different. He needed cash and there was only one way to get it.

He'd lain hidden for almost an hour outside Bannermans Bar in the Grassmarket before a likely candidate staggered into view. A smartly dressed old man carrying a pigskin briefcase weaved towards Jack's hiding place. This one looked like he had a few bob, thought the young lad as he made his move.

"You! I know you," the victim roared, staring into Jack's shocked face.

Fuck, he was a punter! Jack had seen him countless times in Danube Street. Fuck, I'm in deep shit, he thought as he took to his heels.

"Jack Hunter, you will be remanded for a period of twelve months in St. Joseph's Approved School," the chairman of the Children's Hearing pronounced. Thanks to his mother's selfishness and greed, he missed out on the opportunity of a lifetime.

CHAPTER THIRTY-ONE

Fighting Spirit

The borstal system was a harsh, cruel regime and was most definitely based on the survival of the fittest. Despite his street savvy and his ability to fight, the young lad floundered helplessly amongst the inmates, who were for the most, harder, stronger and wiser than him. He was ambushed, beaten and his food was continually contaminated with spit and urine, to the point where he ate virtually nothing. It was worse at lockdown. He could face the brutal exercise and hard work, but being locked in a dormitory with twenty other psychos at night was beyond his endurance. He barely slept for the first two months, afraid to close his eyes, not knowing if he would open them again, or even if he wanted to. For the first time in his life Jack was alone, really alone, with no one to watch his back. And it was only then he realised how fortunate he'd been.

Suicide was rife in the correction centre. At least one inmate a month found it difficult to cope with their sentence and couldn't wait for their release date. The house was permanently on suicide watch.

Two months into his sentence, Jack was on the verge of a serious mental breakdown. Between the lack of sleep and food, he couldn't endure his situation much longer. His spirit was nearing breaking point when, much to his relief, a new face appeared in the house. Jack recognised Billy Martin immediately. He was from his neck of the woods and the lads had boxed against each other in the past.

Billy was a cheerful, happy-go-lucky lad: a seasoned inmate, used to borstal life, having spent as much time in as he had out. He knew how to survive, how to avoid trouble with the top dog and his cohorts and who to leather to gain respect. Shocked at how badly his young sparring partner had been coping, he made it his business to visit the bullies responsible for Jack's state of mind. The hospital wing had a sudden influx of patients, all claiming to have fallen down a flight of stairs.

The remainder of Jack's time in Borstal passed without further incident, thanks to his pal, Billy. Ten months later, on the eve of Jack's release they had their final conversation as cellmates.

"Are you going to be alright on the outside?" Billy asked.

"I'll be fine. I want to get back to training, and hopefully Stella will give me my job back."

"Fuck me. Imagine having a job in the best whorehouse in town. Fuck! I'd go without wages for that job," whistled Billy.

"It's just a job," Jack replied.

"Aye, and Van Gogh was just a painter and decorator."

"Who?"

"Forget it. Just don't forget your pals when you get out."

Not quite as confident as Billy, Jack had no idea what reception he would receive from his mentors. He had been so ashamed and disappointed in himself that he had been unable to look either Stella or Norrie in the face and had refused all their visitor requests.

If only he could turn back time, if only he had swallowed his pride because, as fate would have it, Norrie passed away on the day of Jack's release.

As he stood in the crematorium, amongst the hundreds of mourners, Jack Hunter watched his hopes and ambitions go up in smoke.

With no-one to tutor or mentor him, his dream of becoming a 'contender' vanished in the wind and for a while after his release he resorted to type. Like most of the other neds who hung about street corners, he indulged in a variety of petty crimes, using his fists to get what he wanted.

He'd been hanging around Danube Street for a few weeks, hoping to bump into Stella. Jack missed her and the girls, but more importantly, he missed having a reason to get up in the morning.

Stella had been so proud when Jack was selected for the Games and had done everything she could to help, but she had been equally furious when he ended up inside. In her heart she knew it was thanks to his bloody selfish mother, but he was old enough to know right from wrong.

Just as Jack was about to leave after another bout of loitering in Danube Street, a black cab pulled up alongside him, and out stepped his quarry.

"Hello, Jack, long time no see," Stella nodded to him.

"Yes miss, been nearly a year," stuttered Jack, nervous at finally coming face to face with her.

"How are Jeannie and your grandmother?" Stella made the usual pleasantries.

"My Ma's fine, same as usual. Gran's not too clever."

"Well, give them my regards," Stella said as she walked up the steps to the entrance.

"Can I have my old job back?" he blurted out.

"Your old job back? What job was that? The job I created to keep you on the straight and narrow, to help you get to the top with Norrie, that job, Jack?"

"I earned my keep Stella, you know I did."

"Did you now? Well I can't say you've been missed." She turned on her heel and entered the house, slamming the front door behind her.

"Well, that's my answer I suppose," muttered Jack, disappointed, and turning to leave. As he did so, he heard a voice calling his name.

"Jack, Jack," Kitty called from the basement. "Jack, come down here, I want to talk to you."

Hesitantly, Jack descended the basement steps and entered the warm kitchen. Nothing had changed: pots were boiling on the stove, Dora was over by the sink, tackling the piles of dishes that always needed to be washed and Kitty was buzzing about, doing twenty jobs at once.

The young girl ran to Jack, arms outstretched, delighted to have him back.

"Thank God someone's pleased to see me," he muttered.

"Don't be an idiot," Kitty prodded him. "What did you expect, the red carpet? You've been out for three months and not a sight nor sound of you."

"You know Norrie died? I was gutted and I couldn't think about anything except how I'd let him down. Honest, I was mortified, Kitty, and I didn't think the missus would want me back here," he said with his head hanging down. "Judging by the reception I just got, I was right."

"Of course she wants you back. She's been worried sick about you. Jesus, you're family, just like me and Dora, but that doesn't mean to say she wasn't going to be angry."

"She's more than angry Kitty."

A loud clatter from upstairs interrupted their conversation. "What was that?"

Without waiting for an answer Jack flew up the back stairs with Kitty hot on his heels.

He could hardly believe his eyes. There, rolling about the floor, was his boss, fighting off a man twice her size. Stella was screaming and kicking for all she was worth. She was pinned down by the sheer weight of her attacker who had one arm across her throat and was attempting to rip off her clothes with the other, all the time snarling obscenities at her.

"Don't tell me you don't want it," the drunk growled, leering into her face. "I'll show you what a real man's like," he slurred, fumbling with his trousers as Stella kicked and clawed at him.

Jack leapt at the man and with one punch, a lethal left hook, floored him. Freddie Williams didn't know what had hit him, or fortunately, who. He was out cold.

"Who the fuck is he?" Jack shouted as he helped Stella up. "What was that all about?"

"Old scores, Jack, old scores," said a breathless and shaken Stella, trying hard to recover. "Look, we don't have much time, he'll come round in a few minutes and I don't fancy a rematch," Jack prompted the two women.

"You're right, we have to secure him, get him tied up, or he'll slaughter the three of us. I'll call his brother to come and collect him," Stella answered.

Freddie Williams was not a happy man when he regained consciousness. He struggled with all his strength to loosen his bonds and bellowed at his captors, "Who the fuck did this? I'll fucking kill him. You cunts are dead!"

"Shut up, man! It won't do your reputation any good when folk find out it was me and Kitty here who knocked you out, now would it?" Stella sneered at the hulk of a man straining at his ties. She hadn't practiced bondage for all these years without learning a trick or two.

"Don't talk fucking nonsense. No woman could deck me."

"Do you see anyone else here?" she questioned him. "Yeah, beaten by two women and we've got the photos to prove it." Kitty was busy snapping the restrained man when his brother appeared at the door.

"What the hell's going on here?" Ronnie snapped as he spotted Freddie trussed up like a Christmas turkey.

"Your brother's what's going on. He attacked and attempted to rape me. Thank God Kitty was here."

Ronnie Williams didn't utter a word while helping his brother out to the car. Closing the door on Freddie's rants, he turned to Stella. "I'm sorry about this. I'll make sure he stays away in future."

"If he comes anywhere near me or my business again, it'll be an undertaker who'll be collecting him, is that clear?"

"Perfectly, Stella."

Jack was listening from the stairwell; the last thing he

wanted was to be on the wrong side of the Williams brothers.

"Thank God you were here, boy," Stella hugged Jack in relief. "I think you might just have saved my life."

"I think I did too, so can I have my old job back please?" he grinned cheekily.

"Only if there are no more spells inside, no matter how bad things get with Jeannie. In fact, a spell inside would do *her* the world of good, get her off the gear."

He was back in the fold, back in the bosom of Danube Street.

CHAPTER THIRTY-TWO

Discovery

One way or another Mrs Bruce was going to catch the tenant from the ground floor flat today. The woman owed two weeks rent and whatever the excuse, she wanted her money. It was always the same; the ones the landlady took pity on were always the ones who skipped, leaving her out of pocket. She was determined it wasn't going to happen with this one.

Maria had seemed pleasant and respectable enough, but you could never tell. Mrs Bruce tolerated no loose women in her flats, no men calling late at night, only respectable boarders. This one was supposedly a widow. Her husband had been killed during the war and she had no family ties here. The landlady resolved to catch her as she left for work that morning.

Placing her chair opposite the door Mrs Bruce settled down to wait. The tenant left most mornings between eight and eight fifteen to walk the ten minutes to her place of employment in George Street.

It was almost nine and still no sign of her quarry. Furious at the waste of her time and the non-appearance of her errant tenant, the landlady had the sinking feeling she had been duped again. Disappearing into her own quarters she returned with her husband and the spare key.

"My God, what the devil is that smell?" Mr Bruce asked in the semi-darkness. Pulling back the curtains, he revealed the source of the stench. "For God's sake woman, open the window I can't breathe."

"Well, that makes two of you." Mrs Bruce was standing over the decomposing body of James Royce. "This one took his last breath days ago. You'd better go and phone the police while I have a look around. After all, she owes us rent."

Violet's heart sank when she saw Sergeant Mitchell and a female colleague approach the shop.

"Iris, Sergeant Mitchell is here," she called to her sister, who was busy working out back.

"Morning," said Violet with trepidation. "Is there any news?"

"We're following a definite line of enquiry. Maybe you should sit down."

"Just tell us," demanded Iris, dreading the news.

"I was notified this morning that a body fitting the description of your father has been found in Dalry Road, Edinburgh. His car was also found parked nearby."

"Oh my God," cried Violet. "Are you sure it's him?"

"Pretty sure," answered Sergeant Mitchell.

"I don't think he knew anyone in that part of town." Iris seemed to be taking the news quite calmly.

"What happened? How did he die?" enquired Violet. "Was it a heart attack?"

"I'm sorry, I don't have any more details, other than we know the property was let out to an Italian woman going by the name of Maria Luca."

Both girls gasped.

"Does the name mean something to you?" the WPC asked.

"It's our mother's maiden name," Iris informed the police officer.

"What has she got to say about it?" asked Violet.

"There was no sign of the woman in question. She hasn't been seen for a number of days."

"Unfortunately, someone needs to identify the body," continued Sergeant Mitchell. "Have you a male relative who would be willing to do so?"

"Uncle John, our father's brother, lives at the end of the

High Street, but they haven't spoken in years. I think it'll have to be me," replied the eldest sister.

Iris's legs turned to jelly as a wave of emotion swept over her. There was no doubt that the cold, lifeless corpse was her father; his chiselled features as stern in death as they had been in life. James Royce had left this world long before his time and from what the girls could deduce, their mother was being held responsible.

"No way," Violet protested. "My mother would never strike or lay hands on anyone."

"She didn't have to," protested her sister. "A look was generally enough. Even though she and our father had parted on bad terms, like my sister said, I don't believe she had anything to do with his death."

"Someone did, and until a post mortem has been carried out, all this is conjecture," said Sergeant Mitchell.

"What about a funeral? When can we arrange one?"

"Not until the body is released, which may be some time," he answered.

The brusque Highlander knew from experience that a situation like this could drag on for weeks.

Their next duty was to tell Rosie, and the kind sergeant volunteered to drop them off at her place of work on Danube Street. Duncan Mitchell could no more envisage one of the Royce girls working in the infamous brothel as he could see himself walking naked down the village main street. But work here she did, and according to her naive sisters, it was purely in a domestic capacity. Who was he to judge? But a looker like Rosie Royce was hardly destined for scrubbing floors. There was some talk of a child, but that was none of his business, he refected, as he deposited his charges outside the notorious building.

Neither Iris nor Violet had seen anywhere like it. The

sheer opulence and decadence of their surroundings was overwhelming. Rosie, however, looked awful. Her face was puffy and tear-stained from the days and nights spent crying; she looked so sad and desolate. And surprisingly, Stella was sitting with their sister when they arrived.

"My God, if you've shut the shop something momentous must have occurred," said Rosie sarcastically.

"We have some bad news."

"What makes you think it's going to be bad news?" Rosie sneered. "I take it he's been found, then?"

"Yes," replied Iris.

"Dead or alive?"

With tears running down her cheeks, Iris confirmed their father was dead.

"Good, saves me a job and keeps me out of prison. I hope the bastard suffered," snarled the youngest sister.

"Oh, Rosie."

"Don't you 'Oh, Rosie me'. I will never forgive him for what he did and I hope he burns in the fires of hell."

"Stop it, Rosie, he was our father. He was devastated by mother's antics and your predicament. I'm not excusing him, he shouldn't have done what he did, but he didn't deserve to die."

"Yes, he did," shouted Rosie. "He didn't give a toss about any of us."

"He loved us and would do anything for us. He would have come around eventually."

"Oh, fuck off, Iris. We were just unpaid skivvies. Don't bother letting me know when the funeral is, I won't be going."

"Please come home," both girls pleaded.

"I'll never cross that threshold again."

Stella rose from the bedside. "Leave her for now, she's too upset over Hope to think straight."

"Don't you go making excuses for me," she spat at Stella. "I know you're helping me out and I should be grateful, but you can go fuck yourself alongside that pair."

"Really! There's gratitude for you." Stella rose and said, "Well, if you feel so little for us and all we've done, please don't feel obliged to stay. In fact, you've got till Friday then I want you out." Stella spun on her heels and left the room.

Iris ran after her begging, "Please, Stella, she doesn't mean what she's saying. It's all been too much for her."

"She's not my responsibility. Go home and rest, you both look exhausted. I'll get Jack to take you." It didn't escape Stella's notice the way Violet perked up at the mention of Jack. For God's sake that's all they needed.

Edinburgh Evening News

The body of a man was discovered earlier today in the Gorgie area of the city. A spokesman for Lothian and Borders police confirmed they were treating the death as suspicious and the victim's name will not be disclosed until relatives have been informed...

CHAPTER THIRTY-THREE

Holier Than Thou

"For fuck's sake, not again," Police Constable Cummins whispered to his 'oppo'. "What has he got against Stella Gold? She'll have him for harassment if he's not careful."

"I don't know, but as far as I'm concerned there's a lot worse about town than Stella. You could say she provides a service."

"Aye, and you've been well serviced over the years," Cummins laughed at the thought.

"Listen, buster, if there weren't places like Danube Street there would be even more sex crimes committed."

"You're right, and that's just by the boys in blue," the constable smirked.

"This bugger's on a mission. This is the fourth time he's hit this one house since he took over, and he's only been in the job a couple of months."

"I hate all those holier than thou buggers, always spouting the bible at you. They're usually the bloody worst kind. They make you feel inadequate, dirty, as if you're lusting after anything in a skirt."

"Well, he got that right," Cummins spluttered.

"Shut up, you know what I mean. It's like they're the only Christians and the rest of us are well on our way to hell. All the while they're beating the crap out of the wife and shagging the daughter. I wouldn't trust him or his like as far as I could throw him."

"You're right, mate. These weird Jesus nuts are usually the biggest perverts going. You know the type, live by the bible but would shag the barber's cat."

"I bet it all stems back to some brass laughing at him on

his first go and he's never gotten over it." Cummins burst out laughing, drawing attention from the front of the squad room.

"Is there something amusing, constable? Want to share the joke with the rest of us?" asked Detective Chief Inspector Hamish Ross.

Fuck, thought the young constable. He didn't dare share his thoughts with the rest of the squad, and certainly not with the pious DCI Hamish Ross.

The briefing over, the officers made their way to the waiting vehicles.

"I feel bad about this, but the bugger does it in such a way there's no time to get the word out," Cummins spoke out. "She's alright is Stella, never makes trouble and dishes out a decent Christmas box. There are a lot worse gaffs and a lot worse fuckers running them."

"Funny how he never goes after any of the dosshouses run by the Williams brothers."

"Someone should throw a hand grenade into their places, it might improve the décor. And as for the brasses, you wouldn't touch them with the proverbial barge pole."

"Aye, but they're cheap," replied his mate.

"Cheap? They should be paying you. C'mon, he's getting impatient." The two constables joined the convoy.

"Here we go again," said Cummins. "He wants Stella by hook or by crook this time. She's not to get away, but I'm telling you, I'm not lifting her. Not if I can possibly help it."

The convoy headed for Danube Street.

Detective Chief Inspector Ross knew that most of his men disagreed with his frequent raids on Stella Gold, but would they still disagree if they knew the real reason for his hatred of her? She was the epitome of all that was corrupt and evil. She and her kind bewitched men; good, honest, God-fearing men, who, once in this Jezebel's clutches, were damned forever.

He would do everything as a devout Christian to stamp her and her filthy business out. All within the confines of the law, of course. Or perhaps not. Who would blame him if he bent the rules? After all, that bitch flaunted them without fear or favour. Hamish knew he would eventually win. The voices told him so. He just had to keep the faith.

CHAPTER THIRTY-FOUR

Hamish's Story

Hamish Ross was born into a strict Presbyterian family on the remote island of Inchkillen, the only son of the Reverend Jock Ross and his wife Morag. The reverend was a fierce 'hellfire and brimstone' man who lived as he preached. His wife was a plain, dour woman with nothing attractive about her.

The couple lived a hard, austere life, on a bleak croft in the middle of nowhere, existing on the bare necessities with no other comfort or ease.

Their neighbours and congregation who, whilst respecting the man of the cloth, had no liking for either and avoided contact with the minister and his wife as much as possible. They were seldom invited to social gatherings and never took part in any ceilidhs, the life blood of the islanders. This morose, dour couple could put a damper on any social event simply by attending.

To the amazement of the islanders, ten years into their marriage young Hamish had entered the world. Until then it was joked, Mrs Ross was more enamoured of her award-winning sheep than her husband, and it was they who she took to her bed each night. It was a great source of amusement when the rumours appeared to be true. The evidence was there, they laughed; the bairn had the tightest, woolliest, curly hair imaginable.

Morag Ross despised men and would be the first to agree that she should never have married. Detesting physical contact of any description, she had to steel herself to allow her husband his conjugal rights. Every Sunday after church she had to do her duty, regardless. Sex, according to the scriptures, was for procreation only and the Reverend Jock's demands were, in her opinion, excessive. Worse than that, in her opinion, to desecrate the Sabbath was even more abhorrent.

Her husband was beyond redemption, but not so the child. From the day he was born she bound him to prevent any unseemly contact. There would be no such pleasuring under her roof. She was only sorry that she couldn't have him castrated, as she would any beast. She was determined that the boy not be tempted by the sins of the flesh and watched him like a hawk. If he touched himself she would beat the poor child mercilessly. An innocent act, such as scratching, would bring her righteous wrath down on him.

Hamish was an extremely bright child. He was on his feet, walking at nine months, and his babbling developed into words before his first birthday. He soon dispensed with the childish baby talk of Mama and Papa and could repeat words and verses from the bible. Neither parent considered it ludicrous that a child of that age could do so. It merely confirmed the mother's belief that her way of childrearing was the right way and this was evidence of how pious the reverend and his wife were.

Hamish was threatened constantly with the terrible punishment he would have to endure, should he disobey God or his mother and her relentless bible-bashing. She would make sure he'd never stray from the paths of righteousness, but the beatings stirred in him feelings he could not describe. Hamish could not remember ever experiencing the warmth of a cuddle or being comforted by his mother, but he remembered clearly the euphoria of punishment. Hamish Ross grew into a strange, lonely little boy.

Throughout his early childhood the boy came into little contact with the other kids on the island, only occasionally at church, and this was well supervised by his mother. He was never allowed to run freely along the beach, paddle in the sea, or fetch the cattle and sheep in from the hills. He would watch the other kids enviously but was never allowed to take part. Morag reigned supreme over her son, but that all changed on his first day of school.

The other pupils sensed immediately he was different, so from day one he was relentlessly bullied. Picked on at every opportunity, the little boy drew further and further into himself. He had no escape. Victimised at school and at home, the only physical contact he had was with his father's belt. The Ross's ruled by belt and bible.

At the age of ten, like all island children, he was sent off to the mainland to finish his schooling, an experience which even the hardiest child dreaded, most never having been away from home before. Not so Hamish, he was perfectly self-sufficient. He was more sick of home than homesick. His previous tormentors descended into a pile of snivelling wretches, weeping and wailing, crying into their pillows at night, missing home, much to Hamish's great amusement. How the worm had turned. The young lad seemed to grow six inches overnight. Now it was his turn and he exacted vengeance for all the beatings and mockery he'd suffered at his classmate's hands over the years.

Despite his parent's ambitions that he would follow his father into the ministry, Hamish felt the calling, not to save souls, but to bring justice to a corrupt world. Guided by the voices Hamish enlisted as a Police Cadet.

At first, he was confused. Had he stepped back in time? He seemed to have been catapulted back to a regime of ridicule, persecution and belittlement, however, this time he was prepared. This time he was the tormentor, not the tormented, with God showing him the way.

He was shunned by most of his classmates, but this was nothing new to Hamish Ross. He didn't encourage familiarity, nothing could be allowed to interfere with his mission. He had no interest in weekend parties, drinking or girls. In fact, he had no real interest in any of the usual pastimes a young, red-blooded male would indulge in. Of course, he had feelings and desires, but they were dark and dangerous. It was a test of his faith that kept them under control for most of the time, but he was only human.

Hamish followed a strict regime: a five mile cross country run, followed by a cold shower every morning before breakfast. He heard the sniggers and the name-calling – weirdo, pervert – to name but a few. In the main they had no effect on him, but on a very odd occasion he would retaliate, much to his shame.

Returning back late from his run one morning, he was relieved to find the rest of his classmates had already gone to breakfast. All except one, Peterson, who, he discovered later, had received some bad news regarding his family and been excused from class.

Peterson was a quiet, unassuming lad, who would probably have been the class victim of his year, had it not been for Hamish. Not given to sympathy Hamish ignored the blubbering for as long as he could, but the lad's obvious distress eventually got to him.

Sitting tentatively on the end of Peterson's bed, ready to flee should anyone appear, Hamish awkwardly comforted the distraught boy. For the rest of his life Hamish Ross would have no idea how the situation developed or what actually happened. All he could remember was the exquisite joy of the violent frenzy, and Peterson screaming. As Hamish experienced his first real orgasm, Peterson exhaled his last breath.

Jesus Christ, he was shaking like a leaf, his legs had turned to jelly, he could hardly stand. What had he just done? And with a man! He would burn in hell for this. Down on his knees, Hamish Ross prayed like he'd never prayed before, begging for forgiveness. He was young, he had made a mistake. Surely God would forgive him?

The cadet was straddled across the bed, eyes bulging. This

would be the end of Ross's career in the police force and more than likely a ten-year stretch on the other side of the law.

No-one would come looking for either cadet till after breakfast. That gave Hamish at least half an hour. He had to make this look like Peterson had taken his own life, so he would have to work fast.

Peterson was found hanging from the rafters in the dormitory by one of the cleaners. There had been a number of suicides at the college over the past year and the authorities were extremely sensitive to the situation. No-one, it seemed, had realised how badly Peterson had taken the news of his brother's demise. To save face and avoid any further distress to the family, the whole incident was swept under the carpet. Case closed.

Hamish Ross knew then it was meant to be, he could rid the world of philistines with his master's blessing. God looked after his own 'his will, would be done', the voices told him so.

CHAPTER THIRTY-FIVE

Hunted and Hunting

Jack and Rosie had spent the afternoon flat hunting, but even the landlords of the worst rat-infested slums wouldn't entertain them because they were not married.

"Listen, Rosie, she's determined you're leaving tomorrow and there's no way she'll back down." Jack had been trying all week to persuade her that Stella was deadly serious about her leaving the house, but the stubborn mare paid no heed whatsoever. "Why don't you go home for a week or two? It's your dad's funeral and your sisters need you. You'll regret it if you don't and it'll give me a bit more time to get us a place."

"Let's get a few things straight, Jack, I'm not going back home, ever. I'm not going to any funeral. My sisters have never needed me. And as for Stella throwing me out, she won't do that if I start working for her."

"You don't have to work. I've told you a dozen times, I make enough for both of us. You think you know what it's about, but you'd be swallowed up within days. There would be no going back. Trust me, I've lived with it all my life and I won't let you ruin yours."

"My life's already ruined. What decent man is ever going to take me on?"

"Well, there's me, but maybe I'm not decent enough for you?" Jack answered her sadly.

"Of course you are, but you deserve more. A wife and family. You heard the doctor, there will be no more babies for me. I care far too much to saddle you with all my baggage, Jack, so I've decided to become a working girl, but an exceptionally choosy one. When Stella Gold hears my plan, not only will she not throw me out, she'll give me the best suite in the house."

"I won't let you do it, Rosie. I'll make sure Stella doesn't take you on. You'll thank me for it one day."

After an unsuccessful afternoon they decided to call it a day and return home.

Just as they were about to turn into Danube Street, Jack let out a yell.

"Fuck, Rosie, look what's behind us!" he shouted as he slammed on the brakes. Bringing the car screeching to a stop, he blocked the road to stop the line of police cars heading their way.

"Lock the doors and don't budge, no matter what they say. I need to buy some time and warn Stella," he gasped, jumping out of the car and racing off down the street.

"Move this vehicle!" the driver of the lead car shouted to Rosie. "Shift it or I'll shift it for you."

Having climbed into the driver's seat, Rosie played the helpless woman. "I can't, it won't budge. I don't know what to do, it just stopped," she called back.

The traffic on the main road was quickly backing up over the Dean Bridge towards town. Irate drivers were blowing their horns and threatening all sorts, not in the least intimidated by the presence of several squad cars, two meat wagons and a load of coppers.

"Turn the engine on," the police officer shouted at her, banging on the window.

"I don't know how to," Rosie was playing it up good style.

"What do you mean you don't know how to? Turn the bloody key," said an exasperated officer. "Turn the engine on or I'll have you for obstruction."

"I can't turn the key, there isn't one."

"What do you mean there isn't one? Open this door immediately," the officer exploded, having now been joined by a number of his colleagues and DCI Ross.

"What the hell's going on?" Ross demanded.

"Sorry, sir, but this young lady won't move her car. She says she has no keys and won't open the door."

"I'm not opening the door while you're shouting at me," said Rosie, tears streaming down her face. "It's not my fault my fiancé jumped out and left me."

"What? Why did he jump out and leave you?" asked the DCI.

"He saw you all coming and ran off. I think he thought you were coming for him."

DCI Ross was now aware of a number of pedestrians strolling up Danube Street. Most were scantily-dressed and certainly not in what one would consider appropriate attire.

"Trouble, Detective Chief Inspector? Anything we can do to help?" Stella asked Ross pleasantly.

"What do you want me to do about the traffic, sir? It's backed up all the way into town," his driver asked with trepidation.

Looking back at the chaos and his would-be prisoners cavorting about on the pavement, Ross had no alternative but to abort his mission.

Furious, he turned to Rosie and said, "You tell your fiancé that if I ever come across him he'll be a sorry lad and I'll be the one throwing away the key."

He spun on his heels and marched back to his squad car, Stella's laughter ringing in his ears.

Jack had burst into the house yelling, "Fire! Fire!" at the top of his voice, knowing it was the only thing that would get the house moving.

"What the hell are you shouting about? There's no fire," yelled Stella back at him.

"No, but there's a bloody convoy of police cars coming this way, you need to get everyone out."

"What do you mean a convoy?"

"Don't fucking stand about blethering, woman! Get everybody out."

"Okay, okay. C'mon girls, hurry, the boys in blue are on their way. Let's show them what they're missing." Stella hurried the inhabitants out on to the pavement. She locked the door behind them and 17 Danube Street was closed to business.

Stella and the girls strolled up to where Rosie was holding court.

"Are you alright? Is this big bad policeman shouting at you?" Stella addressed Rosie.

"You should be ashamed of yourself, a great lump like you frightening a poor, defenceless, young lass. Don't cry, girlie. He won't shout at you again, or he'll have me to deal with."

The Sergeant backed away from Stella.

"Good afternoon Mister Ross," said Stella knowing full well this would aggravate the Chief Inspector. "Can we be of assistance?" The Madame faced up to her nemesis. "Your men seem to be causing a bit of a traffic jam."

"Your day will come lady, mark my words," the chief snarled.

"Are you threatening me?" she called after him. "This is police harassment and I have several witnesses. Isn't that so Councillor McNeil?" An elderly man melted into the crowd.

Rosie climbed out of the driver's seat to cheers from the girls and a grateful Stella.

"I take it I don't have to move out just yet?" Rosie laughed at the expression on Stella face.

"Thanks for today, but you're still on borrowed time," replied Stella.

Watching from the other side of the street and taking everything in was Rosie's fiercest enemy, Big Mags. She was still in contact with a few of the older girls and was kept up to speed with the comings and goings of the house.

She had been well aware that her plan to teach Cinderella a lesson had worked. Rosie no longer had her child and was supposedly being kicked out one day soon. Although, that seemed to have been put on the back burner, judging by the conversation she had just overheard. How had the bitch landed on her feet again? Mags couldn't help herself and shouting across to Rosie, she taunted, "Hey, Cinderella, how's the kid? It looks like my phone calls did the trick then."

In a flash, and before anyone could stop her, Rosie flew across the road. Taking the big woman completely by surprise, she jumped on her back. Gripping Mags' straggly bleached hair tightly, she bashed her head, again and again, against the railings.

"Get off, Rosie, there are far too many cops about," Jack yelled, hauling the tigress off her opponent and bundling her down the area steps.

"Get to hell out of here before I let her back at you, along with a few of her mates," Stella shooed her ex-employee away.

"Tell her she's dead. I'll be back and she'd better watch out."

"Aye, you said that the last time and look at you. Bugger off before we get really serious," Stella laughed in her face. "Give my regards to the Williams brothers. I hear they run a real nice gaff."

Mags, beside herself with temper, and seething at Stella's remarks, aimed a punch at her ex-employer, but unfortunately she missed and made contact with DCI Ross's nose. Blood spurting everywhere, he threw Mags into a police car and huckled her back to the station.

"I didn't mean it, it was an accident," the big woman pleaded with the desk sergeant. "I didn't mean to hit the inspector. It was meant for Stella."

"So you admit you did mean to hit someone?" inquired the sergeant.

"I'm telling you it was an accident."

"Well, this is no accident. You're being charged with assaulting a police officer, and as you are currently out on licence, you will be returned to Scorston Prison later today, to serve out the remainder of your sentence."

Mags was led away kicking and screaming.

CHAPTER THIRTY-SIX

Wagging Tongues

Iris and Violet had begged Rosie to attend the hearing into the cause of their father's death, without success.

The coroner's verdict had been returned as 'Death by Misadventure'. Their father's demise had been nothing more than a tragic accident. James Royce had been killed by a blow to the head caused by a fall. However, few members of his family and friends believed the verdict. They all knew it was that Italian vixen who had got away scot-free.

Rosie stood in the graveyard, amazed at how many mourners had turned up on this cold winter's day. It was standing room only in the small chapel, but how many were there to pay their respects to their friend and neighbour? Or had they just come to see if the scarlet woman appeared? Rumours had been rife since news had got out that James Royce had not been found dead in his bed, as any respectable husband should be, but in his estranged wife's apartment which was in a not-so-affluent area of the city.

They whispered it was an accident, but if that was the case, where was she? And what about the youngest girl? She'd not been seen for months and yet here she was, brazen as you like, playing the grieving daughter.

It was Kitty who had finally persuaded Rosie to attend.

"So you got a stay of execution then," the old cook stated, pleased for Rosie, handing her a cup of hot sweet tea.

"Och! I knew something would turn up, it always does,

and I'll continue to help out anyway I can."

"Has she not said anything about you going out front?" Kitty questioned her.

"No, but I've got a proposal I'm going to put to her when things calm down a bit, which might open up another opportunity."

"Well, the missus has a good business head on her, so good luck, but that's not why I wanted to speak to you."

"I'm sure I can guess, and much as I love you, Kitty, it's a no."

"Wait till you hear what I have to say before you make up your mind."

"It'll still be no."

"Tell me something, when you landed in hospital what did your sisters do?"

"What do you mean?"

"I'm asking, what did they do for you? Well, I'll tell you, lass. They defied your da and caught the first bus into town."

"So?"

"So, they dropped everything and rushed to your bedside, despite the grief they got from him. And they stayed with you until you were out of danger."

"I'm well aware of what my sisters did. I've spoken with them and they understand how I feel. I can't go and play the grief-stricken daughter."

"Lass, I understand. Your da should never have done what he did. It was unforgiveable, but he's paid the price and it's not him I'm asking for, it's your sisters. They've stood by you and now it's your turn, Rosie."

"I love them dearly, Kitty, and I would do almost anything for them, but not this."

"Think, Rosie. Those poor lasses have to live and work in that village. People talk, and I bet right now they're all having a field day. First your mum traipses off with a Yank, with not a thought for you girls. Then you disappear without word nor warning, to visit some distant relation. And to top it all, your dad snuffs it in what can only be described as suspicious circumstances. Iris and Violet will never live this down and it's not fair.to expect them to."

"There will be gossip with or without my attendance."

"True, but who'll have to face it? Those two lassies, who have done nothing but right by you."

"I've told you, I can't go and play the devoted daughter, I'm not a hypocrite."

"Of course you can! Do it for your sisters. Go and make sure the old bastard really has gone to his grave. He can't do any more harm from there."

"No, Kitty. I've said all I'm going to say on the matter."

"Well, I thought there was more to you than this, a selfish spoiled child, who won't stand by her family. Go on, get out of my sight."

"My family didn't stand by me when I was kicked out and penniless."

"Maybe, but they came up trumps in the end. Please, Rosie, your sisters need you. Go and pay your respects. Put the wagging tongues to rest."

CHAPTER THIRTY-SEVEN

Double Jeopardy

The DCI was in a foul mood on the way back to the station. Aborting the raid and clearing up the traffic congestion would take some explaining. Hamish Ross knew he was in trouble. Hadn't he already been pulled up over the exorbitant amounts spent on the previous raids? The costs involved in this latest debacle could result in a suspension or a transfer. For the first time in a long while Hamish was a worried man.

Back at the station the two colleagues were discussing the recent debacle.

"I told you it was personal between those two," said Cummins, even more convinced he was right.

"He'll get carpeted for this, mark my words, and he deserves it. What a waste of time and resources to capture a brass. One who'll get off anyway with all the councillors and judges she's got in her pocket."

"I hope he does get booted out and we get back to proper policing and catching real criminals."

"Don't kid yourself. According to him he can't fail. He's got the premier division on his side, a direct line to the Lord God Almighty, and that makes him invincible."

"Maybe so, but he's not getting it all his own way. Did you see his face when the lassie told him she didn't have the keys?"

"I thought he was going to burst a blood vessel."

"Aye, and meet his maker sooner than expected."

On his return to the station Hamish locked himself in his office, striding back and forth muttering. He had to come good. Somehow, he had to have Stella Gold in the cells before word got back to his superiors. They wouldn't accept any excuses this time; she had to be locked up tight.

There was nothing else for it, he'd have to go back to Danube Street tonight, under cover. A softly, softly approach this time. The element of surprise could work. After all, none of those trollops would be expecting another visit tonight, they'd be too busy celebrating his failure. He'd show them.

"PC Cummins, a minute," DCI Ross called over to the two Constables. "I've got a job for you and your partner, a bit of overtime."

"Sorry, sir, no can do tonight. We've got an inter-division football match starting at six." As they hurried off, the two watched as the DCI captured a couple of substitutes.

There was no way the two seasoned PCs were being caught up in their boss's mess.

At just after nine p.m., the three undercover cops turned into Danube Street. Even this early the salon was busy, so how were they to gain entry without giving the game away? He should never doubt his faith, Hamish Ross chastised himself. The Lord, of course, was looking after him. Right on cue, two taxis filled with inebriated coppers on a stag do drew alongside. Ross had been concerned as to how the three of them would carry his mission off. It was a well-known fact that brasses could smell a copper from five miles away, but here was the solution, delivered right into his lap. The three men melted into the boisterous group and slipped in unnoticed.

The DCI recognised a few faces. For starters, the impudent mare on reception was none other than the cause of his failure this afternoon; she would keep. He had only one target in his sights tonight and there she was, holding court, surrounded by a bevy of influential citizens. There was no way she would escape him this time.

It was a few years since Ross had been in this den of iniquity and it was exactly as he remembered. She, too, looked exactly the same – the devils spawn had not aged a jot since the night Reverend Jock Ross met his maker.

"Buy me a drink, mister?" A painted whore interrupted his thoughts. "Want to have a good time?"

"Of course, what's your pleasure?"

"Port and lemon, thanks. Are you with this lot?" asked the hostess, pointing to the boisterous stag party.

"Yeah, one of my lads gets hitched at the weekend. This is his last night of freedom."

"I thought you were all cops," she answered nervously.

"Hey, we're off duty, only here for a good time," Ross placated his companion.

"Thank God for that. We had a right episode this afternoon with some of your lot, but the missus sent them packing."

"Really? Tell me, which one is Stella? I've heard of her but never met her."

"That's her over there. C'mon, I'll introduce you."

"Oh no, she's in company and it sounds like she's had enough of us today. Don't bother her, I was just curious," said Ross, playing his part to the full.

"She won't mind. She likes to meet new clients."

As the girl pushed her way towards Stella, Ross nodded to his two accomplices to follow him.

"Stella, let me introduce you to a new client," the young girl turned. "Sorry, I didn't catch your name."

"Detective Chief Inspector Hamish Ross, and DCs Jones and Kelly. Stella Gold, I'm arresting you on the charge of living off immoral earnings. You are not obliged to say anything but anything you do say may be used in evidence…"

Before Stella could reply, she was handcuffed, marched out of the building and into a waiting police car.

"What the fuck happened there?" Jack said as he made

for the door, but he was too late, the police car had already crossed the Dean Bridge on its way to Gayfield Square.

"Rosie, call Marcus, his home number is in the directory. Tell him it's an emergency, Stella is in custody."

Unfortunately, Marcus was not to be found. It seemed he was on one of his frequent jaunts out of town, no doubt in the company of some young, nubile boy.

He'd done it, he'd snatched her from under their noses. Stella Gold was currently residing in cell number one in Gayfield Square Police Station, awaiting her appearance in court the next morning. He would make dammed sure she would not be returning to Danube Street for some considerable time.

Edinburgh Evening News

The renowned Madame Stella Gold is in police custody. A spokesman for the Lothian and Borders police confirmed she will appear in court today...

CHAPTER THIRTY-EIGHT

Doppelganger

Freddie Williams wasn't used to being kept waiting and today was no exception. All he wanted was to pick up some shirts he'd ordered earlier in the week. Jenner's had the best gents department in the city and because he found it difficult to buy his shirts anywhere else, he refrained from kicking up a fuss.

His departure was delayed by snatches of a conversation he overheard from the fitting room. He was puzzled, he knew that voice, he was sure of it. "Well, bugger me, how weird," he sniggered to himself.

Stepping out from the fitting room, with what looked to be a pile of school uniforms, was none other than Marcus Kramer, the bastard who'd done them over on the Danube Street fracas. Chuckling to himself, he wondered if the old buzzard had ever suspected he, Freddie, was responsible for that slapper Mary departing this world. Not even his brother had an inkling it had been him.

Freddie hated being bested by anyone, and being made to pay for the care and treatment of that fucking slag ate away at him. For once, though, he'd played the long game, fooling them all. His brother never suspected that Freddie could be so devious. He'd always been a 'hit first, question later' type of guy. For over a year he paid regular visits to the nursing home he was funding, which also proved to be excellent cover for his current drugs run. The staff were completely taken in by the big handsome man pining for his beloved.

When a shipment was due, Freddie would collect the

merchandise and drive the five miles to visit Mary. Should anyone be following him or setting a trap, these visits were ideal cover.

He spent time with Mary, talking and watching her, unlike Stella or the care staff who spoke incessantly at her, but paid no real attention. There were slight nuances, an intensity of her stare, just a look about her that made him absolutely positive Mary could understand everything he said. The more he abused her verbally, the more convinced he was that she understood him. Like a cat playing with a mouse, time and time again he threatened to finish her off. He could see the gleam in her eyes, the woman wanted release and who could blame her?

Regularly, Freddie placed a pillow over Mary's face and took her right to the brink of death, to almost her last breath and then he would withdraw. Knowing the torture she was going through, he enjoyed every second.

"Soon Mary, very soon I'll put you out of your misery, but not quite yet."

He was growing tired of the game, though, and with a recent change in the drugs route there was no need for him to visit the area any longer. However, he had a little unfinished business to attend to. He couldn't take the chance on Mary ever regaining consciousness, he had to make sure there were no connections to be made.

On his last visit, he teased and tormented the poor woman beyond endurance. He could see the silent pleading in her eyes, begging him to finish the job and then he heard her.

Christ, was it his imagination? The merest whisper, "Freddie, I'm awake, I'm awake. Help me, please help." Freddie Williams, tough guy, hard man, freaked out for a brief moment. Had he imagined it, had she really spoken to him,? Was she conscious?

There was never any suspicion that the Williams brothers, or anyone else for that matter, had a hand in Mary's death. It was such a pity no-one else had heard her last words when she regained consciousness for the final time.

Only yesterday he and Ronnie had been discussing the prospect of regaining the house in Danube Street and here was Marcus in the flesh, looking decidedly uncomfortable.

Well, fuck me! Freddie was stunned. Who was this little soldier? He'd heard on the grapevine that Marcus had a son and here he was, but this young pup was definitely no kin to the Kramer family.

"Well, well, who do we have here?" Freddie shook the young lad by the hand.

"Oliver Kramer, sir. Are you a friend of my father?" the young lad replied, smiling at the newcomer.

"You'd better ask your old man that question, laddie."

"Parcel these up and have them delivered to my chambers," Kramer senior addressed the shop assistant. Deliberately ignoring Freddie's presence, he hurried Oliver out of the store.

"Who was that man, Father? He was quite scary?"

"A client, son. Not someone you're likely to come across, and certainly not one to be afraid of."

Amused at the chance meeting, Freddie Williams watched as the father and son made a hasty retreat from the store. Boy, oh boy, what a fucking turn-up for the book. There was no mistaking it, the boy was the spitting image of his brother and he was damned sure Ronnie knew nothing about him.

CHAPTER THIRTY-NINE

Eyes Wide Shut

Day after day she lay in bed. Several times a day someone came in and turned her to prevent bed sores and to check on her food. What a joke, a tube of something fed into her stomach to sustain her, why? Why didn't they stop the feed, not bother turning her, just let her die? She wouldn't tell anyone if they neglected her, how could she? What did it matter if the staff didn't do their job properly? All Mary wanted was to leave this living hell.

As time went on and having been transferred out of the city, her visitors dwindled. Good old Agnes (she couldn't, even now, get used to calling her Stella) came religiously on the first Monday of the month. Big deal, one day a month. Why bother? It was a token visit and all it did was remind Mary of everything she was missing, of the life she once had. Why would she want to know about people called Kitty or Dora? Or the news of some councillor caught with his pants down.

If only Mary could talk, she'd soon set the cat amongst the pigeons. She'd spill the beans about Oliver. Oh, she knew that Stella had slept with Ronnie Williams. Stella told Mary everything. Of course she did, there was no way Mary could betray her sordid little secrets. How could these people not see what was staring them straight in the face? If she could communicate it would be a very different story. Stella wouldn't be flaunting her wealth in Mary's face. After all it was Mary who had taken her from the farm and taught her everything she knew.

The only one who understood her situation was Freddie. Her Freddie, who came to visit as often as he could, who tried and tried to help her out of this hell, but being the man he was, just couldn't bring himself to finish the deed. She knew he wanted to, but she was sure he still held the belief that she would one day recover.

A wave of excitement swept over her, he was in the room; she could smell him. A mixture of Cuban cigars and the fresh, distinct smell of Old Spice. Let him open her eyes quickly, sometimes the visit would be almost over before he remembered. She could hear him crossing the room and then came the blinding light. It took a few minutes for her eyesight to adjust. There he was, handsome as ever. He seemed agitated and he was talking to himself, she hoped there was nothing amiss.

"Hello, Mary dear, how are things? Been anywhere exciting since I was here last? Of course not, you've been stuck in that bed, seeing and hearing nothing. Well, you're going on a journey today, my love. This is the last time, until we meet on the other side. I know I'm not going to heaven, but I shouldn't think you will either. So, for the moment, it's goodbye."

He kissed her, she couldn't believe it, he actually kissed her as he placed the pillow over her face.

Please God, make him go through with it this time, she prayed, but just as she could feel herself floating away, he removed the pillow, laughing.

"C'mon Mary, that's too easy. Settle down for a bit and we'll try again."

She was confused, why did he keep doing this? She thought he loved her, so why did he not finish what he started?

"Bye, love," he whispered as he pressed the soft pillow down on her face again.

She was nearly there, she could see the bright light, she was going. It was nearly over. Fuck! He stopped again. What was he playing at? Mary had not felt rage like this since that night, the night she'd been attacked. In a flash of brilliant clarity, she remembered. Christ, it was him, it was Freddie who had put her here and now the bastard was playing games with her. She'd had enough. Mary felt different. In that one moment she was conscious, she was alive, she could speak and it felt like she could move.

"Freddie, Freddie," she said, her voice but a whisper as she feebly clutched the pillow.

It was too late, she had no strength, she could see the light getting brighter. Be careful what you wish for, she thought as the light grew more intense.

Freddie, why? I loved you. Then the blackness descended.

CHAPTER FORTY

Guilty

Stella had spent a number of nights in custody over the years since Danube Street opened. Mostly thanks to some overzealous policing, but it had always been in the company of the other girls.

This gig was a different kettle of fish altogether. Who exactly was this DCI and what was his beef with her? She'd been operating under the radar for years. Even the neighbours had quietened down and accepted her presence. So what was this guy all about? Was he trying to make a name for himself? Surely there were easier ways of ridding the city of crime? Why didn't he clear up the girls who worked the streets and the docks, or the other houses in the city? A punter was more likely to catch something off them than any of her workers. Nor were they likely to be mugged by pimps in the process. This was something personal, but what? Where the hell was Marcus, why had he not been in touch? Instead she was left to languish in this shit-hole.

Rosie had brought a change of clothes for her, knowing the press would be out in full. Stella being Stella, she wouldn't appear in public looking anything less than her best. But where was her brief? Marcus had never let her down in the past, no matter what he was doing. He would drop everything for Stella even though relations between them were strained. No-one could contact him and time was marching on.

With only minutes to go before she was taken up, and despite a request for a postponement, Stella was appointed a duty solicitor to act on her behalf.

"How do you do, Miss Gold? My name's Nigel Sheridan. I'm here to represent you."

This lad looked as if he had just graduated high school, thought Stella, but she had no choice.

"I see you've been charged with 'living off immoral earnings' and from the charge sheet, you are classed as a habitual offender. At your last appearance in court, earlier this year, you pled guilty. And received a caution and were fined."

"That's correct. I want you to do the same, get it over and done with. I've spent long enough in this disgusting hole."

"Are you sure you don't wish to enter a plea of not guilty until you can consult with your usual legal representative?"

"Plead guilty and let's get it over. I'm sure my usual brief would tell me to do the same. I can't think what's happened to him."

"I would recommend you plead not guilty, just to be on the safe side."

"That means this could drag on for months. No, enter a guilty plea."

The public gallery was full to capacity; the girls were all out in force, along with several members of the press. It wasn't often they had such a celebrity in their midst. Stella, despite her worries, smiled and waved to her public.

"Please rise. Judge Bernard Turnbull presiding," announced the clerk of the court.

Watching the elderly judge take his seat, Stella was delighted to see old Bernie. He was a valued and regular client, she was on home ground here.

"I promise to tell the truth, the whole truth and nothing but the truth, so help me God."

"You are Miss Stella Gold of Danube Street, City of Edinburgh?"

"I am," answered Stella.

"Miss Gold, you are charged with living off immoral earnings. How do you plead?"

"Guilty your honour."

Judge Turnbull looked up and, staring straight at Stella, asked, "Are you sure, Miss Gold?"

"Yes, your honour."

Having been through this procedure several times in the past, Stella just wanted to be home, in a hot bath and with some of Kitty's chicken broth.

"You do understand, Miss Gold, that this charge can carry a custodial sentence of up to two years?"

"I do, my lord."

"I'll ask you once again, Miss Gold. Do you wish to change your plea?"

"No, your honour, I just want this to be over with."

Judge Turnbull was in a quandary. Here before him was one of the most infamous madams in the city, also a great friend of his, pleading guilty to a charge for which he had no choice but to impose a prison sentence. He had already compromised his position by not admitting he knew Stella and interfered with due process by questioning her plea.

"Counsels please approach the bench."

"Before I pass sentence have either of you anything to say?"

Counsel for the prosecution was adamant, given the history of the accused, that she be given a prison sentence. The defence asked for leniency on the basis she had not wasted the courts time and proposed a heavy fine.

Judge Turnbull did, in his opinion, the best he could for his old friend. It was a shame Marcus Kramer was not in court, he would have tied the prosecution up in knots, but there was little else the judge could do.

"Stella Gold, I hereby sentence you to six months at Her Majesty's pleasure."

There was an audible gasp from the gallery. The missus was going down. Jesus, what would happen to them? The reporters were going mad, light bulbs flashing frantically.

"What?" exclaimed Stella. "That's not right. I get a fine!

I've always only got a fine! I want to change my plea. I want a retrial."

"Order, order." The clerk of the court was unsuccessfully endeavouring to restore calm.

"I'm sorry, Miss Gold, the bench gave you ample opportunity to change your plea," the clerk addressed her. "Take the prisoner down."

Stella was furious with herself. How could she have been so stupid? Why hadn't she listened, and why had Marcus not been in court defending her? And as for that stupid old goat, why on earth had he not just whacked a bloody great fine on her and closed the case as usual?

Marcus arrived at court looking dishevelled and anxious, just as Stella was being led down to the holding cells. Despite their differences, over the years Marcus would always have her best interests at heart, or so she thought.

"I need a word with my client," he addressed Judge Turnbull.

"It's not usual practice, but there are obviously extenuating circumstances," said the judge, noting Marcus's appearance.

"Where the fuck have you been?" his client fumed at him.

"I'm sorry, Stella, I've been in the hospital all night with Oliver."

"What's wrong with him? Why is he in hospital? My God, Marcus, is it serious?"

"He's been off colour for the past week, but I thought it was the flu. Things took a turn for the worse yesterday and he was admitted to the children's ward early evening."

"What's wrong? What do the doctors think? Stella was becoming more and more distressed.

"Polio, they think he's contracted polio."

"Oh my God," Stella wept.

The disease was rife in Scotland and the mortality rate was terrifyingly high. Few families escaped the vicious disease.

"How bad is he?" a panic-stricken Stella asked.

"Bad." Marcus replied. "He's in an iron lung to help with his breathing, but he's not responding to treatment. Look, Stella, I can't stay. I have to get back to him."

"Of course. Marcus, is there any chance we can get this overturned so that I can get out to be with him?"

"Right now I've no idea. Why on earth did you plead guilty?"

"I always plead guilty and it's over and done with."

"You knew if you appeared again it would be a custodial. The judge told you so."

"I know, I know, but when I saw old Bernie I thought I was home and dry."

"Trust me, you were. He did you a good deal. Anyone else would have put you away for at least twelve months."

"He could have given me a fine, Marcus, Christ, he's a mate."

"Yes, he is, and he should have declared an interest. You owe him a decent drink for that. He put his neck on the block for you."

"Never mind him, can you get it over turned?" Stella's anxious face spoke volumes.

"I don't know, and sorry, but right now my boy is my main concern."

"Of course, but don't forget he's my son too." Stella stared him straight in the eye. "Please keep me posted. If there's any change, get word to me."

"I will, I promise."

"Any chance I could have a word with Jack?"

"He's just waiting for me to leave."

Right on his heels came an anxious Jack, "Oh Stella, what a bummer. I thought you were going to get away with a fine when I saw old Bernie."

"Me too, Jack, me too."

"What happened to Marcus? How on earth did you end up

with that dingbat? Fuck, I would have been better representing you. It's a fine time for Marcus to go walkabout."

"His son is ill. He's been at the hospital all night and he's on his way back there now."

"Shit! Sorry for the boy and all that, but we needed him too."

"I just said his son's ill," snapped Stella. "We're the last thing on his mind."

"Sorry, of course you're right."

"Do you think you could hold the fort for a bit, till I get things organised?"

"Yeah, sure, there's nothing much I've not dealt with and Marcus can keep me right."

"I don't think he'll be about much."

"Is the lad that bad?" asked Jack.

"I'm afraid so."

Were those tears? He didn't think Stella knew the boy all that well. Maybe she was shaken by her present circumstances.

"Don't you be concerned, we'll be fine and I'll visit as often as I can."

Hamish Ross was in the witness room when he heard that the bitch had pleaded guilty. He couldn't believe it. God did work in mysterious ways. He was a bit disappointed she only got six months, a measly six months. Still, he should be grateful he'd managed to get her put away. Who knew what could befall her in such a place?

DCI Ross lived with the anger and shame of his father's fall from grace every day. He could still picture him cavorting with that whore. What was worse, he was by no means the only minister enjoying the company of these harlots; the salon was full of them – disgusting, two-faced hypocrites, purporting to be god-fearing Christians.

Hamish had never loved his father, but the young man had

had the greatest respect for him. He was a righteous man, a man of his word. He lived by the commandments and tried his best to have his family and congregation follow suit. Until that moment Hamish truly believed the reverend Jock was a true man of principals, but not so.

Having just graduated from training college, Hamish Ross's first placement was in St. Leonards, a large station on the south side of the city. During his probationary period, he was called to a disturbance at the infamous address in Danube Street.

When Ross and his partner arrived at the scene, the two adversaries had already been ejected from the premises and staggered off arm in arm, blissfully unaware of the profound effect their skirmish was about to have.

The two young constables, eager to experience their first call to such a renowned address, were not giving up the opportunity to prolong their visit and entered the premises to take witness statements from both clients and hostesses, much to the annoyance of the doyenne.

"There's nothing to tell," she insisted. "We managed to get the two guys off the premises and other than myself and a passing stranger, nobody saw a thing."

That was not quite true, Hamish Ross saw something. Something so shocking he couldn't believe his eyes. A sight he would never have believed possible.

Descending the wide staircase from the rooms was none other than his pious, god-fearing father, arm in arm with one of those painted whores. Laughing and jesting, so engrossed with his companion, the Reverend Jock failed to notice the young policeman standing open-mouthed, shocked to his very core.

"Let's go, there's nothing to more to be done here." PC Ross addressed his sidekick.

"No way, man, I'd rather spend the next half hour in here than pounding the streets in the pouring rain," answered his partner, appalled at the prospect.

"Do what you want but I'm out of here," Ross was adamant, desperately trying to pull himself together.

My God, his father in a place like this! He couldn't believe it. What were the chances of him catching the old rogue out? This wasn't even his usual beat. No, it was definitely not a coincidence that he had arrived at this den of iniquity to find his father and his contemptible associates.

He had to be punished. It was the Lord's wish. What other reason would there be for his son to find him? He was nothing more than a hypocritical, lying heathen, ruling his family and congregation as a religious despot when he was nothing but a lying, cheating whore-master who would soon feel the wrath of God.

Edinburgh Evening News

The body of an elderly man was found in the water of Leith this morning. It is thought to be that of a missing clergyman, attending the General Assembly. Police are treating his death as suspicious…

CHAPTER FORTY-ONE

Clean Up

Word had certainly got around, the salon was packed to capacity. Most were regular punters, concerned that Danube Street was still in business. Few could believe Stella was actually in prison or that she had pleaded guilty. There was a certain amount of gloating amongst the legal eagles in attendance, smugly assuring anyone who would listen, that had she come to them, the Madam would not have been spending the next 180 days confined, courtesy of Her Majesty. It was hard to believe that the great Marcus Kramer had not woven his usual magic. Rumour had it she'd sacked him; others said that he had refused to represent her. Whatever the reason, it was hoped things wouldn't change; the house would remain the same, although most doubted it.

It wasn't just the clients who were fearful, Jack was equally concerned. Concerned that he could meet the challenge he'd been set. Could he maintain the business? After all, it was Stella who was the attraction, who was the allure and drew the punters in. Could he really carry this off?

"It's been a bit of a shock," Jack confided in Rosie. "Let's just get through the evening and see what the options are tomorrow."

"I know you don't want to let her down, but it's a hell of a job to take on, Jack. Of course, I'll help and do anything I can to assist, but truthfully, I'm not sure if I'd be more of a hindrance than a help."

The words were hardly out of Rosie's mouth when Claire, one of the most popular girls, grabbed hold of Jack pulling him out of the salon.

"Jack, I didn't do anything bad, honest, he just collapsed."

"What are you talking about, Claire? Who just collapsed?"

"That old geezer, the judge. I think he's done for Jack."

A soon as he opened the door Jack could smell the amyl nitrate. His eyes watering, he turned on the girl. "You've been using poppers, don't deny it, I can smell them. For fuck's sake, you've given him a bloody heart attack. He must be seventy if he's a day, you stupid fool. Get back out to the salon and keep your mouth shut. I mean it, or you're in big trouble. Fetch Rosie and remember, keep your trap shut."

"For fuck's sake, Rosie, lift! Get your end up."

"I can't, he's too heavy," the young woman whined. "I can't move him, we'll never be able to do this without help," she replied.

"Fucking brilliant, why not go out into the salon and ask for volunteers? Hey, anybody willing to help shift the dead body next door? It's only the illustrious Judge Bernard Turnbull. Yes, that's the one! The same judge who today sentenced Stella Gold, the owner of these premises, to six months at Her Majesty's Pleasure."

"Keep your voice down," Rosie bit back at him. "We didn't finish him off. The silly old fool shouldn't have been shagging at his age anyway."

"I agree, but he also shouldn't have been given a popper by some greedy tart, but he was, so we still have to get him out of here. If we report it, guaranteed we'll be shut down, probably for good." Jack was trying desperately not to lose his temper with both the struggling girl and the fat old sod, half-naked, straddled across the four poster bed.

"The salon is heaving with nosy buggers dying to know the gossip. The last bloody thing we need is the occupants of Gayfield Square Police Station knocking at the front door."

"What do you suggest? I can't move him an inch, never

mind along the passage and out into the back yard, and what do I say to the girls? They all know something's gone down."

"Never mind those nosy tarts, they'll make up stories no matter what we tell them. But you're right, we can't do it ourselves. Maybe we should call Gayfield, Square? On second thoughts, we could get a clean-up squad in. They would have it done and dusted in less than an hour. We've been struggling with the fat old git for almost that now and there's no-one looking after the shop."

"Jesus, Jack, on our first night looking after the place, surely there's another way?"

"If you know of one, be my guest, otherwise shut up and let me get on with it."

Jack was right, once they had called in the squad, it took precisely one hour for the removal of the body and the room to be put back to normal, ready for business. Jack had to admit the Williams brothers certainly took care of the situation.

Wandering round the salon for the first time in years, Freddie Williams couldn't believe it was the same place. The change in Danube Street was nothing short of miraculous, nothing like the shabby dosshouse it had been when they owned the gaff.

Six months. Stella Gold certainly had old Turnbull in her pocket. A pissing six months, and it was highly unlikely she would serve more than half that time. Anyone else would have copped for at least twelve. So that's why the old coot would have been in celebrating tonight. A little 'thank you', maybe?

Stella would have a bloody fit when she found out he had his foot back in the door, and by the time she got out he planned on being well and truly ensconced. He laughed to himself, yes, he was back where he'd always known he belonged.

"Thank you Judge Turnbull, may you Rest in Peace," chortled Freddie Williams

CHAPTER FORTY-TWO

Holding the Fort

Jack and Rosie were closeted in Stella's office. "How we got away with that last night, God only knows."

"No matter what you think, Rosie, we couldn't have done that on our own and hey, they don't come cheap. That operation cost a monkey. The biggest cost, though, is the prospect of having that mad bugger on the premises whenever it takes his fancy."

"Is he that bad?" asked Rosie.

"You better believe it. Christ, I nearly fucking died when I saw him walk in. I never for a moment thought either would come in person. I presumed they'd send a couple of men to do the job."

"Maybe he wanted to know who was running the place since Stella had gone down," Rosie ventured.

"I need to hire a couple of doormen, not that that would stop the Williams brothers if they fancied a visit, but it might deter any other pretenders."

"We also need to hire another bartender. You can't be behind the bar and keep on top of what is going on in here."

"You're right. I'll get on to that tomorrow."

"You'll think I'm losing my marbles, but what about Kitty?"

"Eh? You are losing them."

"Dress her up, make her look respectable. She doesn't have to be Miss World to serve drinks and keep order."

"That might work. Let's face it, the punters won't hang around the bar while she's on."

"Do you really think this is going to work? Would it not be better just to close till Stella gets out?" Rosie asked doubtfully.

"Don't be so pessimistic, girl. We have to give it our best shot. The punters will still come, even if it's just to see if the place has fallen apart."

"Freddie Williams scares me. Did you see him strutting about the salon as if he owned it?"

"Well, he did at one time. I don't know the full story, but Stella got the house off them in payment for a debt or something. As I said, I don't know all the ins and outs, but I do know she's going to be mad as hell at us for bringing them in."

"Forget 'us', it was your idea, I was dead against it."

"Fuck off, Rosie, we'd still be struggling with him now."

"I suppose so," she conceded. "Anyway, you paid them, so there's no need for them to come back."

"Mm, I hope you're right."

An almost identical conversation was taking place in Chez Williams, concerning the surprise call from Danube Street.

"Hey, what about last night, bro? I swear to God I couldn't believe they had the fucking balls to call us. Pity you were otherwise engaged."

"You should have sent a couple of the lads, not got personally involved. You knew it wasn't Stella, she's banged up for the next six months."

"Of course I knew. Wasn't the stiff the judge who put her away? It certainly opens the door for us. Seriously, Ronnie, you should see the place. I say it's takeover time. Who's going to stop us?"

"That smart-ass lawyer for a start. He'll slap an injunction on us so fast our old man will feel it. We won't be allowed within a hundred yards of the place."

"We don't have to be on site to be running the gaff."

"Look, brother, we've waited this long, another few months won't make any difference."

"Doesn't it bother you how long she's been coining it in? Fuck, it was one of our best gaffs, stolen from under our fucking noses by her and Kramer."

"Sure, but remember how our old man got it in the first place."

"Shit, are you going soft? He won it fair and square."

"Fair and square?" laughed Ronnie. "I would hardly call pointing a gun at a punter's head and forcing him to flip for the family home, exactly fair and square."

"So, he shouldn't have gambled."

"You're right, but you can't blame Kramer for wanting revenge."

"Kramer? What the fuck's he got to do with it?"

"It was his father."

"His father what?"

"It was Kramer's father who lost the house and two days later blew his brains out."

"Fuck!"

"I thought you knew."

"No, that's news to me."

CHAPTER FORTY-THREE

All Good Things Come to Those Who Wait

So, he could be human after all, was the consensus of opinion by Hamish Ross's men, as he joined them in the pub at the end of the shift. The squad had never seen him in such good humour; maybe they had misjudged him? He was certainly a dedicated cop. Once he got the bit between his teeth he wouldn't let go until he had solved the case. He was certainly pleased with the outcome tonight, and despite his misgivings, it was the right thing to join his men for a celebratory drink.

Hamish allowed himself the odd treat when a mission was completed, but alcohol usually played no part. Therefore, after a couple of obligatory drinks and dressed in his civvies, the DCI drove down Leith Walk towards the docks, seeking out Jeannie's spot.

As a rookie policeman, he had made the acquaintance of Jeannie Hunter many years ago. In fact, it had been on the very night his father met his maker. The euphoria of doing God's will and achieving his blessing led Hamish to Jeannie. This was his reward, the voices told him. She was there for him.

He was one of those rare breeds who could find satisfaction with either sex, but only when he deserved it. God knows he had worked for his reward that night.

Jeannie could spot a headcase a mile away and this guy certainly fell into that bracket. He was a sleazy fucker, always spouting passages from the bible and insisting on more than he paid for. But as far as Jeannie was concerned, he was no worse than most and he had been one of her regulars for years. She might see him once a week or he'd go AWOL for months.

The prostitute had had her suspicions from the beginning about Mr Sleazebag, as she and Jack nicknamed him, away in the dim and distant past. She was convinced he was a cop, the hair and the shoes being a dead giveaway. No young guy nowadays had the short, back and sides of their fathers and certainly no one wore highly-polished boots but cops. She couldn't have cared less if he was the fucking Police Commissioner, as long as he paid her and didn't give her any grief.

Hamish hadn't been down this way for some time, but there she was. Shivering in the cold air, her tits out on display and skirt up to her arse, she almost defied description. She was like a demon, a vicious angry demon, there for him to consume.

Hamish never used a rubber, despite Jeannie's profession. He was safe, the Lord would not have provided her if that were not the case. Jeannie always made the point that they should use one, but Hamish refused and she wasn't giving up the money for his stupidity. If he had to visit the VD clinic once in a while, so be it.

"Hey, big boy, long time no see. What are we celebrating tonight? Catch Herman Goering then?"

"What do you mean? Why would I be catching anyone?" Hamish turned and walked back the way he came.

"Give me a break, I was only having a bit of a laugh. I don't give a fuck what or who you do, I'm just here for the money, honey."

"No more remarks about what I do, or I might just do you."

The voices were clamouring in his ear, maybe he should pass on this tonight? No, he was all worked up and he was here now.

For once Jeannie's flat was warm, and as inviting as a hovel could be. Her punter, not the most personable of creatures at any time, was even weirder than before. The man was jabbering away to himself. From the tone of the conversation, he appeared to be chastising himself for some actions which he seemed to have no control over.

Over the years Jeannie had come across all sorts, she'd even taken a few beatings, but never, not once, had she ever offered a punter his money back. This one was way off beam, though.

"Look, pal, I'm not up to it tonight. I've just come on and it wouldn't be right. Another time, okay?"

He threw Jeannie down on the brick-hard bed, tearing at her skimpy clothes, all the while calling her every contemptible name imaginable. She was a she-devil, he was going to cleanse her, free her from sin and lead her to paradise.

Jeannie couldn't decide whether to play possum or fight back; this lunatic was having his money's worth, regardless, as he rode harder and harder, calling all the time for redemption and for his sins to be washed away.

The bastard was off his head. Jeannie couldn't shift him.

"Repent!" he screamed at her. "Ask the lord for forgiveness." He began slapping her, wrenching out clumps of her hair.

"I repent! I repent, Lord!" shouted Jeannie. She fucking would, if the Lord she was calling on got her out of this mess. "Forgive me, Lord," Jeannie begged.

The seasoned prostitute was terrified he was going to finish her off, that she wasn't going to get out of this one alive. By now she was screaming at the top of her lungs.

A loud bang on the door and voices out on the landing brought her ordeal to an end. Thank fuck for nosey neighbours, she thought as she breathed an immense sigh of relief.

"What the fuck's going on in there?" shouted her next-door neighbour.

"Jeannie, you okay?" called another. "I'm phoning the cops."

"No, I'm okay. Fuck off the lot of you. Can't a girl have a party once in a while?"

"A fucking party?" replied the neighbour. "Don't fucking invite me to your next one, ya mad cow."

"Right, you," Jeannie snarled at her attacker. Never one to miss an opportunity, she demanded, "You're going to cough up fucking double what you've already paid or you won't get out of here alive." Jeannie, shaking like a leaf, couldn't pass up on the chance for a bit extra and she reckoned she had more than earned it.

Counting out the extra money, Ross apologised again and again to the woman he had half-killed. "I'm sorry, Jeannie, I just got a bit carried away."

"A bit carried away? Fuck off, ya psycho bastard, and don't ever come back. I might still be tempted to call the cops. Though I'm sure your lot would just cover up for you. Now fuck off and don't come back."

Tentatively opening the door, he had no choice but to run the gauntlet of neighbours still chatting on the stairway.

"You better not have hurt her," said one bruiser of a man, squaring up to him.

"Give him a dig anyway," said his wife.

Hamish knew he couldn't fight his way through the throng, and Jeannie had already sussed he was a cop, so his best bet was to flash his warrant card and make a quick getaway.

The neighbours melted away, like snow off a dyke and DCI Ross vanished into the night.

"Who the fuck did that? Tell me, Ma, I'll fucking kill him," Jack ranted and raved the following morning. He had been spending nights in Danube Street, mainly for security, but hoping to make it into Rosie's bed too.

"Och, Jack, I've had worse. It's all superficial and it'll be fine in a few days," Jeannie dismissed her son.

"Ma, it's time to stop. For fuck's sake, you could have been really hurt, killed even. You're too old for this malarkey."

"Cheeky fucker, I'm not that old."

"You're too old for this caper."

"Aye, sure. I'll get a job in Lyons tea shop in Princes Street. Can you see me now, wearing a neat wee uniform and lacy mob cap? Aye, I'd be the bees' knees. With a coupon like mine I'd turn the fucking milk sour. I know you mean well, son, but it's not going to happen."

"You don't have to work. I can help out. Think about it, Mum, please."

"I will admit I was a bit shaken up. He was a mad fucker alright, but he's been coming to me for years. I've always thought he was a rum one, but not dangerous, just a creep."

"Not that sleazy fucker I nicked the money off all those years ago?"

"Aye, son, that's him. I'd forgotten about that. Christ, he was mad. I hit him over the head with a vase."

"It was the best fish supper I think I ever had. Why didn't you call the cops, Ma?"

"A lot of good that would have done. They're not going to ride to the rescue for the likes of me. Anyway, I have my suspicions about him and if they're right, I would only have made things worse."

Looking at Jeannie, Jack's heart went out to the poor battered soul facing him. She was a sorry sight and he knew deep down she was right. Jeannie's path had been chosen years ago, there was no going back.

"So, what do you suspect, Miss Marple?" Jack laughed at his mother's expression.

"He's a cop. I'm positive, and I think he's quite high up too."

"So that's why you wouldn't call them?"

"Fuck, Jack, I wouldn't call the cops even if I was being murdered."

"You fucking well were being murdered," Jack spluttered.

"Well I'm not fucking dead yet, am I?" Jeannie snapped back at her son. "Change the record, for God's sake. How's your boss? I heard she got sent down."

"You don't miss much, do you?"

"No, thanks to you. How's she coping?"

"I'm off to visit her this afternoon so I'll find out then."

"This is your chance, lad, don't fuck up, and certainly not over that bit of skirt you've been chasing lately. She's a beauty, no denying, but she's trouble. Trust me, I know what I'm talking about."

"I know you do, Ma, but you needn't worry on that count, she's made it quite plain that we're just friends, no more."

"That won't stop you sniffing about though, will it?"

Jack could still hear his mother's laugh as he skipped down the steps out into the cold sunshine.

CHAPTER FORTY-FOUR

Counting Sheep

S hit, that was all she needed, thought Stella when she saw who was at the head of the welcoming party. It was only two days since she'd last set eyes on the ugly big woman.

"Fuck, Mags, I didn't know you cared that much for me," grinned Stella. She had to face this out, make a complete idiot out of her in front of these women or she'd be dead meat. "I never thought you'd be so worried you'd get yourself banged up just to keep me company. You really needn't have bothered, we're all going to be such good friends, isn't that so, girls?" Stella acknowledged the group of prisoners, agog at this pantomime.

Mags, her face burning in a mix of embarrassment and temper, lunged at her enemy who deftly stepped aside, leaving the big woman sprawled across the floor. Stepping over her, Stella addressed the assembled cons, "Hello, ladies. In case you didn't already know, I'm Stella Gold, and that," she pointed at the retreating figure of Mags, "is an ex-employee of mine. I have to tell you, she was as good a brass as she is a fighter, so you can understand why she is an ex. Now, can someone show me to my suite?"

The laughter rang in Mags ears. How did she do it? How did that fucking whore always manage to come out on top? Well, round one to Gold, but Mags wouldn't underestimate her a second time.

Stella paced her cell, back and forth, the first night of her sentence, much to the annoyance of her cellmate.

"For fuck's sake, woman, will you give it a break? You're

driving me up the fucking wall. I've hardly closed my eyes," Stella's cellmate grumbled from under the covers.

"Shut up or I'll close them for good," Stella snarled at her new companion.

"Listen to me, girl, you're not dealing with that halfwit from this afternoon," said the old woman sarcastically. "Get back into your bunk and let's get some sleep."

Stella ignored her cellmate and continued pacing back and forth.

"What's wrong with you? It's surely not being in here that's getting you in this state?" Pat, her cellmate, asked.

"No," Stella answered dismissively. "Although there are hundreds of places I'd rather be."

"You don't say," replied Pat.

"It's personal."

"No such thing in here, dear. Your life is an open book once you enter these gates."

"It's my son, he's ill."

"Is it serious?"

"Very. He's just been diagnosed with polio and he's not responding to treatment."

"Oh my God, lassie, that's a fearful illness. No wonder you're about off your head with worry. Look, have a wee drop of this and try to get some sleep, things might look better in the morning."

"What is it?" Stella sniffed the bottle.

"It's just a bit of something I make to keep the chill out my bones. It won't do you any harm, but it might let you get some shut-eye."

"I know this request is out of the norm, Ma'am."

The governor had been apprised of Gold's situation and the confrontation on her arrival, but even she couldn't believe the request. She'd been in the place less than twenty-four hours.

"My son is seriously ill and I have to see him," Stella begged the governor, tears streaming down her cheeks.

"For goodness sake, woman, you've only just arrived. It's not possible. The best I can do is send for the prison chaplain. Take her back to her cell," the governor addressed the guard accompanying Stella.

"Give it a bit more time, Gold," the screw sympathised. "The guv's okay, it's just timing."

"Time's the one thing I don't have," Stella sobbed.

"Look after her," the screw instructed Pat, as they returned to the cell. "She's had a bit of a let-down."

"She refused your pass. I thought it was a bit of a long shot. It's to let you settle in, the same reason you don't get visitors in the first week, other than your brief."

"Shut up, Pat, I'm not that fucking green. I know the rules, but I have to see my boy."

"For Christ's sake, don't show any weakness in here. You'll be slaughtered. There are a few not quite sure about you and if word gets round that you're a soft mark, you're finished."

"I don't give a toss how anyone in here perceives me, I have to see my son." Throwing herself on the bunk, Stella turned her face to the wall, blocking out everyone, but the vultures were circling.

The first foray was at breakfast the next morning. Pat had gone on ahead fearing there would be an attempt, and she was right.

There were two main factions on the wing: one run by the powerful, vicious Franny Brogan, a forty-something lesbian, serving two life sentences for the brutal murder of three members of her family, a woman with nothing to lose. The other was Brogan's arch rival, Nettie McGraw, wife of the infamous James McGraw, aka The Bishop. Nettie had no beef with Stella, in fact they'd come across one another a few years back. When one of Nettie's sisters was on the run, Stella had helped her out. But it was dog-eat-dog on the wing and unless

Stella joined someone willingly, she would be the trophy for whoever captured her.

Pat watched as the lines formed. Shit, she couldn't go and warn her, she'd have to create a diversion. Quick as a flash, Pat smashed her tray down on the head of the con opposite her. It just so happened that Vicki, the recipient of Pat's breakfast, was one of the most volatile girls on the wing. She could easily laugh it off or create bedlam, she was certainly not the sharpest knife in the drawer.

Standing up in the middle of the canteen, yelling at the top of her lungs, covered in porridge, eggs and whatever else Pat had on her tray, Vicki let fly at the diner sitting to her left. After pummelling her mercilessly, she then set about the one to her right. All this time Pat was watching out for her cellmate, who had failed to show for breakfast.

There had been no need for Pat's intervention – Stella had been called to the governor's office.

Fearing the worst and without waiting to be asked, she sat down in front of the woman.

"Have I lost him? Please don't tell me he's gone."

"Calm down, Gold, it's good news. I've just had a call from your brief. Your son is over the worst. I don't know all the details, but he is certainly on the mend."

"Thank you, Ma'am, thank you. Is there any possibility I can visit him?"

"I'm sorry, I don't think that's likely, but I promise I will look into it and keep you posted. In the meantime, go back to the dining hall and grab some breakfast, if there's any left."

"I'm not fussy about food, thank you again Ma'am." Stella left the governor's office.

"Where the hell did you get to?" Pat grabbed her as soon as she appeared.

"What happened here?" Stella surveyed the debris.

"I sent my breakfast back," she chuckled.

"What?"

"The gangs were ready to pounce and I couldn't warn you."

"I was with the governor, my boy's on the mend."

"Thank goodness, but you've got problems here, sister. You either go with Nettie, she's okay by the way, or you lie down to Franny. Either way you'll take a beating."

"I don't think so. I've not lasted this long in my game without learning a few tricks."

"Well, my advice is to go with Nettie McGraw, she'll protect you."

"I don't need protecting, Pat. I can stand my ground with most of this lot."

Pulling a nylon stocking from her pocket and lifting the cue ball as she passed the billiards table, much to the annoyance of the players, Stella made her way across the recreation room to Franny Brogan's mob. Without stopping, she marched straight up to Franny and smacked her with all her force. The woman's nose exploded while Stella rained blow after blow on her opponent. Eventually Franny Brogan lay bleeding on the floor. Stella had always believed in taking her enemy by surprise and in most cases, it worked. She'd certainly taken that snivelling mob by surprise.

"Anyone else fancy a go?" she shouted at the crew. "Feel free, I'm just in the mood. I missed my breakfast and that always makes me cranky. What about you, big yin? Are you ready to take me on?" Stella shouted at Mags. "No, I didn't think so."

"Fuck, she's only been in the place two days and already put Brogan out of action and the other one is eating out of her hand," Mags muttered to herself. Now was not the time to challenge the bitch. She would watch and wait. Her time would come.

Nettie McGraw walked over to Stella. "Well done, girl. You'll get no bother from me, but you've made a helluva enemy there, watch your back."

How prophetic those words were to be!

CHAPTER FORTY-FIVE

Cut and Dried

"We'll do our best," Iris promised her young sister. "The lawyer thinks we have a reasonable chance."

"Fingers crossed," ventured Violet.

"Fingers crossed!" snapped Rosie. "It's not a fucking Pekinese you're fighting for, it's my baby."

"Calm down, Rosie, you're not helping things. The girls are nervous enough without you having a go. Everyone will do their best," promised Jack.

Only days after Stella had been jailed, the two oldest Royce girls had been summoned to attend a children's hearing which had been convened to decide the fate of baby Hope Royce.

Since the death of her father and no sign of her mother, Iris, the eldest at eighteen, was deemed to be 'in loco parentis'. An associate of Marcus had offered to present their case at the hearing but it was cut and dried, a mere formality. The fate of the child had already been decided. The baby was a ward of court and a petition for adoption was granted.

It was Kitty who finally roused Rosie from her bed. The girl had returned from the hearing, spoken to no-one, locked the bedroom door and stayed there, refusing any nourishment for days. Jack was at his wits end.

"Rosie, open this door now," Kitty called from out on the landing. "Did you hear me? Open the door. If not, I'll get one of the boys to break it down and you'll pay for the bloody thing. You've no right to be in this room. It belongs to the missus, so get yourself out now."

The old girl could hear movement on the other side of the door. "Are you bloody deaf? I said open the door."

For once Rosie did as she was told.

"My God, take a look a look at yourself! Christ, you stink to high heaven."

Rosie was still wearing the clothes she'd worn on the day she'd gone to the hearing. She paid no heed and flung herself back onto the unmade bed.

"Oh no, my girl." The wee cook dragged her into the adjoining bathroom and turned the taps on full.

Kitty scrubbed the girl from top to bottom, paying no heed to the curses and oaths spewing from her mouth.

Eventually, with the fight knocked out of her and sobbing quietly, she allowed Kitty to finish bathing her and shampooing her matted hair. Kitty threw her a drssing gown and called for one of the girls to fetch the light lunch she'd already prepared.

"You'll feel better with some food inside you, lassie," she said as she virtually spoonfed Rosie.

"I'll never feel better, not till I get my daughter back."

"A lot of good you'd do her now, if you did get her back."

"Shut up, Kitty, you've no idea what you're talking about."

"Is that a fact?" Kitty snapped at her. "As I told you once before, you're not the first to lose a bairn and you won't be the last. I know it's a shame, but what exactly could you give Hope? Answer me that."

"I'd give her everything."

"Really? And how would you do that, girl? Get some mug to take you on and bring up another man's bairn? You were quite prepared to let Jack do it and if not, go on the game like the rest of us mugs. That's okay when you're young. But do you really want your kid brought up in a brothel, no matter how nice the wall paper is?"

"I'd get a place of my own," answered Rosie.

"You weren't doing too well with Jack the other day. Face it, Rosie, she's better off where she is."

"She's mine!" Rosie shouted at her inquisitor.

"She is, and you should want the best for her. She'll be with a family who have waited years for a baby and who will give her everything."

"They can't give her a mother's love."

"Don't talk rubbish, lassie. There's no denying you want your bairn, but what about the times you want to go out on the town? Because you will. In God's name, Rosie, you're still a kid yourself. You'll resent her for keeping you back."

"I'd never do that."

"No? Well, you'll be the first. Now, no more nonsense. You have to put the wee lass to the back of your mind and get back into the land of the living. We've got problems here and though it pains me to say it, you're the only one bright enough to sort them."

"Me?"

"Aye, get dressed and get downstairs, we need to talk."

"I think you've talked enough for one day, don't you?"

"I've not even started. You've got fifteen minutes or I'll be back to haul you down."

Despite the tongue-lashing, Rosie felt better and was intrigued as to what problems were so bad, only she could solve them. It was surely a ploy to get her out of the missus' bedroom.

Rosie was shocked at the difference a week had made. She had never seen the salon look so dirty and unkempt. The same applied to the girls, most of whom were gathered on the sofas, looking grubby and very unappealing. Not the glamorous creatures associated with Danube Street. Stella would have a fit if she saw her precious salon as it was now.

"What's going on?" she asked. "Why is the place in such a mess, and why are we not open for business?"

"It's in a mess 'cause me and Dora have only one pair of

hands. As to why we're not open, ask that lazy bunch of tarts."

"Don't you call me a lazy tart," shouted Angela, one of the older girls.

"Nor me," added her sidekick, Evelyn.

Those two had been in residence the longest and had definite ideas about their status in the house.

"I see what you mean, Kitty, but I'm not the one to solve this, they'd never take orders from me. Probably not from Jack either."

Just then, in walked a harassed Jack and at the very same moment a fight broke out between two of the younger girls over a scarf. Hair, teeth and nails went flying everywhere. It took both Jack and Rosie to separate the vicious cat-fight.

"I'm not having this," shouted Rosie. "You wouldn't try this on if the missus was here. We're not taking that kind of shit in her place. You two can collect your stuff. You're fired."

"Fuck off. Who do you think you are? You're not the boss of me," one of the youngsters shouted.

"That goes for you too," Rosie told her partner-in-crime.

"You can't sack us," said the blonde, menacingly, right in Rosie's face.

"Oh yes she can," answered Jack. "Now gather your things and get out."

The two combatants left the salon in tears.

"As for the rest of you," Rosie addressed those gathered, "Jack went to visit Stella yesterday and it's her intention to close the house down till she's released."

A loud gasp met this news.

"She would rather close the place than have it run into the ground. What do you say to that?" Rosie faced them up.

"What about us?" Angela called to her.

"What about you? You didn't give a damn five minutes ago, when you were mouthing off about what you would or wouldn't do. Why should Jack, Kitty and I have all this grief for a bunch of ungrateful bitches? Have a think and let us

181

know what you want. If we shut, so be it, I for one won't lose any sleep, but you'll all have to find new jobs and somewhere decent to stay. There's nowhere this cushy in town, but it's your decision."

"You pulled a blinder there, Rosie," Kitty smirked. "I knew you'd think of something, but shut the place down? Fuck, they nearly shit themselves."

Rosie and Jack exchanged glances, little did Kitty know that shutting the place was very much on the cards.

Stella was in half a mind to close down Danube Street. It would give them a chance to refurbish and open up afresh on her release. It wasn't that she didn't trust Jack and Rosie, it was their youth and lack of experience.

Back in the office, answering a knock on the door, Kitty showed the two sparring youngsters in.

"We're really sorry, miss, we shouldn't have spoken to you disrespectfully, and we won't ever fight again if you give us another chance."

"Honest, miss, we're truly sorry. We'll do anything, even help Kitty. Just don't send us away, please, we've got nowhere else to go."

"If, and I say if I give you another chance and you break the rules again, you are out, lock stock and barrel, do you understand?" Rosie stood firm.

"Yes, miss, we understand."

"Take your things back to your rooms and report for work at six o'clock, dressed, made-up and presentable. No man's going to pay money for something that looks worse than his wife."

Next at the office door was Angela. "If we agree, does that mean the missus will stay open?"

"We can't guarantee she won't change her mind, but surely it's worth a try?" Rosie answered her. "You're not going to find somewhere else this good."

"We'll give it a try," Angela reluctantly agreed.

182

"Look, don't think you're doing us any favours, Angie. If you can't take orders from Jack and I, just pack up and go elsewhere." Rosie knew she had to keep the upper hand.

"We'll work for you, just as we did for the missus."

"Good, I'm glad you agreed. First things first, we have to get the salon ready for business, everyone dressed, made-up and sexy. I expect record takings tonight. As you know, if the house earns, so do you girls. Second, I'm going to be depending on your experience, Angela. For the first time, officially, Danube Street has a head girl. That means for the extra work you'll be paid commission, how much depends on you."

Trying desperately hard not to look delighted, the Head Girl left the office thinking, Wait till Mags hears about this.

"Stepping over the mark a bit," said Jack, not quite sure what had just happened.

"Look, she'll make plenty for the house, it'll take the pressure off us and we've got a reasonably happy workforce. Winners all round."

"Still, you should have run it past me." Jack was slightly peeved.

"What would you have said? Yes or no?"

"Yes, I suppose."

"There you are, we think the same way. Problem solved." Rosie winked to Kitty.

"You've got him eating out of your hand, lassie."

"Not really, Kitty, I just know what buttons to press. It's for his own good."

CHAPTER FORTY-SIX

Reap as Ye Sow

Nettie McGraw had been right about one thing, Stella had certainly made a helluva enemy in Brogan. The top dog didn't take kindly to being bested, and certainly not by Stella Gold. From morning until lockdown, Stella had to be on her guard.

Prison life was not as grim as she had imagined it to be. It was no walk in the park, but she hadn't always lived in the lap of luxury and hard work didn't faze Stella. She was put to work in the prison gardens and, being the daughter of a farmer, this was no hardship. It was ironic that it had been the hatred of the farm that led to her present circumstances. Labouring eight hours a day gave Stella plenty of time for reflection.

Her main concern was her son, as there was every possibility that Oliver could be left with permanent disabilities. The level of his recovery would not be known for some time and it was more than probable he would require nursing at home. Who better to do this than his mum? Marcus had done a splendid job of rearing him up to now. From all accounts he was a clever, polite little boy, but Marcus must see that this was a second chance for both of them. Stella had been so young when she agreed to the arrangement, but there had not been a day gone by when she hadn't regretted her actions.

Like it or not, things were about to change and she hoped they could be civil, but Marcus Kramer was used to getting his own way. For the present, Stella couldn't do much, but she wouldn't be inside for ever. She spent time most evenings writing, outlining her plans for the future, presuming Marcus would go along with her. She was quite confident that her husband would agree with her decision. If not, divorce was on the cards. Between them they could give their son a full and rich family life. There seemed to be no dissention in Marcus' weekly bulletin from the hospital and this gave Stella confidence that he agreed with her.

She intended to make a new life for herself which included her son and soon came to the momentous decision that she was going to retire. There were several options open to her, such as selling the business as a going concern. But, she thought wryly other than the Williams brothers, how many other individuals would invest in a brothel? Albeit, a most successful one, but still a whorehouse. She could lease the house, or perhaps engage a manager. Whatever, Stella Gold, Madam extraordinaire, would soon be officially no more.

Dear God, the fucking woman was delusional. Every day these ridiculous missives would arrive, full of unadulterated nonsense, advocating life with Mummy and Daddy. Mummy and Daddy indeed! Could she actually believe that he, Oliver's father, the person who had walked the floor when he was teething, who heard his first word, been there when he took his first step, would even contemplate handing over the care of his son to her? What was she to Oliver? A womb, nothing more. She was living in cloud-cuckoo-land with her illusions of a happily married couple, taking their place in Edinburgh society. Marcus couldn't believe how wrong he'd been about Stella. He could only assume she had been so affected by her incarceration that she'd gone stir-crazy. He was determined to prevent her having any input in his son's life. To this end, Stella Gold must never leave prison.

Three weeks into her sentence Stella had her second visit from Jack.

"You look well, Stella," the young man complimented her.

"What were you expecting? That I'd disintegrate into some poor, snivelling weakling?"

"Of course not, sorry I mentioned it," Jack laughed at his boss.

"Well, how are you and the delectable Rosie coping? Is the house still standing?"

"It's more than standing, the house takings are up considerably. We've been packed every night."

"See, I told you, there is no such thing as bad publicity."

"You're right, as usual," Jack shifted uncomfortably in his chair.

"Okay, what's happened? Don't lie, I've known you far too long, Jack Hunter, not to know when you're trying to hide something from me."

"We had a problem, a big problem, the first night you were banged up."

"And it's taken this long for you to tell me?"

"I was hoping I wouldn't have to, and I couldn't get a visiting order till now."

"So what happened?"

"We had to call in the Williams brothers to help clear up a serious incident."

"For fuck's sake, not them, Jack. Tell me you're kidding. Nothing could have been that bad."

"Listen, Stella, let me explain," Jack nervously faced her.

"This had better be good."

"Judge Turnbull died in room one."

"What does it matter what room the old fucker died in? Why did you let that pair of bastards in?"

"Stella, he died on the job. He'd come to see Marcus, but of course he wasn't in. Anyway, I gave him a few drinks, as a sort of thank you, next thing I know Claire is screaming her head off that some old guy has popped his clogs and she couldn't move him."

"Why didn't you just call an ambulance? They would have carted him away."

"I didn't think of that, I was convinced we'd get shut down. Maybe I panicked. I just wanted him out with no cops. Rosie and I tried to move him, and the only thing I could think of was to get the boys in to do a clean up. I didn't know what else to do."

"I might have guessed she'd be in the mix somewhere."

"She pleaded with me not to get them, it was all my doing."

"She's got more sense than I gave her credit for. Fuck, I don't know what to say."

"I'm sorry, Stella, I did what I thought was best at the time."

"Well it's done now. Have they been back since?"

"That's the problem, Freddie's never out the place. He's causing ructions every night. He strolls in about eleven with a couple of his boys, usually roaring drunk, picking fights with anyone who crosses him. Last night it was Councillor McNeil, fortunately Kitty got in between them. I don't know what to do about him."

"He'll always come mob-handed, that's his style, and if you challenge him, you would be taking on all of them. Now that he's got his way back in, he'll be hard to shift."

"I'm not afraid of him, but no way can I take on all of them." Jack didn't tell the missus that they also had a new Head Girl, but he did let slip that Kitty had been tarted up and was working the bar, much to Stella's amusement.

"She certainly could handle a bar, but I can't for the life of me imagine what she looks like."

"Like Boris Karloff in a frock!"

"Better looking than I thought," she chuckled. "I'm surprised she's not got rid of him."

"Even she's wary, remember, he's her old boss."

"You said she's on the bar most nights."

"Yes, she is."

"She could spike his drink. If I remember correctly, it used to be a large scotch. Get Kitty to crush sleeping pills into it. That should knock him out."

"That takes care of one night, but what about the next visit, and the one following that?"

"His brother will soon get fed up having to collect a comatose Freddie every night."

"Surely they'll get suspicious?" Jack argued. "That would give us a bigger problem."

"I don't think so. No matter how suspicious he gets, Ronnie won't want it put about that his brother can't hold his drink."

"It's worth a try. He's bad for business and I haven't any better ideas."

"Look, Jack, if he gets that bad, shut the place. I'm not going to be responsible for anyone else getting hurt, and believe me, I know exactly what Freddie Williams is capable of. He might not take me on face to face, but you lot are sitting ducks."

"As I said, we'll do our best. How are things in here?"

"So, so. It's not the Ritz or the Savoy, however, I made my mark at the beginning, so for now I'm pretty much left alone, except for Big Mags."

"Big Mags, what has she got to do with it?"

"She's banged up in here as well."

"Jesus, Stella, watch your back with that one."

"Don't worry, it's under control."

"What about Marcus, have you heard from him? Is there no way he can get this overturned?"

"It doesn't appear so. He's been in to see me a few times, but there's nothing more he can do."

"Are you sure? Maybe I should pay him a visit, let him know exactly what's going on."

"I don't think it will do any good, but hey, it's worth a try," replied Stella.

"I'll keep you posted about Williams. Take care, Stella, we all miss you." Jack stood up to leave.

"I meant it, Jack, don't take chances."

Stella was in the recreation room penning yet another missive to Marcus when she became aware of a change in the atmosphere. It had gone decidedly quiet and the hairs on the back of her neck were standing up. Looking up from her writing, she saw she was surrounded by Brogan and her posse. Right behind her aggressor, surprise, surprise, dripping poison into her ear, was none other than Mags. Much to her amazement, since the day of Stella's arrival the woman had kept quiet and out of her way, but that was obviously about to change.

During her work in the prison garden, Stella had come across a broken, metal prong from a fork. Knowing it would be useful to have a weapon, over several days she had sharpened the weapon until it had a lethal, razor's-edge finish. She was never without it, carrying it everywhere, taped to her leg. She had always known the time would come when she'd have to protect herself and it looked like the time was now.

Brogan leant threateningly over the table, almost nose to nose with her. It was imperative that Stella remain calm. She reached down and ripped the sharpened tool from its hiding place.

"Can I help you?" Stella smiled into the scarred face of her rival.

"You and me need to have a wee chat," responded Brogan.

"Oh, I don't think so," she answered.

Holding Brogan's gaze, Stella slammed the weapon with all her might, right through the woman's hand, bone-crushingly pinning her to the table, straight through a vein. There was blood everywhere and Franny Brogan passed out, with her hand secured firmly to the table.

"I always think actions speak louder than words," commented Stella.

More than one prisoner was on the verge of fainting at the sight of Brogan's injuries, including Big Mags. Gold wasn't going to be the pushover she had thought.

Stella calmly stood up from the table and walked back to her cell as the screws arrived on the scene to attend the wounded prisoner. Franny Brogan lost the use of her right hand that day; she also lost her position of top dog. Stella Gold was left well alone, for the moment.

Of course, no-one saw a thing. Not even the victim.

CHAPTER FORTY-SEVEN

Karma

"It was good of you to see me at such short notice." Jack shook hands with Marcus.

"I'm due in court in an hour, so we will have to make it quick."

"I went to visit Stella yesterday, which has left me worried on a couple of counts."

"Stella Gold can more than take care of herself," Marcus replied reassuringly.

"Under normal circumstances I would agree with you, but her circumstances are anything but normal. First of all, I think she's in serious danger from one of our ex-girls. My second concern is the house and Freddie Williams."

"Williams! What has he to do with anything?"

"I had to call him on the night Stella was jailed and now we can't get rid of him."

"Dear God," exploded Marcus. "I've managed to keep them at bay for ten years and after just one night you let them back in? Seriously, I don't know what to say. They're bound to reckon we're quits now. How you're going to keep them out, God only knows."

"Stella has a plan."

"You better make sure it works, or close the place. What's the other problem?"

Jack explained the situation exactly as Stella had told him.

"Look, as I said, she can look after herself. I wouldn't worry too much about this Mags. Come to think of it, wasn't she one of your dalliances?" Marcus quizzed.

"We had a bit of a fling a while back, nothing serious."

"Are you sure? You should never shit on your own doorstep,

laddie. Anyway, leave this to me. I'll see what I can do."

Jack left the chambers believing the lawyer was doing his best.

"Your brief's here to see you," the screw called over to Mags.

"My brief? I think you've got the wrong person." The woman continued to play cards.

"There's a well-dressed gent, carrying a brief case, waiting in the interview room for a Margaret Black. Is that you?"

"Yes."

"Well, your brief is waiting to speak to you."

Full of curiosity, Mags followed the prison officer.

"Hello, Margaret, I'm Marcus Kramer. Have a seat."

The woman was bemused. She had known right away who he was, but what the hell did this top barrister want with her? Maybe Gold was bringing further charges? Whatever it was, it was unlikely to be good news for her.

"I take it you know who I am?" he asked.

Mags nodded. "Whatever she's accusing me of, I didn't do it."

"By her, I presume you mean Miss Gold?"

Mags nodded. She was saying nothing.

"Tell me, Margaret, can I call you that?"

"Mags, I get called Mags."

"Well, Mags, I have a proposition for you."

"You can get me off?" The woman sat up in her chair.

"No, sorry I can't, but I can make your stay in here worthwhile."

"What? Can you get me my own suite?" she sneered.

"No, but how about enough money to set you up for life?"

Having caught her attention, she asked, "So what do I have to do?"

"We'll get to that in good time. I need to know a bit more about you, make sure you're the right person for the job."

"For the right money, I'm the right person."

Marcus looked around the room, double-checking there were no cameras or listening devices, and whispered, "I want someone taken out."

"What?" The woman laughed at him. "Haven't you noticed I'm in prison. No guns, no sharp objects, nothing. If I can take someone out with a bar of soap or a dish cloth, then I'm your woman, otherwise forget it."

"What if I could get you a weapon? Have you got the nerve to carry it off? Tell you what, let's leave it for now. I'll come back next week and we can talk again."

"Yeah, okay, it's not like I'm going anywhere. But tell me, who is it you want taken care of and how much is in the pot?"

"I'll tell you next week. Meanwhile, keep this between us, don't go blabbing because I will find out and believe me, you don't want to be in my bad books."

The brief took his leave and Mags, well, all she could think about was how much money she could squeeze out of him.

CHAPTER FORTY-EIGHT

Alice is in Wonderland

Both Rosie and Jack's misgivings about maintaining the level of customers proved to be unfounded; if anything, Danube Street became even more infamous. The only fly in the ointment was Freddie Williams.

Despite flashing his cash, none of the girls would entertain him. He was a vicious, mean bastard and had roughed up a couple of the less experienced girls who were too frightened to complain. He'd also refused to pay on more than one occasion, definitely not good for business.

It was usually about ten thirty, just after the pubs closed, when he would stroll into the salon and, depending on how inebriated he was, either act as a genial host or take offence at the slightest thing and strike out at the most placid of punters.

This particular evening, the conspirators hoped he'd had a skinful before arriving and that one drink would see him off. Kitty had everything in order, the large measure of Scotch had been spiked with pills in plenty of time, to avoid detection.

It was the usual Friday night crowd and the salon was full to bursting. There was a constant stream of customers in and out of the rooms. Girls not otherwise engaged were hustling the punters for drinks. The bar was three deep when the Williams party arrived.

Immediately Kitty knew this was not going to be as easy as it had seemed in the planning. Freddie and his three companions were all drinking large Scotches. How on earth was she to pull this off and make sure it was Freddie who drank the spiked whisky? She couldn't take any chances. Jack, watching from the sidelines, saved the day. Banging into

Freddie, he knocked the drink right out of the unsuspecting villain's hand.

"Sorry, Mr Williams, I'll just get you another."

Diving behind the bar, Jack retrieved the prepared drink and shot back to Williams who downed it in one go.

"We'll have drinks all round, boy, and put them on my tab," he laughed at Jack. "Hurry, you don't want to keep my friends waiting, it might not be good for your health."

Jack was fuming, he wanted to punch this ignorant pig in the mouth, but he kept smiling, hoping it wouldn't be too long before the pills worked.

Three rounds of drinks later Jack saw his chance. Freddie was beginning to sway and his companions, now scattered around the salon, were paying no heed to their host.

"Are you feeling alright, Mr Williams?" he enquired.

"Fuck off, I'm fine. I want a shag, send your best bitch out to me," the drunk snarled at Jack.

"Sure, just you wait here while I see if Alice is free. You'll like Alice, this girl does things that should be illegal."

Freddie was teetering, swaying back and forward. It was only the promise of the fictitious Alice that kept him on his feet.

"Alice works next door, Mr Williams. We can't have her working in the main house."

"Next door? What the fuck are you talking about, boy?" Williams slurred.

"It's where we take special clients. Only those and such as those get to go next door."

"Take me there now," the big man demanded, swaying precariously at the front door.

Jack led him down the front steps to the pavement. He turned left, opened the wrought iron gate to number nine and heaved the sixteen stone Freddie Williams down the basement steps to land, with a sickening thud, on the concrete below. Jack sprinted down the stairs after him. He removed everything from the drunk's pockets, making it difficult to identify him and to give the appearance he'd been mugged. Williams was still breathing when Jack left him, but only just.

The victim lay in the Royal Infirmary for two days before he was identified. It was not unusual for Freddie to go off on a bender and disappear for days at a time, his drinking sprees were legendary. However, there were none of the tell-tale clues; usually he left a trail of destruction in his wake. Nor had he caused the mayhem normally associated with these episodes. Ronnie couldn't help but be anxious about his brother's disappearance. There was something not quite right. The city was changing and the brothers, while still the major force to be reckoned with, had as many enemies as they had friends, and Freddie certainly had enemies. A few hours after Ronnie had put the word out, news of Freddie's whereabouts surfaced.

"We're keeping your brother sedated, Mr Williams, he's sustained a major head trauma and we won't know how much damage has been done for some time. We had to repair his skull by removing shards of bone from his brain and replace the damaged area with a metal plate."

"He is going to be okay, doc?" Ronnie asked with some trepidation. Thoughts of Stella Gold's partner, Mary, flashed into Ronnie's mind. What goes around, comes around, he thought.

"We don't know, it's a waiting game. Almost all patients experience some difficulties, personality changes or loss of motor functions. This can be temporary, but it's too soon to tell."

Fuck, a personality disorder? He was a raging fucking psycho before landing a smack on the bonce, what was he going to be like now? Ronnie didn't want to even consider the possibilities.

He wasn't going to make Freddie better by hanging around the hospital. There was something not right here and he was going to find out what had happened, and who was responsible.

Freddie had been discovered early the next morning by the milkman making his rounds. At first glance he thought the man was dead, especially having lain out in freezing temperatures. He had a pulse, very faint, but he was still in the land of the living when he was carted off to the infirmary.

Ronnie's first port of call was Danube Street. Someone there must know what happened to his brother. Freddie wasn't a character you could miss easily.

"I was on reception that night," ventured Rosie. "I remember your brother arriving with three other men," she told Ronnie. "The salon was packed as usual, it was Friday night. I never pay any attention to who leaves, only those coming in. But we know he was here for a time, his bar bill shows three rounds of drinks, the last one served just after midnight."

"You put the time on the bill?"

"Always," Rosie showed her inquisitor a few examples. "It saves arguments later."

"Good idea," Ronnie murmured. "So you're saying you didn't see him leave?"

"I was in and out the salon as well as on the desk."

"And you, I don't suppose you saw anything either?" Ronnie Williams challenged Jack.

"All I know about your brother being in here is that someone spilt his drink, he was about to kick off, so I replaced it. I didn't speak to him after that. Surely the guys he came in with can tell you what happened?"

"They say the same, they didn't see him leave."

Back in the car, Ronnie pondered over his visit. They were

just too glib, he thought, like a well-rehearsed script. He knew, better than anyone, what a fucker Freddie could be. He may have decided to go on elsewhere, it could have been an accident, but Ronnie had a lingering niggle. Had Stella been at home, he would have been far more suspicious. But these two, there was no way they could have carried this out; it looked like a genuine accident. If the truth be known, Ronnie had always known Freddie would come a cropper one day. He was a wild fucker as things were, what kind of madman would he be if his wiring was fucked up?

"What if Freddie remembers?" Rosie was completely unnerved by Ronnie Williams' visit. "He'll be back. I'm telling you, we haven't heard the last of this."

"There's no way that big arse will remember anything. He could barely remember his name by the time I got him outside, so stop worrying. Whatever happens, he's out of action for the foreseeable."

"Christ, Rosie, what did you think would happen?" Kitty asked. "Of course the brother was going to arrive on our doorstep. Now don't panic, the cops will be here soon as well, looking for answers."

"But I thought it was meant to be an accident."

"Aye, but only if we can convince them. All you have to do is deny seeing him leave. And that's not a lie, you didn't see him go."

"Where am I?" Freddie asked his brother groggily. "What happened?"

The medical staff had slowly brought the patient round from his induced coma. Only now would the extent of his injuries be known and what his future held.

"You're in hospital, Freddie, you had an accident."

"Accident? What kind of accident?"

"You fell down some steps and knocked yourself out."

"Steps," Freddie was having difficulty processing the information. "Where? Did I fall down at home?"

"No, we think you were leaving a club."

"Eh?"

"Look, don't worry about where and how, just concentrate on getting better."

"Somebody pushed me, Ronnie. Who did this to me? Who was it?" Freddie challenged his brother with a maniacal glint in his eyes. "I'm telling you, I'll fucking do them in."

Freddie Williams had certainly not taken news of his condition, either quietly, or lying down. The medical staff had no choice but to keep him under sedation, they had never encountered anyone like Freddie Williams.

CHAPTER FORTY-NINE

All in the Preparation

For Stella, life in prison was not so bad. She was constantly on the watch where Mags was concerned, but for whatever reason, the woman kept out of her way most of the time. Stella had gained the respect, and possibly the fear, of most of the women on her wing. Life inside, whether it was a male or female institution, was very much 'dog-eat-dog' and although Stella hated violence, she knew she could hold her own. It was not being able to see Oliver that was the greatest strain, now that she had decided the path she was going to follow.

Stella grudgingly agreed with Marcus that until she was back on the outside and the lad was fully recovered, there would be no dramatic changes to his life.

The disease had left him with a weakness in his right leg. He would be required to wear a metal calliper to strengthen the muscles, but worse, like many children subjected to weeks in an iron lung, he was now chronically asthmatic. Even the slightest exertion brought on an attack.

This condition just further confirmed that she could not return to her previous lifestyle, but should devote her time to Oliver's well-being. The limited information she could glean from the prison library suggested that many of the leading experts recommended treatment similar to those suffering from tuberculosis. Time in a cold, crisp climate, and it was her intention to take the boy to Switzerland for a spell.

"Don't you think you're getting a bit ahead of yourself?" her cellmate said on hearing Stella's latest proposal. "Can you really see that Marcus one letting you trip off to Switzerland for a couple of months with his son?"

"He's my son too." Stella snapped back. "I've every right

to spend time with him."

"I'm not saying you don't, but I think you're heading for a big disappointment if you think he's going to hand over the lad's care to you."

"It's for Oliver's good. Anyway, Marcus would never stand in the way of any treatment if it were to improve his health. There is no way he would be able to look after him 24/7 when he's discharged. So why on earth would we hire a nurse when I can look after him?"

"I hope you're right," Pat sighed, not at all convinced.

She was sure Stella was in for a big let-down. If the lawyer was in favour of her cellmate's plan, where the hell was he? He had only been to visit once, and that was just after her trial. That didn't bode well for Stella's plans as far as Pat was concerned.

If only Pat knew how near to the mark she was. Marcus Kramer had no intention of letting his wife anywhere near their son. When he read her latest missive, he laughed out loud at her latest proposal. She was going to take the boy to Switzerland to 'take the air'. Take the air? She really was mentally deranged. How could she suppose for one minute he would subject their pure, innocent son to a woman of her morals?

"Your brief is back again," the prison officer called over to Mags. "Jesus, he's certainly earning his fee, and he doesn't look like he takes on many legal aid cases."

"It's none of your business why he's here to see me," Mags marched off ahead.

"Thanks, officer," Marcus addressed the guard. "We won't be too long, will we Mags?"

"No."

"So what's your decision? Is it a goer or not?" Marcus asked.

"It depends on who it is." Mags still had no idea who the

lawyer wanted her to dispose of.

"It's Stella."

"WHAT?" Mags was astounded, "I thought she was your partner, your best client?"

"She was, but things change and now she's making life very difficult. So, are you up for this or not?"

"Christ, I'd thought of everyone bar her. I'm up for it alright, I hate the bitch, but it depends on how much." If he only knew she would do it for free.

"Five thousand," Marcus offered. "Half up front and the balance after the job's done."

"You must be kidding. It's Stella Gold we're talking about, probably one of the most well-known cons in the country. That's not nearly enough. Think about it. I'd get a minimum fifteen years if I was caught. I want at least double."

Marcus had suspected she would want more than his opening offer. Was it worth that amount to get rid of Stella? Definitely!

"So what's the plan?" Mags asked, all ears now.

"You have to befriend her," Marcus explained. "She has to trust you in order for you to get near her."

"There's no chance. She bloody well hates me as much as I hate her."

"Just think of the money."

"But what if she doesn't bite?"

"You've got to make her, otherwise the plan won't work," replied Marcus. "The weapon will come in via Brogan's pet screw, the night before her release. It will disappear the same way, after the deed's done. Any questions?"

Meanwhile Stella was eagerly awaiting Marcus' arrival, desperate for news of her son. She was oblivious to the fact that the double-crossing brief had spent the last hour with her enemy.

"He's doing well, the asthma has improved," Marcus

reported.

"That's why I want to take him abroad. They have wonderful clinics in Switzerland."

"I'm sure they have, but don't you think you need to get to know him first, before you go traipsing across Europe?"

"What better way to forge a bond between us?"

Marcus stood up and walked away from the table with his back to her. He daren't let her see how difficult it was, keeping his temper in check. How stupid was she? he asked himself.

"Wait until you get out. Do your time and we'll see what the future holds."

"I'm fairly sure I know what it holds for me. For a start, I'm not going back to Danube Street, I've decided to retire," Stella informed him.

If he'd harboured any doubts about her fate, then this had secured them.

Stella had to go.

Freddie spent most of his days in a drug-induced stupor, drifting from hour to hour. It had proved impossible to keep him in a mainstream ward or free from sedation. He was vicious, violent, disruptive and completely unpredictable.

During his first weeks in the ward he had viciously assaulted two female nurses, scarring them both for life. He had bitten off the earlobe of one of the male orderlies and threatened most of the vulnerable patients he came into contact with. It was a bad state of affairs, but there was no reasoning with the man. Whether it was a result of the brain injury or his previous psychosis, no one could determine. Whatever the cause, Freddie Williams had to be kept under lock and key and sedated at all times. He was one very dangerous man, waiting, always waiting for the opportunity to exact revenge on anyone.

CHAPTER FIFTY

Welcome Party

A huge banner was strung out across the entrance and bunting hung from the first floor windows to the railings, announcing the homecoming of the missus. The house was spick and span and the inhabitants equally so. The atmosphere was electric.

Jack and Rosie were closeted in the office, going over the accounts for the last time. Since they had been in the driving seat, profits had soared and both were sure Stella would be pleased with the few changes they had made.

"I can't believe we'll be handing all this back tomorrow, Jack."

"Me neither," he answered.

"I have to say, I don't know how I'm going to handle not being in charge," said Rosie. "When I think how terrified I was at the start and all that carry on with Freddie Williams."

"Kitty was right, you took to being in charge like a duck to water. No-one questioned your age. Even I forget how young you are sometimes."

"It's daft, I always knew that we were only caretakers, but it's only tonight it feels real. I hope she's pleased with what we've done." Rosie said wistfully.

"She was damned lucky to have us. Can you think of anyone else who would have taken over and not royally screwed her?"

"We make a good team, Jack. I'm really going to miss here."

"What?" Jack was completely taken by surprise. "What do you mean, miss here? Where are you going?"

"I've not quite decided yet, but with the missus coming

back, I want to do something else."

"Stay with me, Rosie, please," said Jack. "You know how I feel about you and you just said it, we make a good team."

"Shut up, ya daft bugger. You know I care for you, but we're far too young to be tied down. C'mon, let's put the finishing touches to the welcome home party. What time are you going to pick her up?"

"Eight o'clock," said a sad and dejected Jack. "But I won't give up, Rosie."

CHAPTER FIFTY-ONE

Insomnia

Stella Gold would have been extremely surprised if she'd known how many sleepless nights she was causing. It was ironic that on her last night in prison sleep evaded her also, when usually, she slept like a baby.

Lying in the dark, she mulled over the past months. The woman leaving in the morning was very different from the one who'd arrived. She had made friends, and of course, enemies, but none that she couldn't handle. Her time would have been much tougher if she hadn't had Nettie on her side. She and Stella had forged a friendship which would extend way beyond these walls. The greatest surprise though, had been Mags, the bane of her life. Out of the blue, she had extended an olive branch, endeavouring to make her peace.

Doubtful to begin with, Stella had been suspicious of the woman's motives, but, as the weeks had gone on, she could find no fault and it definitely seemed that Mags had turned over a new leaf. Stella came to enjoy her droll sense of humour and despite Nettie's warnings, let down her guard.

Surviving her sentence had given her the confidence to walk away from Danube Street. She was still a young woman, the world was her oyster, and she was considerably richer than when she and Mary had started out. Then there was Oliver. One look at the boy and his parentage was obvious. Stella wasn't fooling herself that it would be easy. Marcus wouldn't give in to her demands without a fight, but she knew far too much about him and his practices not to be taken seriously. If necessary, she would involve Ronnie, but whatever it took, she would get to know her son.

It would soon be dawn, she had survived. Life could only

get better, she thought, as she drifted off to sleep.

No matter what was going on in DCI Hamish Ross's life, he too, normally slept like a baby. The sleep of the just, he would say, but tonight was different.

It had come to his notice, earlier in the day, that his old adversary, Stella Gold, would be let loose in less than eight hours. Back, polluting the environment with her vile trade. How time flew. What was he to do to get rid of her once and for all? He was annoyed at himself; he had taken his eye off the ball, missed an ideal opportunity to finish her off. It wasn't his fault; he was a busy man and the world didn't stand still on Hamish Ross's account. It had been a case of out of sight out of mind. He had been too engrossed in his latest crusade, to rid the city of the scum plying their trade around Calton Hill.

Edinburgh was plagued with immoral young boys preying on vulnerable members of society. He had disposed of another evil fiend this evening, not that he expected any gratitude from his peers, who were more intent on rehabilitation than punishment. For Hamish, knowing he was doing the Lord's work and there was one less deviant on the streets, was gratitude enough.

Edinburgh Evening News

The body of a young boy was discovered last night in the Calton Hill area of the city. This is the fourth such incident in the past year and police are appealing for witnesses…

Marcus Kramer also tossed and turned as sleep evaded him. Hopefully, by tomorrow everything would be over. That bloody woman would have no more hold over him, nor could she interfere with the boy's future.

It was a pity it had come to this, he mused. He liked and admired Stella. With grit and determination, she had created a successful and profitable business, making him a ton of money into the bargain. If she had just stuck to their arrangement, things could have continued just fine. But no, like all women, she had changed her mind; shifted the goal posts. He couldn't imagine how Oliver would react, finding out his mother was alive. Stella was determined to play a part in her son's life and Marcus was determined she wouldn't.

No, it had to end now.

CHAPTER FIFTY-TWO

Lock Down

"Oh shit," muttered Jack as he turned into the cul-de-sac to see all the occupants of the house and a number of reporters standing outside on the pavement, forming a welcoming committee.

"Where is she?" Kitty asked, peering into the car. "I knew it. I'll bet she's off to the beauty parlour. She would want to look her best, you know what she's like."

"No, Kitty, she's not at the beauty parlour. I don't know where she is," said Jack.

"Eh? I don't understand," said the old girl. "Did Marcus get there before you and she left with him?"

"There was no-one about when I arrived, but there was definitely something big going down, that's for sure. The place was crawling with cops. About eight o'clock, one of the screws came out and told me and two reporters that the prison was on lockdown, there was no point in staying as no prisoners would be released today."

"What a shame. I bet it's a jail-break," said Angie. "Fancy them picking her release day."

"They can't do that," shouted Kitty. "I've made all her favourites. I've been up since six this morning and now they'll go to waste."

"Well, there's bugger all I can do." Jack ushered the girls back inside.

"Phone the prison and see if you can get any information," Rosie spoke for the first time. She had a really bad feeling about this.

*

At roughly the same time Kitty had risen to prepare for the homecoming, the duty officer had gone to waken Stella.

"Wake up, Gold. Don't you want to go home?" Miss Jones, the screw in charge of Stella's landing, barked at the still half-asleep, soon-to-be-released prisoner. "We'll wait until the others have finished their ablutions then I'll take you round."

"Can't I go just now?" Stella asked.

"Sorry, this can be a bad time for some, especially the lifers. It's also the last time for some scores to be settled."

"I think if someone wanted to settle a grudge they would have done it by now."

"You'd be surprised."

"I'll be fine, miss."

"I'm sure you will, but rules are rules."

Stella wished she could say goodbye to her cellmate, but Pat had spent the night in the sick bay with one of her migraines. Instead, she'd run the gauntlet of ribald comments and good wishes as she made her way to the shower block for the last time.

"Quick, get into the cubicle and don't come out till you hear me say I'm going to give her some privacy."

Mags did as the screw instructed and sat waiting for her victim to arrive.

Should she go ahead with the contract? Mags pondered. After all, she was five grand up as it was, she could just walk away with no comeback. Let's face it, it was unlikely Kramer would shop her; he would be just as guilty as she was. Should she give it up? Too late, she decided, she could hear voices.

"Okay, Stella, I'll leave you alone, give you a bit of privacy." The screw left the shower block.

That was it, the signal. Stella was on her own. Mags gave it a few minutes to psych herself up. This wasn't the first time she'd taken a life, but that had been in self-defence. This was different. Did she really have the nerve to carry it off? Well, she'd soon find out. She seached for the weapon which had been planted in the cistern earlier. It was now or never.

For once the water was at least tepid. As she shampooed her thick hair, Stella became aware of a presence outside the cubicle.

"Who's there? Is that you, miss?" Rinsing the suds from her eyes, she was surprised to see who was standing before her. "Mags! You gave me quite a fright. I'll be finished in a few minutes, be a doll and hand me a towel."

"This isn't a social call, Stella. I've got a message for you, from Marcus." Big Mags sneered.

"From Marcus? Why the hell would Marcus send me a message through you?"

"Oh, he and I are great pals," Mags replied sarcastically.

"Really? Just how long have you two been buddies?"

"Since he stopped being buddies with you," Mags replied.

"What?" Stella was genuinely perplexed.

"Don't you want to know what the message is?"

"Officer! Officer!" Stella screamed, seeing the glint of steel in the woman's hand and realising she was in big trouble.

"Don't bother shouting, you're wasting your breath. Your fans are too busy preparing a farewell surprise, but it's nothing compared to the surprise I've got for you."

Stella was helpless, there was no escape. The knife entered just below her ribcage.

The world stopped. All around was deathly quiet. What had happened? What had that mad woman done? Oh my God!

Her last thoughts were for her child. "Oliver!" she cried to herself. She would never know him now. Please God take care of my baby, Stella prayed.

She lay in a pool of blood. Someone was calling her. She recognised the voice, a voice from the past. It was Mary. Mary had come for her.

"Christ, how much longer is she going to be?" one of the inmates asked impatiently.

"Maybe she's changed her mind, decided to stay a while longer," quipped another.

"Somebody go and hurry her up, before the candles burn out."

There, on the table, in pride of place, was a pink iced cake with six candles, marking her time inside.

"Stella, what the fuck are you doing?" shouted one of the girls.

Her screams could be heard all over the wing.

A single, fatal stab wound to the heart was all it had taken.

Having carried out her mission successfully, Mags wasted no time in passing the knife to the waiting screw. It was pandemonium, but by diving in to help no-one noticed her wet shoes or damp clothing.

The alarm had been raised, but by now the crime scene was irretrievably contaminated by both inmates and screws. Mags was pretty much home, if not dry.

"I don't think it was a breakout, Jack. They would have had the tracker dogs out right away and you'd have seen or heard them."

"What the hell does it matter what the incident was? It's mucked up all our plans."

"Not necessarily," answered Rosie. "Maybe they'll let her out later today. I don't see how they can keep her in if she's done nothing."

"I'm going to phone again, see if they answer this time. Good morning, I want to speak to someone about the release of a prisoner."

"I'm sorry, sir, there's no one available."

"What do you mean there's no-one available? I've just left the prison and there were dozens of police and prison officers around."

"I'm sorry, sir. As I said, there is no-one available to take your call."

"When will there be someone available?" Jack was becoming quite aggravated by the telephonist.

"I'm not sure. I would suggest you call back later today when we may have more information." The line went dead.

"Well, that was a lot of good," Kitty snorted. "What exactly am I to do with all this grub?"

"For Christ's sake, Kitty, stop moaning," challenged Jack. "What's a bit of food going to waste compared to the missus being stuck in there another day. If you're that bothered donate it to the Sally Ann."

"Huh! I can just see all those jakies down the Grassmarket stuffing their faces with smoked salmon and lobster." Kitty marched back inside, ushering the rest of the household before her.

"Why not call Marcus? Maybe he can find out what's going on." Rosie suggested.

"No, I'll leave it for a bit and then do as she said, phone back later. I don't really like the man," Jack confessed. "The less I have to do with him the better."

The call from the prison officer to confirm the deed was done came just after eleven. Marcus had been on tenterhooks until then. Although he was confident that his plan would work, it didn't stop him from jumping every time the phone rang. Strangely enough, he felt incredibly sad at the news, even though it was he who had instigated her death. He had had no choice; Stella wasn't the kind of woman to be fobbed off. It would only have been a matter of time before the cat was out of the bag and Marcus couldn't allow that to happen, but he had genuinely cared for her.

Life would be duller without Stella, but now there would be no guilty secrets to hide and probably no more Danube Street. He hadn't really considered what would be done with the place. Maybe he could restore it to its former glory? There was time enough for that decision.

"What the fuck was going on now?" DC Cummins grumbled to his partner, "My head's bursting and I feel like shit."

"Well, you did put away a few last night."

"You can talk! You sunk a few pints yourself."

"I can hold my drink." Cummins' oppo laughed at his sickly pallor.

"God, I hope it's not something gruesome or I'll spew. I feel hellish."

"Morning, men" Ross addressed his squad. "We've just had a report in that there's been an incident at the woman's prison. A body has been found in the shower block – a stabbing. The victim is believed to be Stella Gold. After serving six months she was due to be released today, but someone got to her before she was discharged."

"Fuck, if I didn't know better, I'd think that bastard had a hand in this."

"Shh. For God's sake don't let anyone hear you say things like that. He'll run you out of the force personally."

"He's a fucking wanker, I can't stand the man," Cummins muttered under his breath. "Look at him, he's fucking gloating. What did she ever do to him? I'd love to find out."

"Keep your mouth shut. I'm warning you, he's lethal. I'm glad we're still on the Calton Hill cases, I don't want to work alongside him," DC Cummins told his partner.

"Especially with a hangover."

"Fuck all to do with my hangover. I've got a bad feeling

about this, but let some other bugger figure it out."

DCI Ross read out the names of those officers assigned to the new murder case.

"Sir, you're forgetting we're on the Calton Hill case and are following a positive line of enquiry," DC Cummins addressed his chief.

"I want you two on this case. Hand over your notes to DC Brown, fill him in on what you've got up to now."

"Can't we finish our enquiries and then transfer over?" Cummins was hoping against hope to come up with something to avoid working with the DCI, but his luck was out.

CHAPTER FIFTY-THREE

Secrets and Lies

As soon as Rosie saw the two police officers approaching the front door, she knew something was very wrong.

"Jack," she called downstairs. "We've got visitors."

A loud knock on the door confirmed their arrival.

"Good morning, can I speak with the person in charge?" the young policewoman addressed the pair.

"That would be me. I'm the manager, however, the owner, Miss Stella Gold, is due back at any time, if you want to call back?"

Rosie had never seen Jack this nervous.

"Can we have a word in private, sir?"

By now the landings and stairwell were host to every female in the house, eager to discover what was going on.

"Of course," answered Jack, leading the two into the salon.

"I'm afraid we've some bad news, sir. We have to inform you that Mrs Kramer is not on her way back. Unfortunately she was found dead this morning."

"Who's Mrs Kramer?" Jack said relieved. "It's Miss Gold who is the proprietor. Mrs Kramer would be the wife of her brief, Marcus Kramer, and nothing to do with here."

"The victim was Mrs Stella Kramer née Gold, spouse of Marcus Kramer. There is no mistake, sir."

"Oh my God, what happened? How did she die?" The young man was completely at a loss.

"I'm sorry, sir, we don't have any further information on the incident, but we'll be in touch."

Rosie showed the officers out and went to fetch Kitty.

"What's up?" Angela asked.

"Is there something wrong with the missus?" asked another.

"Girls, could you go back to your rooms just for the minute? I promise I'll come and get you shortly."

Jack could hear the old lady chattering away as she came up the stairs.

"Sit down, Kitty. Pour her a brandy, Rosie," Jack instructed.

"What did they want?" Kitty demanded. "What trumped up charges have they come up with this time?"

"Kitty, hush for a moment. The police were here to deliver some bad news, the worst in fact. It's Stella, she's gone from us."

"Gone? Gone where?" asked a puzzled Kitty.

"She's dead, Kitty. Apparently she was found in the shower block early this morning."

The girls on the upper floor heard Kitty's grief, the sound of a wounded animal, a low, deep, primitive sound.

"Take her downstairs, Jack, while I speak to the girls."

It was only right that Rosie take over. Jack and Kitty were devastated, unable to fathom the loss of their friend. Although Rosie had had a great affection for Stella and appreciated all the woman had done for her, she didn't have the deep sense of loss those two were experiencing and the girls had to be told.

"Girls, girls," she called.

A silent file of women made their way into the salon.

"As you know, we had a visit from the police a short while ago. I'm sorry to have to tell you the officers came to bring news of Stella's death."

Rosie's statement was met with loud gasps, cries and a barrage of questions.

"I've no further information, but I'll keep you informed. I would ask you to respect Jack and Kitty's feelings and of course, the house is closed until further notice."

"I don't want to sound callous, but what about us? We all need some where to stay and work. How long will the place be closed?" Izzy asked.

"I have no idea, but I would think you can stay here for the immediate future. What happens after that, I don't know. I'm sure Marcus will have answers for us."

"Jack, what about Marcus, do you think he knows?" Rosie asked. "Should we contact him?"

"You're not going to believe this, the police told me she was his wife," Jack blurted out.

"His what? I have to say I find that hard to believe. They did have a peculiar relationship, though. I know it wasn't quite personal, but it was a bit too personal in other ways. That still doesn't answer my question, should we contact him?"

"I would suppose, given their relationship, he already knows." Jack stated.

The sound of footsteps outside signalled the man in question's arrival.

"I take it you've been told?" Marcus asked with obvious relief. "I can't tell you how much I was dreading having to break the news to you all."

"The police were here earlier. What happened to her, Marcus?"

"I only know what the police reported. She was found stabbed in the shower block."

Kitty broke out crying again.

"What do you want to do about here?" asked Rosie. "Obviously we are closed for now and I've told the girls they can stay on for the moment."

"I have no idea what's going to happen."

"How's your son?" Kitty asked through a veil of tears.

"He's on the mend," replied Marcus. "I brought him home a couple of weeks ago."

"It's a shame she didn't get to see him up and about, she was very worried about him."

The old woman had a sly look on her face, which unnerved Marcus a little. What could she know? Nothing, absolutely nothing. There was no way Stella would have confided in this mongrel. He had never understood why she took her on, or kept her on for that matter. Marcus left, saying he would be in touch.

"Jack, I need a word in private." Kitty led Jack back through to the office. "I have to tell you something, and for now, it has to remain between us."

"You know you can trust me, Kitty. What's bothering you?"

"I have Stella's will. She didn't trust Marcus Kramer with it, so she visited a brief down the coast when Mary was ill."

"Who's Mary?" Jack asked puzzled.

"I'll tell you another day, but for now I think we should contact Stella's solicitor, just in case. If she didn't trust that slimy toad, then I don't think we should."

Kitty was distraught. Her friend, her rock, was gone. The old woman couldn't comprehend never seeing Stella again. What would she and Dora do? The missus had always said she would take care of them, but she wasn't expecting to die, not at her age.

Edinburgh Evening News

Reports of a disturbance at Scorston Women's Prison resulted in the death of Stella Gold, a well known businesswoman in the city. A spokesman for the prison service confirmed that the incident is under investigation…

CHAPTER FIFTY-FOUR

The Party's Over

It had been a long hard day. There had been almost a hundred inmates to be interviewed, as well as all the staff. A complete search of the wing uncovered nothing. This had been a well-executed hit and the weapon would be gone by now. Any evidence was contaminated by the time DCI Ross's officers arrived. The fact that there were so many witnesses and no one saw a thing was par for the course in prison life.

Shame about Jeannie, he could seriously do with her company tonight. Although after their last run-in, Ross thought it may not be such a good idea. Oh ye of little faith, he repeated to himself as he drove through Leith. He'd recognise that swagger anywhere. There, bold as brass, was the object of his desire.

He rolled down the window, "Hello, Jeannie, jump in." He'd never brought his car anywhere near the area before, but he was quite confident the Lord would protect him now.

An unsuspecting Jeannie leaned forward, opened the door and came face to face with him.

"Fuck off, ya mad cunt," she snarled. "I mean it, fuck off or I'll phone the cops."

"No point, my dear, we are here already," Hamish laughed at her.

What the hell was she going to do? She was only a few yards from her home but there was no chance she'd outrun him. The noise from the Port of Leith bar gave her an idea. She ran across the road and into the crowded bar. She headed straight for the public telephone and called Jack. Looking through the bar mirror, she spied her pursuer searching for her.

"Jack, it's me, your mum. I'm in trouble, son. I need your help."

"Oh, Mum, I can't leave here. Stella was found murdered this morning and I have to make arrangements."

"Listen to me, boy. I never ask for your help and if you don't get here pronto, you'll be arranging another funeral."

"What's wrong? What do you need me to do?"

Jeannie had never called on Jack for help and he knew it must be serious.

"That was my mother. She's in trouble and I have to go," Jack told Rosie and Kitty.

"Go, we'll be fine."

Replacing the receiver, Jeannie watched as the sleazebag searched for her. Thankfully, she knew the barmaid on duty, one of the few in the area she hadn't upset or fought with. She signalled to the woman to let her out the back way; a route often used by working girls as an escape from punters and pimps. Jeannie arrived at her flat with only minutes to spare.

Not wishing to upset the neighbours, Ross knocked quietly on the door, remembering he had not come off best after his last encounter.

"C'mon, Jeannie, let me in. I'll behave. I got a bit carried away the last time. I'll pay double, c'mon, open up, be a good girl."

"Fuck off, there's no chance I'm letting you in."

Jeannie heard sounds of a scuffle outside.

"Ma, it's me. Open the door," Jack shouted.

"Is he still there?"

"He's out cold, open the door."

There, laid out on the landing was DCI Hamish Ross.

"For fuck's sake, Ma, do you know who he is?" Jack asked, astounded.

"Fucked if I know," replied Jeannie. "I don't want to know either. He's a fucking basket-case and after his last visit he can go find another mug."

"He's a fucking detective inspector. He's the one who had it in for Stella."

"What happened to her, by the way? How did she cop it?" Jeannie asked.

"I don't want to talk about it just now. We need to decide what we are going to do with this fucker. You could be in big trouble, Ma."

"He's as mad as box of frogs, Jack, always praying and quoting the bible. Honest, son, I'm sure he's on something."

"No way, not at his level."

"I'm telling you, he can be okay and then within minutes he's off his face."

"If he is, which I doubt, then all the more reason to get as much on him as possible. Check his pockets."

"There's a warrant card, a notebook, a wallet containing twenty pounds and a small twist. Fuck me, you're right."

"I knew it! I've seen all sorts in my time, son, but he's way off the scale. It also explains the stuff about the bible and thinking he's God."

"He's going to be coming round shortly. Get your camera."

Having taken a series of very compromising shots, Jack woke the sleeping policeman by dousing him with a jug of cold water.

DCI Ross jumped to attention, rubbing his chin. "You're under arrest, my lad, for assaulting a police officer."

"Fuck off, ya wanker. Do you think you're dealing with a pair of idiots What you had in your possession would put you away for at least a year. How do you think you'd last in prison, with all the guys you've put away?"

"What are you talking about, laddie? All I had on my

person was a couple of aspirin."

"Okay, swallow them. If they're only aspirin, get them over your neck. Two aspirin won't harm you, but two tabs on top of what you've already had will have you leaving here in a box."

Ross grabbed the twist and threw it on the floor. Before Jack could stop him, the police chief ground the contents into the lino.

"You were saying?" he smirked. "As for your photos, behave yourself! All they'd show is me with two aspirin. So, if you don't mind, excuse me, I've got a case to solve. A friend of yours, I believe. Couldn't have happened to a nicer tart."

Jeannie, grabbed hold of Jack and saved her boy from making matters worse.

"I'll get you for this, Ross,' Jack swore. "One way or another, I'll get you."

Jack had followed Stella's instructions and contacted the solicitor She'd engaged, a small family business out of town. Mr Cameron arranged for the documents to be collected by a courier to ensure safe delivery.

"Are you sure we did the right thing?" Kitty asked Jack as they sat by the kitchen fire. "What do you think Marcus will say when he finds out?"

"You can ask him yourself," replied Jack, as the lawyer barged through the door.

"What the hell are you playing at?" Marcus roared, his face bright red, evidently barely keeping his temper in check.

"What are you on about, man?" Jack stood up to face the irate lawyer. "Don't come barging in here, shouting at an old lady."

"Keep out of this, it's nothing to do with you." Marcus dismissed Jack and turned to Kitty. "Why did you keep back documents belonging to Stella when they should have been given to me?"

"I didn't keep anything back on purpose," said a distraught Kitty. "It was such a shock. Stella gave me the envelope years ago. To tell you the truth, I'd forgotten all about it until the solicitor called."

"You should still have directed everything through me," continued Marcus.

"Why? The envelope was addressed to Cameron and McCluskey Solicitors, and Stella gave me precise instruction that it was to be hand-delivered to Mr Cameron, so I didn't think I was doing anything wrong." Kitty sobbed into her apron.

"You've no idea how this complicates matters." Marcus stormed up and down the kitchen. "I would have made provisions for you, made sure you were taken care of, but you can say goodbye to that now. In fact, I'm giving you notice to quit the house. You have fourteen days to find alternative accommodation."

Kitty pulled herself together and turned to the lawyer "I don't think you can do that, Mr Kramer."

"Are you questioning my authority, Mrs Murphy? Surely you must realise that you and this assortment of scallywags wouldn't be able stay here rent-free forever?"

"Of course not," the old lady answered. "But I don't think you ought to be giving us notice until the missus' wishes are made known."

Red-faced, the angry lawyer stormed off furiously. "Shit, maybe we should have given the letter to him?" Kitty said.

"So he could dispose of it? No, Kitty. We did the right thing, and don't worry, if Stella Gold said she would take care of you, she will have."

"I hope to God you're right."

They'd know soon enough what Stella had in mind for them. The reading of the will was to take place the day after the funeral. Both he and Kitty had been invited to attend, as, they assumed, had Marcus.

Much to the disappointment of her friends and clients, the announcement in the Evening News intimated that Stella was to have a private requiem mass, held in the church of Saint Mary Magdalene, with family flowers only.

Marcus, who had made the arrangements, hadn't reckoned on Stella's popularity and the need for those she touched to pay their respects. The small chapel was packed to capacity and the perfume from the floral tributes was carried on the breeze for miles. The mourners came from all points of the compass and all walks of life; representatives from the city council, the clergy, even members of the police force, who, unlike DCI Ross, held the Madame in the highest regard. She had what was known as a 'good turnout', a measure of a person's standing, in life as well as in death. Thinking back, it was a far cry from poor Mary's where he and Stella had been the only mourners.

The old house had seen some parties over the years, but nothing compared to the wake held in Stella's honour. It went on into the wee small hours. Although tinged with sadness, the mourners were there to celebrate her life. And what a life. Stella had been a strong, determined woman who had forged success in a man's world. Fearless and enterprising, full of surprises, and for a few present, there were still some to come. The revellers were all aware that she was the last of her kind and there might never be anywhere the likes of number 17 Danube Street again.

Edinburgh Evening News

The funeral of the colourful character and businesswoman, Stella Gold, took place today. Representatives from the city

225

council, police and members of the clergy were in attendance. The service was held in St Mary Magdalene's followed by a graveside sermon...

CHAPTER FIFTY-FIVE

Last Will & Testament

What the hell was he doing here? thought Ronnie Williams, shifting uncomfortably in the rickety wooden chair. The request from Stella's solicitor had come completely out of the blue, following the news of her murder which had almost floored him. He was devastated, nor had he seen it coming. He'd managed to get her through her sentence without too much trouble or cost, although she'd done none too badly without his help. To be beaten at the last hurdle, told he'd never see her, kiss her or hold her again was more than his brain could compute. He wanted to take hold of someone, anyone, and inflict on them the pain he was suffering right now. Hard though it was, he had to keep it together, he was pretty sure no-one knew their secret.

For years he had managed to keep her safe. He had ensured no-one had encroached on her territory or threatened her livelihood, all without her knowing. She may have suspected, but it was never spoken of. They had been lovers for almost several years. The first Monday of every month she would leave the city to visit her solicitor, after which he'd pick her up and make the short drive to their cottage by the sea. As often as they could, they would spend the night together. These opportunities were few and far between, red letter days, days to be cherished. No-one had ever suspected.

Their longstanding affair had begun soon after the house opened. Stella was easy pickings for the gang leaders in the city, a babe-in-arms. The most dangerous aspect of her situation was that she was totally unaware of her predicament. Ronnie put out the word that Danube Street was under his jurisdiction and woe betide anyone who disregarded his decree.

They had met again quite innocently at a dinner thrown by the Lord Provost. Neither attended civic functions as a rule, however, as personal guests of the provost, it would have been rude not to go. Seated next to one another, the mutual attraction had been almost palpable. Had they been anywhere other than the city chambers, either one would have ripped the clothes off the other. Ronnie was fascinated by this creature. He, who could have his choice of almost any female in the city, was totally smitten. She was his soulmate and he hers, but sadly, circumstances had prevented their relationship from ever progressing. Her bête noir was Marcus; she was married and no amount of cajoling would encourage him to release her. And of course, there was Oliver.

Ronnie's own bête noir was Freddie. He could never let his brother know that Stella was in his life. He'd known since he was a young lad that one day he would have to put a stop to Freddie's rampages, but he could never choose between the two and he would be forced to if Freddie ever found out about Stella.

The request to attend the reading came as a complete surprise to Ronnie. Surely after all these years together she wasn't going to 'out' them, or Freddie. What would be the point? His brother had spent the last few months banged up in a high security hospital for the criminally insane. At last the authorities had seen sense, locked him up and thrown away the key. So there was nothing Stella could add to make Freddie's situation worse; he really was a lifer.

So why was he here? Ronnie pondered. There was no way she was going to leave him anything in her will, theirs had been a clandestine affair. One which would never have survived the glare of publicity. It was pure curiosity that brought him to this dingy, dusty room in the depths of the Law Society for the reading of a will belonging to someone, who in the eyes of the public, he hardly knew.

Jack and Kitty arrived shortly after Marcus, who deigned to acknowledge them with a nod.

"I hope you don't have great expectations," the lawyer smirked at the two. "Stella wasn't a great saver."

Jack made a move towards Kramer but was stopped in his tracks by the voice of Edinburgh's most notorious villain.

"Now, now, ladies, have some decorum, please," Ronnie Williams drawled at the two.

Whether it was the shock of seeing him, or being mocked, both Jack and Marcus stopped in their tracks.

"What are you doing here?" Kramer quizzed Ronnie.

"The same as you, probably. I'm hoping she's seen fit to leave me her business," Ronnie sneered at the two standing before him.

"I wouldn't think so, you were hardly her favourite person. Seriously, what are you doing here?" Marcus persisted.

"Well we'll soon find out," Ronnie replied as Mr Cameron entered the room carrying a huge sheaf of papers.

"Good morning, gentlemen. You too, madam," he smiled to Kitty. "I've asked you all here as beneficiaries of Mrs Stella Gold-Kramer. I have been acting on behalf of Mrs Kramer since shortly after her marriage. The original will was written at that time and since then there have been several changes and codicils, the latest being on the 18th of September of this year."

"She was in prison in September," snapped Marcus.

"That is correct," replied Mr Cameron. "So, if you would allow me, I will begin."

"Wait, what proof do we have that it's Stella Kramer's will. I dealt with all her business and know nothing of any will." Barked Marcus.

"It has been witnessed by the Governor of Scorston Prison and I hardly think she would be duplicitous in such a matter.

So, as I said, I will commence with the reading."

There were a number of small bequests, mainly to charities and past employees. She bequeathed five thousand pounds to the roof fund at St. Mary Magdalene's, two thousand to the baby unit at the Simpson Memorial Hospital. There was also a donation to supply carrots and sugar lumps to the various dray horses who had delivered to the house over the years.

The first shock was the bequest to her mother for ten thousand pounds, apologising for not being a good daughter in life, but hoping her parents would forgive her and that she would make up for her misdeeds in her passing. She hoped the money would be used to bring some comfort into their lives. Kramer was the only one present who was aware that Stella's parents were still alive. Mr Cameron read on.

"The sum of twenty thousand pounds to be given to Roderick McLeod, the biological son of Mary Wallace, to give the boy options in life.

The property at number one Wellington Place, North Berwick, its contents and the sum of ten thousand pounds to Kathleen Murphy, in thanks for her loyalty and friendship over the years.

A ten-year lease on the property at number seventeen Danube Street with the option to buy at the end of the tenure, together with the sum of ten thousand pounds bequeathed to Mr Jack Hunter for his unfaltering loyalty.

The remainder of my estate comprising of properties as detailed overleaf. The portfolio of stocks and shares held by my broker, Philips and Sons, the balance in my personal accounts with the Royal Bank of Scotland, together with the Bank of Zurich and any other properties or assets which may have been accrued are bequeathed to my son Oliver Kramer.

I also appoint as guardians and executors of this estate, Mr Cameron of Cameron and McCluskey and Mr Ronald Williams. It is my belief that my son will need their help and protection. This concludes the wishes of Mrs Stella Kramer."

"For your information," the lawyer added. "There is a breakdown of the estate attached to your copy of the document. We estimate the value of Mrs Stella Kramer's estate to amount to just over 1.3 million pounds."

All four people present gasped out loud.

First to speak was Marcus. "I cannot believe this, it's ridiculous. I'm the boy's father, his next of kin. I refuse to allow this person," he pointed to Ronnie, "to have anything whatsoever to do with my child. He's scum, a low-life criminal."

"Be careful, Kramer, very careful," Ronnie growled across the table at Marcus.

"Please, Mr Kramer, this is no way to conduct yourself. Mr Williams can only exercise his duty over your wife's estate, nothing more. There was a conflict of interest here between your family and your profession. Surely you understand why she did this?"

"The bitch did it on purpose! She did it to make sure my son knew who she was, despite the fact she abandoned him, wanted nothing to do with him. She sold him to me when he was only days old. I'll contest this fabrication, drag it through every court in the land."

"Don't be ridiculous, Mr Kramer, the will is incontestable. You would be wasting your time and money, but that, of course, is your prerogative." Mr Cameron had no time for this jumped-up barrister making a show of himself.

"As for you," Marcus turned to Jack. "You're nothing but a glorified pimp, the spawn of a dockside whore. I'll burn the place down before you get near it," Kramer screamed at him.

"I don't think that's a good idea, Kramer, making threats like that before witnesses. I don't know why your wife appointed me and quite frankly, I want nothing to do with either you or your son," said Ronnie.

"If he is your son." muttered Kitty to Jack.

"Hush, Kitty."

"What you do or don't do with your son's inheritance is entirely up to you, but cross me or speak to me in that manner again and you'll regret it. I promise you, I don't make threats I don't keep." Ronnie about-turned and walked out.

What the hell was the stupid mare thinking? Ronnie knew he shouldn't speak ill of the dead, but she had to be out of her bloody tree to dream up this half-baked scenario. No matter how much he dismissed the situation, he knew deep down there could be only one reason she would involve him.

The boy had lived with the belief that Kramer was his father and his mother had died in childbirth and it was too late to change the story now. Ronnie wasn't sure he'd want anything to do with a kid reared by Kramer, there was no telling what kind of nancy-boy he'd turn out to be. Fuck. What if Oliver ever came in contact with Freddie? He'd shit his lacy underpants. No, he was better well away, but he couldn't help wondering. Damn Stella Gold. She was still causing him problems, even from the grave, but God, how he missed her.

The value of Stella's estate hadn't been the only shock that morning. How in the name of Judah had she managed to amass such a fortune? thought Marcus. One of his many failings was to ignore the fact that there were smarter folk than him out there. Not for a moment would he have believed how astute Stella had been. How she never missed an opportunity, no matter how small, to grow her fortune. She had listened to those in the know and acted accordingly. Grudgingly, he had to admire her. Despite his anger at the executors, he also had to admit Oliver was well and truly a man of means, which would open many doors. But why the hell had she involved Williams? Stella knew the history between them and he would have thought the last person on earth she would have trusted would be Ronnie Williams. He saw from the copy of the will, that Williams had only been recently included. Why? She couldn't have known of his plans, so why introduce Williams to the mix?

CHAPTER FIFTY-SIX

Visitors

While Kitty and Jack were off attending the reading, Rosie had some unexpected visitors – her sisters. She was delighted to see the girls, she hadn't realised just how much she'd missed them.

"My God, you look knackered," she sympathised.

"So would you, if you were working day and night to keep the business going." Iris flopped down on a sofa. "I swear to God, I could sleep for a week."

"That's what we're here about." Violet glanced at her older sister. "There have been a few developments since we last saw you."

"Well, don't keep me waiting," Rosie was intrigued.

"You can see how exhausted we both are. We never realised how much hard work the bakery was. Dad had help and he didn't have to serve in the shop after baking half the night."

"True. I'm not sure if I could cope," Rosie sympathised with the two girls.

"Well, we've had an offer. Uncle John wants to buy us out, lock stock and barrel."

"That means we get shot of the place and get our lives back," Violet said gleefully.

"I don't care. I've no interest in the bakery, do what you want with it. But if you sell up where will you live?"

"That's the next piece of news we have for you, go on, Iris, tell her."

"I'm getting married," blushed Iris.

"Married? Who to?" Rosie asked, puzzled.

"Sergeant Mitchell."

"Jesus, Iris, he's ancient."

"He is not, he's thirty. And I don't care what you say, I'm going to get wed. It could be the only chance I get."

"Sorry, that was rude. I do like him, he was really good when Dad went missing. Where does that leave you, though?" Rosie asked Violet.

"I'm going to stay with them in the station house for the present. So, what do you say to our news then, Rosie?"

"I say well done the Royce girls."

"Where are Jack and Kitty?" enquired Violet.

"They're at the reading of Stella's will. We've had notice to move, so I might be joining you in the police house," laughed Rosie.

"Oh, Rosie, it's not big enough," Iris said, somewhat embarrassed.

"I'm joking, you twit. Jack and I will find something, I'm sure."

"Are you two officially an item?" Violet asked her younger sister.

"Well, yes and no. He wants me to move in with him," Rosie replied.

"And?" asked both sisters.

"I refused. I love Jack but I'm not in love with him. He needs someone who will look after him and give him babies."

"What did he say to that?" Violet blushed to the roots of her hair.

"Not much," answered Rosie, curious at her sister's reaction. "Heavens, why did I never see this before? He'd be just the man for you. That's it, you marry Jack."

"Stop it, Rosie, don't be daft. Anyway, I'm not having your cast-offs."

"It's a change from me having yours," Rosie exclaimed.

The conversation was interrupted by the noisy return of Kitty and Jack.

"Rosie, Rosie," called Kitty. "Oh, Rosie you'll never guess, you'll never guess in a million years what the missus did for us."

"Calm down, Kitty, or the whole street will know your business."

"I don't give a hoot," said the old woman, grabbing Dora and dancing round the kitchen.

"My, there's been some excitement in here today," Violet said, thankful for the change of subject.

"Listen, Rosie, you know I always said the missus would take care of us, well she did. She's only left me and Dora a cottage in North Berwick and ten thousand pounds. Ten thousand pounds! Like I told Jack, I've barely ever had ten bob, never mind ten grand."

"That's fantastic, Kitty, you're made for life. No more six o'clock starts and twelve o'clock finishes. You can be a lady of leisure."

"What! Are you fecking daft? I may be made for life but I'm not ready to hang up my boots yet. Tell them, Jack. Tell them what she did for you. Rosie, you're not going to believe this. I know we shouldn't be celebrating, after all, it's what we used to call blood money, but I've never had anyone give me anything in my life."

"Shut up, Kitty and let Jack speak, you're going nineteen to the dozen."

"Sorry. It's just so unbelievable"

"Well, Jack, c'mon. Don't keep me in the dark. What's your good news?" Rosie asked.

"She left me the lease on here and the same amount as Kitty," muttered a subdued Jack.

"You don't seem too happy at your good fortune."

"What's the point? I can't do this on my own, not without you and you're planning on leaving."

"Leaving? Who's leaving?" asked Iris. "Why would you want to leave here? I never thought the day would dawn when I'd say this, but you're great at this job. The girls all like and respect you. Jack's right, without you the place will fall apart. Don't be stupid, Rosie."

"I know what this is all about," said Violet, taking Rosie's hand. "It's all about Hope. You have to move on with your life, Rosie. You're young, you have to get over her and the best way is hard work."

"She's right, Rosie. Your only salvation, my girl, is get your head down and make this the best little whorehouse in the east." They all laughed at Kitty's repartee.

"It's true, Rosie, you'll never forget her but you can still have a life." Lifting her cup of tea, Kitty toasted, "Here's to the next chapter for Danube Street."

CHAPTER FIFTY-SEVEN

Prayers Answered

Hamish Ross had prayed frantically for a solution to his recent mission. It was all very well being a self-appointed 'Avenging Angel', but he still had to provide answers. Fortunately, on the seventh day the Lord had delivered, in the guise of Raymond Smith.

Smith had walked into Gayfield Square at five o'clock on the 2nd of November and confessed to the murders of four young men on Calton Hill.

Hamish Ross had almost leapt out of his chair with relief at this confession. If ever he had received confirmation that the Lord was truly on his side, this was it.

Smith had recently been discharged from the Royal Edinburgh Psychiatric Hospital and had nothing whatsoever to do with the case, or any of the other twenty or so he had confessed to over the past five years, a mere detail that DCI Ross omitted to disclose.

Desperate for a result to take the heat off his squad and increase his conviction rate, Hamish leaked the information of the arrest to the press.

"What the fuck is that idiot up to now?" Acting Sergeant Cummins questioned his one-time partner.

"God knows, but you keep well out of it. Make waves and you'll be acting alright, acting the fucking goat."

"I know, but it gets right on my tits. Why can no-one see through this fucker? He acts all holier than thou yet he's the biggest cunt in the station."

"Everybody knows Ray Smith is no more the culprit than

the station cat. He's just bought the chief some time, nothing else."

"Naw, this stinks, there's something else going on, mark my words."

"I think you could be right, however, for now, your job is just to book him in and keep hold of your stripes."

Duty Sergeant Cummins booked Ray Smith into one of the holding cells. It was a Friday night and as usual the station was full. Most occupants were loudly protesting their innocence, all except one. There was no sound coming from Smith.

Opening the spyhole, Acting Sergeant Peter Cummins saw his career vanish before his eyes. Raymond Smith was hanging from the ceiling by his belt. The belt the sergeant had checked in together with the rest of his possessions. How the fuck had that happened? This belt was not easily forgotten, with its distinctive silver horse head buckle. Cummins knew he'd checked it in, so how had the prisoner got hold of it? Someone had it in for him and he knew who that someone was. Cummins had no defence, he was done for.

Raymond Smith was pronounced dead by the duty doctor and four murder cases were marked closed and filed away.

One day, Cummins vowed. One day he would have his revenge. He would expose DCI Ross for the murdering bastard he was.

Edinburgh Evening News

A spokesman for Edinburgh and Lothian Police Force reported a man arrested in connection with the 'Rent Boy Murders' was found dead in his cell. The police are treating this as suicide…

CHAPTER FIFTY-EIGHT

Treachery

Jesus, he needed a drink. It was always the same after a visit with his brother. It was the most dismal, dreary place, no wonder few of the poor buggers recovered.

Alone in the stark visitor's room, Ronnie had watched his once fit and healthy brother come shuffling along the corridor, chained to a warden. It was hard to believe this poor creature was Freddie, a pale shadow of the man he'd once been. A bag of skin and bones, but still he exuded a menacing air. Flickering just under the surface was that devious, treacherous devil, waiting to pounce.

Ronnie could hear him muttering under his breath.

"He pushed me, he pushed me, but I'll get him." Freddie repeated this mantra over and over then, out of the blue, he would fire a random question, catching his brother off guard.

On Ronnie's last visit Freddie had been obsessed with Mary, the girl he'd almost killed years ago. He laughingly insisted he had been responsible for her death, gleefully confessing he'd smothered her. Maybe, somewhere in his subconscious, he was feeling remorse, although he'd never shown any such emotion before. Ronnie certainly wouldn't put it past him but he was fairly sure Freddie was, for once, innocent. Maybe he had sent the poor woman on her way. If so, it was the only favour he'd ever done her!

"You promised we'd get it back," he shouted at Ronnie.

"Get what back?"

"Danube Street. You said when she got out of prison we'd get it back. You lied to me."

"When who got out of prison?" asked Ronnie.

"The woman, we had to wait till she got out." Freddie

stamped his foot in temper.

"Stella, the woman was called Stella and she's dead. The place belongs to someone else now."

"I don't care! You said it would be ours. I want it when I get out of here, okay?"

"I'll do my best," Ronnie endeavoured to placate him.

"What about your son? Is he still with that nancy-boy, the lawyer?" Freddie watched his brother slyly from under his eyelashes.

"I don't know what you're talking about. I've got no kids and well you know it."

"Don't treat me like some kind of div. I might be a psycho but I'm not stupid."

Freddie's maniacal laughter chilled Ronnie to the bone. His brother really was mad, no doubt about it.

Thankfully the visitor's bell rang. Ronnie couldn't get out quick enough. Jesus, these visits were hard work. Freddie might not mention Stella or the boy for months, or he could just as easily take up the conversation where it left off, next time.

Along with most of Edinburgh elite Ronnie received an invitation to the opening of the newly renamed and rebranded Seventeen Danube Street. The town was buzzing in anticipation and the rumour factory was in top gear. It was said to have cost a small fortune to kit the place out. Italian marble tiles for the foyer were brought direct from Milan and fabulous crystal chandeliers, worth thousands, were just two of the extravagant purchases made for the house.

Ronnie was undecided whether to attend or not, he had had a gruelling day and he was still reeling from his visit with Freddie. No doubt there would be constant reminders of the previous Madame, which he could well do without. However, curiosity won in the end. Nor could he let the good citizens think he hadn't been invited.

The partners were doing the final walk through before opening to their guests. Jack and Rosie had never worked so hard in their lives but boy, it been worth it. The results were overwhelming. The occupants of number sixteen had decided to sell up. They'd had enough of living next door to the busiest whorehouse in Edinburgh. So, with a great deal of haggling and a distinct lack of any other interested parties, Jack and Rosie had doubled the size of number seventeen for a song. Thanks to their many contacts in high places, they procured a gaming licence allowing them to open the new addition as a casino: The Gold Room, dedicated to the memory of Stella.

"Jesus, Rosie, it's fabulous. I can hardly take it in," said Jack, catching his breath. "Can you believe we are actually responsible for creating this?" He was almost overcome with emotion.

"It's fabulous, magnificent. I love it," replied an excited Rosie, overawed at the splendour of their achievement. "What do you think she would make of it?"

"She'd love it, love the style, and everything about it."

The original business was still carried out discreetly but now they had a piano bar, a restaurant and of course, the new casino. It had become chic to be decadent.

"God, Jack, what if no one comes? It'll all be for nothing." Rosie had a fleeting panic attack.

"You have to be joking, look outside, look at the line of cars."

To her delight, anyone who was anyone was in attendance. Included in the guest list, apart from Ronnie Williams, were Marcus Kramer and DCI Ross. Neither Jack nor Rosie had seen or heard from Ronnie or Marcus since the day of the will reading and did not think either man would attend. Ross was a different kettle of fish. Jack had delivered the invitation in person to the Chief Inspector, who was left in no doubt that failure to attend would result in several compromising snapshots being distributed amongst the guests and members of the press. "Will that not encourage him to go after us even more?" Rosie worried.

"He can hardly criticise the place when he has enjoyed our hospitality. I've primed the bartender to make sure he is kept topped up," Jack reassured her.

"What about Marcus?" she asked.

"We've offered him an olive branch. If he refuses, so be it. But this property ultimately belongs to his son, so surely it's in his best interest to keep a watch on the place?"

"Mm, maybe. And Williams?"

"He'll come to see how much protection money he can squeeze out of us."

"I always found it strange that Stella didn't pay anyone."

"She paid in other ways, I think, but leave that for now, let's get this show on the road."

First of the three to arrive was Ronnie Williams and it was evident to him that the new owners had come up trumps. The place was magnificent; each room was spectacular, he thought.

Glamorous hostesses, dancers on podiums and fullsize portraits of Stella Gold were scattered throughout the rooms. Like a punch to his solar plexus, Ronnie gasped at how beautiful she had been and how she still affected him. Swallowing his drink, he headed back to the bar, and ran smack bang into Marcus Kramer.

"I must say I'm surprised to see you here, I wasn't aware you mixed in polite society," Kramer drawled.

"Fuck off, Kramer. Don't piss me off, I'm not in the mood."

"So? Why would I give a damn?"

Rosie, who had been watching from the sidelines, stepped

in between the two sparring partners. "Gentlemen, gentlemen, it's a party. Take your disputes outside. Please don't make me ask you to leave."

"Sorry," murmured both men, turning in opposite directions.

No sooner had she dealt with them when a fracas at the entrance drew her attention.

"Tell them who I am," roared the bleached-blonde creature. "You can't keep me out," Jeannie swung her large, heavy handbag, catching the security guy a hefty blow to his temple. "It's my son's gaff, you have to let me in."

Catching sight of Rosie, Jeannie got even louder and the handbag cracked a few more heads.

"It's okay, boys, Mrs Hunter should be on the list. Can someone go and find Jack for me?"

There was no way Rosie could refuse Jeannie admittance, but shit, she couldn't let her loose amongst her guests either.

At that precise moment DCI Ross arrived, looking extremely annoyed.

"Well, fuck me," Jeannie yelled at the newcomer. "Actually, you have, several times."

The raucous laughter could be heard throughout the house, stopping Jack in his tracks.

It couldn't be, could it? There she was, drunk as a lord and abusing the chief inspector, much to the delight of several guests. Jack scooped his mother up and carried her upstairs to one of the empty rooms. Dumping her unceremoniously on the bed, he flew downstairs to stop Ross who was on the point of leaving.

"Oh no you don't. I'm sorry about Jeannie, but let's face it, it's your own fault. Now come and socialize and make like you don't have a problem being here."

Ross was seething. Not only did he not want to be there, but to be embarrassed in front of all these onlookers was humiliating to say the least.

"Hazard of the job, old boy. I presume you've put her away at some time?" the Lord Provost appeared at Ross' side, making conversation.

Ross looked around Was the capital's most senior official speaking to him?

"You must get that sort of thing everywhere you go, especially with your record of arrests."

"Not that often," Hamish replied, "and certainly not so vociferously."

The Provost chuckled, and finding the situation most amusing introduced a few more guests to their conversation.

Hamish was unused to this level of recognition. Normally people gave him a wide berth, but not tonight, and for the first time in years he was actually enjoying himself. There were no voices telling him what to do. How strange, and how refreshing.

CHAPTER FIFTY-NINE

Hope's Story

Everything changed on the day of Hope Robert's eleventh birthday. The day of her party was as clear to her as if it were yesterday. There were egg and cress sandwiches, jelly and ice-cream, and a pink iced cake with candles. She had on a beautiful new dress and black shiny shoes with pearl buttons. Her mummy had tied her long blonde hair in rags the night before, to make it wavy. She was a princess. Everyone told her that, so it must be true. She was the only child of Donna and Michael Roberts.

The party had been a great success and now Mummy and Daddy were clearing up while she opened her gifts. There was a book from Auntie Joan and Cousin Sheila, a hula hoop from Thelma and Patrick, her other cousins. A beautiful scrapbook with angels and cherubs and lots more gifts. She was a lucky girl getting all these wonderful things. Life would have been perfect, except for one thing: 'the secret', the secret between her and Daddy. If she told she would be sent away, away from Granny, her aunties, uncles and cousins. She definitely didn't want that, but she hated the secret, it was wrong.

"Come and sit down, Hope, your dad and I have something to tell you," said her mum.

"I've been a good girl today, Mummy, and I said thank you to everyone. I've not been naughty, not once."

"No, precious, you've not been naughty, but we have something to tell you. Did you notice Auntie Pearl? Did you notice anything different about her?"

"Do you mean about her having a baby?"

"That's right, she's going to have a baby and the baby is growing inside her tummy until it's ready to come out."

"Is that how you got me?" Hope asked curiously.

"No, not quite. That's what we want to speak to you about. You didn't grow in my tummy like Auntie Pearl's, you grew in another lady's tummy. A lady who couldn't keep you kindly gave you to us."

"Why couldn't she keep me?

"I'm not sure, maybe she wasn't well."

"So you're not my real mummy and daddy? Do I belong to the other lady?" The little girl's chin was trembling. "Will I have to go and live somewhere else?"

"No, chicken, you are our special girl and always will be, but we have some good news to tell you. After all this time Jesus has sent us a miracle. I've also got a baby growing in my tummy, so do you know what that means?"

"You're going to send me away when the new baby comes." Hope wouldn't be comforted.

"You're not going anywhere. It means you'll have a new brother or sister."

"I don't want a brother or sister, I want it just to be us."

"Go and play with your new toys and don't worry, everything will be just fine."

But Hope did worry, she worried that she would be sent away and she worried about her Daddy coming into her room at night. So what he said was true, if she told, she would be sent to the other lady.

Six months later, a beautiful bouncing boy arrived in the Roberts household.

"What the hell am I going to do with her?" an exasperated Donna Roberts asked her husband. "That's the second time I've caught her with a pillow over his face. The poor little soul has so many bruises on him I'm terrified the health visitor will think he's being abused."

"It's just sibling jealousy, she'll grow out of it."

"For God's sake, Michael, I can't leave her alone with him at all, in case she harms him. What are we going to do? Because this can't go on."

A scream brought both parents running into the other room. Hope appeared to be engrossed in her book while a bright red mark was appearing on her brother's cheek, where he had evidently been pinched.

"It wasn't me," Hope shouted defiantly.

"Well who the hell was it?" Her mother was at a loss as to what to do. "What's wrong with you, why do you behave like this? We've given you a beautiful home, lovely clothes, toys and the best of everything."

"No you haven't, he gets everything. You don't want me now you've got him. I've heard you saying you wish you'd never picked me."

At the end of her tether, Donna snapped back, "You're right, I do wish we'd never picked you. Not when you are being such a nasty little girl. Now go to your room and stay there until I tell you otherwise. There'll be no tea for you tonight."

The moment the words were out, Donna regretted her outburst. Of course she loved Hope and wouldn't send her away, but something had to be done. She couldn't work out what was troubling the child, it couldn't just be her baby brother.

"I wish you would back me up with her," she snapped at Mike.

"Hey, this is your ballgame. I didn't want to adopt in the first place, but I'll tell you this, if that little monster harms my son again, you'll have me to deal with."

"Don't say that, Mike, you were just as thrilled as I was when the adoption was approved. She was wonderful when she was little. It all seemed to change when we told her I was pregnant."

"Rubbish! I went along with this to keep you happy, but now she's more trouble than she's worth." Mike knew exactly when things had changed.

Listening at the door, the anxious little girl overheard the angry exchange between her mummy and daddy. It was the last straw for Hope, she hated him. She wouldn't wait to be sent away, she would go now and see how they liked it. She'd run away and then they'd be so sorry.

Packing her favourite books, a few clothes and her birthday money, nearly twenty pounds, she sneaked out the back door. As she jumped on the bus into town, Hope knew exactly what to do. She'd been on the bus loads of times. "Single please."

The bus lady looked questioningly at her. "Going somewhere nice?" she enquired.

"Yes, to my Granny's."

"Are you not a bit young to be on your own?"

"She's waiting at the bus station for me."

"If you're sure. I wouldn't let my kids travel on buses by themselves," was the conductor's parting shot as she handed Hope her ticket.

Hope plonked herself down on the bench to decide what her next move would be, the very same bench Rosie had sat on all those years ago. But no Knight in shining armour was about to come to her rescue.

The bus depot was a treacherous place, a veritable melting pot of seasoned travellers, bewildered souls and many nefarious characters. Unfortunately for this naïve little girl, she'd been spotted by two of the depot's most prolific opportunists. Kylie and Chelsea were well known around the area and worked the depot daily on the lookout for fledglings. They spied Hope not long after her arrival. Easy pickings, they both agreed.

Hope was wary of the two girls who approached her. "Hello, little girl, are you waiting for someone?" the taller one asked her, ever so politely.

Hope had been told never to speak to strangers, but these weren't strangers, they were just big girls.

"No, not really," Hope replied trustingly.

"Not really? Where are you going?" the chubby, smaller girl asked.

"I haven't decided yet." She didn't want to look stupid.

"Don't tell us," the big girl laughed. "You've run away from home?"

"How did you know that?" Hope gasped.

"Well, a lot of little girls run off and end up here in the bus station with nowhere to go."

"What happened, what was so awful that you ran off?" Chelsea asked.

"I don't want to talk about it. I think I should maybe go home, my mum will be worried about me."

"Just your mum? What about the rest of your family, will they be worried?" Kylie asked, sitting on the bench beside her. Noticing Hope's slight hesitation, she continued. "Will your daddy not miss you?" She put a comforting arm round Hope and nodded to her accomplice over the little girl's head.

"You can tell us, maybe we can help?"

"So why won't your daddy be worried? Does he smack you?"

"Oh no, of course he doesn't. I think I'll just get the bus back home." Hope stood up to leave.

"Don't rush off, let's go have some hot chocolate in the station buffet, then you can get the next bus."

There didn't seem to be any harm in that, and she was hungry.

Over their hot chocolate, the two girls, Kylie and Chelsea, managed to wheedle out of Hope part of the reason she had run away. The girls agreed it was rubbish having a baby brother and being told she was adopted. She had every right to give her mum and dad a scare.

"I tell you what, why don't you come and spend the night with us, like a sleepover? We can phone your mum so she doesn't worry and then we'll put you on the bus tomorrow."

"I'm not sure," Hope's bravado was wavering.

"It'll teach them a lesson, especially your dad. Maybe it'll stop him doing dirty things to you."

Hope almost choked on her drink and her face turned bright red with embarrassment.

"He doesn't do nasty things to me," the little girl spluttered. How could these girls know?

"Don't stick up for him, Hope, he's a bad man. He should take your brother and go and live somewhere else. Just leave you and your mum. We'll tell her that when we take you home."

How many times had Hope dreamt of that scenario? Just her and her mum living together, no dad, or the brat.

"I'm not sure, maybe it would make things worse?" Hope was confused, but these girls were her friends and they wanted to help.

"Do you want him to stop or not?"

"Stop," she said in a tiny voice.

Big Mags handed them a fiver for this piece of prime meat. She was ideal. She looked young for her age and Mags had more than one eager customer willing to pay top dollar for a juicy little peach like this.

The ex-brass had not looked back since her short stint in prison. It hadn't been her first visit, but she was damned sure it would be her last. For the first time in her life she had struck gold. No more selling herself or being at the beck and call of psychos. No. With her ill-gotten gains she'd invested in a small bed and breakfast in the Port of Leith. Catering to the less fortunate in the community, she rented rooms by the hour. Shoplifters traded from her kitchen table, drug dealers stashed their goods in this safe house, while she supplied young bodies to a very particular clientele. Big Mags was a very busy woman.

Hope woke the next morning feeling sick, and her head hurt. She wanted her mummy. Most of last night was a blur. She remembered getting on the bus with the two big girls to visit their auntie. Hope didn't like the auntie, or her smelly house, but she was far too polite to say. The auntie said she had phoned her mum, threatening her with all sorts, but mainly 'the social'. The young runaway had no idea what 'the social' was, but it sounded bad. The auntie said she had told her mum about the bad things her daddy did, but her mum didn't believe her and told her that Hope was not to come home, she wasn't wanted. How could her mum say those things? Hope had cried for a while, until the auntie gave her some medicine which she said would make Hope sleep.

She was a bit shaky as she rose from the smelly, damp bed. No matter what they said, she was going home.

The bedroom door was locked! She knocked and knocked and called out, but no-one came and now she needed to pee. She danced up and down, desperate for the toilet. Finally, the frightened little girl could hold it in no longer. To her immense embarrassment, she had what her mum would call 'an accident'. What would these people say? Imagine peeing herself at her age? She crawled back into the stinky bed, crying to herself, waiting for someone to come.

A young girl has gone missing from her home in West Calder. Hope Roberts was last seen at three o'clock yesterday in the High Street Edinburgh. Police are appealing for any information...

CHAPTER SIXTY

Coincidence

Strolling along Princess Street, Rosie Royce was completely unaware of the admiring glances she was receiving from the many passers-by.

"I'm sure she's a film star," said one Edinburgh worthy to her companion as they came abreast of her.

"Ask for her autograph," said the other.

"No, you ask her," she said but the opportunity had gone as Rosie nipped into Jenner's, Edinburgh's most prestigious store. She had a number of gifts to collect to celebrate her and Jack's tenth anniversary in business.

She could hardly believe ten years had passed since she and Jack had taken over Danube Street officially. It seemed like only yesterday Stella Gold had left the business in Jack's hands. The ten-year lease was almost up and the opportunity to purchase was on the table. Never, all those years ago, had she or Jack believed there was even the slightest possibility that could happen. But here she was, on her way to meet with Jack and their silent partner to conclude the deal. Today marked the culmination of all their hard work and enterprise.

From day one Ronnie Williams had seen the potential in Danube Street and made them an offer they couldn't refuse. Protection, racketeering and money laundering were rife in the capital, but with one of the Williams brothers in their corner they were invincible.

What a decade it had been. Both her sisters were settled and happy. Iris had married her beloved police sergeant and produced a boy and a girl, both of whom adored their Aunt

Rosie. Violet had presented Jack with twin boys three years ago and was about to pop another one out any day soon. At any family gathering, Rosie always laid claim to the fact that she had set the couple up.

Danube Street was still at the centre of their business empire, but they had seized every opportunity to expand. And with a fleet of taxi cabs and a string of beauty salons throughout the city, Jack Hunter and Rosie Royce were doing quite nicely, thank you.

Over the years Rosie had embarked on a few affairs, but as she constantly declared to her sisters, she was not the marrying kind. The truth being she had never met any man who could compete with her. She was stunningly attractive, always impeccably dressed and as smart, if not smarter than most of the men she came in contact with. She was a real tough lady. There was a hardness in Rosie, an icy core that, sadly, no-one so far had come near to melting. Few men would go against her in business and those who did usually regretted doing so. Rosie was content enough in the world she had carved out for herself. There was only one thing missing, the one constant that never changed: her desire to find her child.

Hope would be almost twelve now and ready to enrol in senior school, pondered Rosie. Would her daughter be academic, artistic or musical like her father? Whatever, Rosie would give everything she owned for a glimpse of her daughter and to know she was happy.

Over the years the desperate mother had spent a small fortune hiring numerous private investigators, even a psychic, to trace the girl. Each one had promised the earth, but so far none had delivered. Hope was out there somewhere and although Rosie had exhausted all the conventional routes, she stubbornly refused to give up.

"Why don't we have a word with Hamish Ross?" Jack suggested one morning over coffee.

"I can't see him doing us any favours," replied Rosie.

"He certainly wouldn't help for free, but for the right price, he might be tempted," answered Jack. "It's worth a try, leave it with me." He certainly didn't want to raise her hopes only to have them dashed, but if anyone could ferret out information, Detective Chief Superintendent Ross could.

Ross was now the youngest superintendent in the force with a success rate second to none; he had galloped up the promotion ladder. Portrayed as an honest, god-fearing, dedicated police officer, the citizens of Edinburgh were glad to have him. He might use somewhat unorthodox methods of policing, but if he got results that was all that counted. His was the face continually on the front pages of the local newspapers. Ross knew exactly how to handle the press.

Jack had seldom called on Ross's services, but Rosie needed a bit of luck where the kid was concerned and nobody had the contacts or access to information that DS Ross had at his fingertips.

Back on Princes Street, Rosie, making her way to the offices of the Law Society, was enjoying the glorious sunshine. The city was in the midst of its annual International Festival and Princes Street was teeming with colourful performers handing out flyers advertising the various performances.

As she neared the West End Rosie stopped dead in her tracks. She couldn't believe her eyes. There, plastered over a huge billboard, was the face of someone she remembered only too well. It couldn't be him, she thought in disbelief, but there, for all to see was the father of her child, her first and only love: Toni Francitti, lead singer with The Brooklyn Boys, appearing at the Usher Hall.

"Are you alright, Miss?" a young man asked, coming to her assistance.

"Yes, yes thanks. I just felt a bit giddy, it must be this heat," Rosie replied.

"Are you sure? Can I fetch you some water or get you a cab?"

"No, honestly, I'm fine." She wished he would just go on his way.

"If you're sure. I could walk with you?"

"No, I'm only going a short distance, thanks," Rosie said firmly. She had to recover herself before her meeting.

The young man walked off leaving her staring at the face from the past. Francitti had barely changed. If anything he was even more handsome. She had to see him.

Turning around, all thoughts of her meeting gone, Rosie arrived at the Usher Hall only to find all performances of The Brooklyn Boys sold out. Even the touts outside had no tickets left, such was the group's popularity. She was going to have to pull some strings.

As she gazed at his likeness on a poster outside the theatre, she felt the old, familiar fluttering in her stomach. Feelings she hadn't experienced since she was fourteen. Reluctantly, she turned and headed back down Lothian Road towards the offices of the Law Society. She was almost thirty minutes late for her meeting.

Rosie was full of apologies when she rushed into her meeting, only to come face to face with the young man who had come to her assistance an hour earlier.

"Goodness me," he smiled at her. "It's a small world."

"Rosie, this is Mr Oliver Kramer, son of Marcus and Stella." Rosie's lawyer introduced the pair.

She knew who Oliver Kramer was, but what was he doing at this meeting? she thought as she nodded at the other two men present: Ronnie Williams as co-executor of Stella's will, and Jack.

"I asked Oliver along today because he is almost twenty-one and will very soon inherit Danube Street, along with the bulk of Stella's estate."

"Does this alter the conditions of Stella's will?" Rosie asked.

"Only if Jack declines to purchase the property, in which case we would have to renegotiate a lease. However, since that does not appear to be the case, this meeting is merely a formality."

"Can I ask what the value of the property is, and who carried out the valuation?" the young man interjected.

"Of course. The property was surveyed and valued by an independent company and it is currently on offer at sixty-five thousand pounds." Jamie Cameron handed over a copy of the survey. "Mr Hunter has offered the full asking price."

"I take it that this meets the criteria of my mother's bequest?"

"It does."

"That's fine. I have no objections," said Kramer junior.

While Jamie Cameron was conversing with Oliver, Rosie was struck by the similarities between Ronnie and the boy. They were like two peas in a pod. She couldn't believe no-one else had noticed.

It took some time to complete the documentation for the purchase but at last, it was theirs.

"I've booked a table in the George for lunch. I hope you'll all be my guests?" Jack offered.

"Sorry, no can do," replied Cameron. "I've still got some work to do on the conveyancing. Maybe another time?"

"It'll be a long time before we make a purchase like this one," Jack laughed. "You'll come, Ronnie? And you too, Oliver?"

"If I'm not imposing," young Kramer accepted.

"As long as you are paying, Jack," smiled Ronnie.

What a day, pondered Rosie. Of all the folk in Princes Street to bump into, Marcus Kramer's son, and then to come face to face with the father of her child. She didn't believe in coincidences, but today seemed to be proving her wrong.

258

CHAPTER SIXTY-ONE

Under Lock and Key

Hope banged on the door for hours, crying relentlessly. "I want to go home, please let me out. I want my mummy."

It was dark before the auntie eventually came to check on her. "Look at the state of this place," she said, slapping Hope's legs. "Have you peed yourself, you mucky little madam?" She administered another stinging slap. "No tea for you tonight, my girl," she slammed the door behind her.

"I need to go to the toilet again," Hope called through the door. "I have to go, and not for a pee."

The door flew open and she was dragged bodily from the room. Hope had never seen a toilet like this. At home they had a nice pink bath and a crinoline lady that covered the spare toilet paper, a far cry from this room. She couldn't think of words to describe it. There was no crinoline lady, in fact there was no toilet paper, just scraps of newspaper on a string. However, toilet paper or not, she had to go. Whether it was as a result of the drugs she'd been fed or the disgusting soup she'd devoured, Hope managed to soil herself. She was sure the auntie would be mad at her.

"Please can I go home? I don't feel well and I want my mummy," she began sobbing once more.

"Didn't you hear me last night? Your mummy doesn't want you. You're an orphan, nobody wants you and if you keep behaving like a baby I'll send you to the Humbie Home for bad girls. Do you want that?"

"No. I want my mummy. I want to go home."

There was no consoling her and Mags had had enough. Being anything but maternal, she thought another dose of 'medicine' should do the trick. This one was proving to be a bit more difficult than usual. Mags would need to increase the dose till she got it right.

CHAPTER SIXTY-TWO

On a Promise

"What are the chances of getting me tickets to see the Brooklyn Boys? They're appearing in the Usher Hall this week," Rosie appealed to Jack over lunch.

"You've no chance, tickets for their shows are rarer than hen's teeth." Her business partner laughed at her.

"I take it that's a no?"

"I'm pretty sure I can get tickets and a couple of backstage passes," Ronnie offered, "For a price."

"We all know what that would entail. No thanks, I'll try elsewhere," Rosie rebuffed him.

"Well the offer stands if you change your mind."

During lunch, young Kramer and Williams appeared to get on like a house on fire, which was most unusual given their backgrounds. If asked, Rosie would have sworn they were related in some way, but from what little she knew of the situation, it was extremely unlikely.

"What do you plan on doing in the future, now that you're a man of means?" Ronnie asked the boy quite candidly.

"I don't know, but one thing's for sure, I'm not joining the family firm. I'd like to take a year out and travel."

"Well you certainly have the means," said Ronnie.

Oliver was determined to get away from Edinburgh. Having gained a First in Law he had been expected to join the family firm, but no way was that happening now. He had been devastated to discover his father had been lying to him for years, allowing him to believe his mother had died in childbirth, when in fact she was the infamous Madame, Stella

Gold. He could never forgive his father for depriving him of the chance to know her. No matter Stella's lifestyle, she had still been his mother and he'd never had the opportunity to know her.

Ronnie Williams was an imposing man who intimidated most people, but not so Oliver Kramer. He didn't scare him one iota, in fact, Ronnie appeared to be more intimidated by Oliver than the other way round.

"Well good luck with your venture. I hope the next ten years are as profitable. Maybe I'll pop by the next time I'm in town," the young man said as he stood, ready to leave.

Seeing the two standing side by side, it was impossible for Rosie not to see the remarkable likeness between the two men.

"Ronnie, have you any family connection to the Kramers?" Rosie blurted out.

"Definitely not," Edinburgh's top dog replied.

"The likeness is remarkable. What do you say Jack?"

Not wishing to be brought into the conversation Jack hesitated before admitting, "They do look alike."

"Alike? It's incredible."

Both men sat back down at the table.

"We're not just talking about some similarities. Everything about you both, your tone of voice, the way you walk, all your mannerisms. This is not just a passing likeness," Rosie insisted.

"You're getting a bit carried away, Rosie," Jack tried to divert his partner. "I will admit they do look a bit alike."

"What are you getting at?" Oliver looked very uncomfortable.

"I'm not sure," answered Rosie. "What have you got to say, Ronnie?"

"Nothing. No matter how alike we may look or how we hold a tea cup, I'm nothing to this young lad. It's purely coincidental. Now, if you'll excuse me." Ronnie Williams left the table.

"Look," commanded Rosie. "Look at how he walks. It's almost a swagger and you, my boy, do exactly the same."

"Maybe so, but my swagger as you call it is the result of a bout of polio when I was young, not some inherited mannerism. Sorry to disappoint you," Oliver replied.

"I'm still positive there is some family connection," Rosie was adamant.

"I may not have known who my mother was, but I sure as hell know who my father is."

"I wouldn't be so sure, lad. I wouldn't be so sure."

Rosie tried everyone to procure a ticket for the concert without luck before admitting to herself that Ronnie was her only chance.

"Hi, it's Rosie, how are things?"

"Fine, what can I do for you?" Ronnie was sharp and to the point.

"I'm hoping you still have those tickets to see the Brooklyn Boys."

"I have, and the deal still stands."

She could hear the humour in his voice. "Hey, I wouldn't want to shorten your life, old man. I'd be far too much for you."

"I wouldn't put a bet on that if I was you."

"Seriously, Ronnie, I'm desperate. I've tried everyone."

"Why so desperate? Have you got a schoolgirl crush on them? Cream your skimpy lace pants when you hear them?"

"Yeah, something like that," answered Rosie. "Is it a yes or a no?" She wasn't one for playing games and Ronnie Williams knew that.

"I'll think about it. I might get a better offer," he laughed as he hung up.

Bastard, she thought, knowing he'd keep her hanging until the last moment.

CHAPTER SIXTY-THREE

Missing Persons

The bar was empty this early in the day which suited both men, neither wishing to be seen in the other's company.

"I need a favour."

"So this isn't a social call?" The police superintendent smiled sarcastically at his host.

Smart-arse, Jack thought to himself. He really disliked this man. He was a smarmy, condescending prat, but Jack knew Ross was probably their best chance, so he'd play along.

"I need help tracing someone."

"Try the Salvation Army." Ross replied.

How Jack would like to smack him. Ross definitely brought the worst out in him. "I want information on an eleven-year-old girl who was adopted as a baby. I want to know her whereabouts. All the information I have on her is in here." Jack pushed the yellow folder across the table to Ross.

"Someone's been busy. Why do you want this information, and what do you intend doing with it? If, and I say if, I can obtain it."

"Nothing sinister. She's Rosie Royce's daughter. She had the child when she was fourteen and to cut a very long and complicated story short, the child was taken into care. Rosie has never got over it and I would like her to know that the girl is in good hands."

"It'll cost."

"Let's see what you come up with first."

"If I was going to screw you I would have done it long ago."

"Maybe so, but let's see what you deliver."

*

Hope had no idea how long she had been in the room, she was allowed to the toilet twice a day, any accidents and she was slapped. Food came at random times. She might be fed twice a day, or not at all. She existed from dose to dose of her medicine.

Big Mags had been using this method of breaking down her protégés for years and she knew from experience the girl would be ready soon. Word was out and she had a number of clients bidding for the pleasure.

Today, as she cowered in the corner of the room, Hope was astonished Auntie wasn't yelling at her.

"Would you like to go to a party?" Mags asked the child kindly.

"Oh, yes please, but I've got nothing to wear," Hope fingered the rags that she'd been wearing since she arrived. "I can't go like this, people would laugh at me," said the little girl, almost in tears.

"You're right, we'll have to do something about that. You just leave it with me."

Mags being nice caught Hope off guard.

"Can I have a bath and wash my hair?" Everyone knew you had to look your best at parties. Hope had a lovely blue, frilly dress with rosebuds at home for such occasions.

"Of course. I'll send Kylie and Chelsea to help."

Hope hadn't seen the big girls since the night they arrived. She was looking forward to seeing them, they were her friends.

Later that day the two miscreants were enrolled in the preparations for Hopes 'party'.

"For fuck's sake," Kylie exploded on opening the door to Hope's prison.

"She's fucking rank." Chelsea gagged at the stench emanating from the room.

Hope, so used to the foetid smell, had no idea what was bothering her friends.

"She must be crawling" said Kylie, backing away.

"Get Mags, she can do this one herself. I'm certainly not going near her."

"What's wrong? You've got to make me nice for the party," Hope said in a small voice. If they wouldn't help her she wouldn't be allowed to go.

"No offence, hen, but you're stinking. God knows how we're meant to get rid of the smell," Kylie complained.

Hearing their moaning, an exasperated Mags took over. She threw the girl into a bath of freezing water and with a scrubbing brush, attacked the grime and dirt. Hope screamed in pain as the rough bristles removed skin as well as dirt. It took two baths, each full of freezing water to get her clean, and a further dousing over the sink to wash her tangled, matted hair. Each time Hope squealed, Mags smacked her. By the end she was in such a state that even Kylie and Chelsea felt sorry for her.

"Bring me the scissors," Mags commanded. "I've had enough of this." She grabbed Hope firmly and chopped off her long blonde hair.

Her beautiful hair had been Hope's pride and joy but she'd rather be scalped than suffer the torture she'd endured for the past hour.

"Stand up, girl." Mags ordered, as she examined every inch of her body.

Her skin was red raw from the scrubbing. Mags noticed a few delicate, pubic hairs. These had to go and were none-too-gently plucked.

Satisfied the girl looked the part of one much younger, the woman threw a pink, lacy dress onto the soiled bed along with socks and shoes.

"I can't wear that," Hope protested. "It's far too small."

"You wanted a dress. I've brought you one."

"But it's too small," the girl cried, seeing her outing fade away before her eyes.

"Get dressed before I really lose my temper."

266

Hope was right, the dress was at least two sizes too small and barely covered her bottom. With no underpants and her hair cut like a boy, she was too embarrassed to come out of the room.

"Come on, don't be shy. Let's see you," Kylie called to her.

"You look ace," Mags smirked.

"I can't go out like this," sobbed Hope, trying desperately to pull the dress down to protect her modesty.

"You ungrateful little bitch. No party for you today."

"Please. Please let me go," Hope pleaded, grabbing her soiled pants from the heap of rags on the floor.

"We'll see, but I wouldn't bank on it," the auntie growled at her. "You two," she addressed Kylie and Chelsea. "Keep an eye on her. I don't want her skipping off."

A pitiful Hope, perched on the end of her soiled mattress, pleaded with her two friends to persuade auntie to let her go. She was starving and there was always nice food at parties.

"Listen, Hope, it's a big person's party. You have to be brave and when it's finished you'll get a treat," Chelsea tried warning the youngster.

Hope didn't care what kind of party it was, as long as she got fed. It was a shame about the dress, but at least with the knickers, she wasn't showing off her front bottom. Her mum would have gone ballistic if she'd gone out like that. Auntie said she had spoken to her mum recently and she was still angry.

It was party time and she jumped up and down with excitement. She was allowed to go as long as she behaved.

"Here, take this before you get too carried away," Auntie dished out the brown liquid. "Okay girl, now behave yourself. No nonsense. Do what the nice man says and you can have fish and chips for tea and maybe some chocolate. Do what you're told, or else."

"What man, Auntie, what man?"

"Hush."

Mags led Hope up the stairs to the top of the house, and into a small attic room. A strange man was standing in the middle of the room doing dirty things, touching himself. Hope clung to Mags desperately and she had to prise the kid free.

No, no. I don't want to be here, this isn't a party, Hope screamed in her head.

"Hello, little girl, come to Daddy."

The world went black.

CHAPTER SIXTY-FOUR

Escapism

The world had mainly forgotten Freddie Williams. Apart from monthly visits from his brother, who was convinced each one would be his last, and the occasional hurriedly scribbled note from Big Mags, informing him that yet another of his crew had departed this mortal coil, it seemed as far as the rest of mankind was concerned Freddie Williams could well have been dead also

Days merged into weeks, weeks into months and months into years, and any vestige of the wicked, fun-loving extrovert had long since disappeared. Freddie Williams was one truly evil psychopath, detested and feared by screws and inmates alike. No one was brave or stupid enough to ever turn their back on Williams.

He spent his waking hours obsessively plotting his escape and how he would extract revenge for the many scores he had to settle.

At the time of his detention, Mags had been his woman of the moment. In the beginning she would visit regularly as she revelled in the notoriety of being his bird and the kudos it merited amongst the criminal fraternity. However, the years had taken their toll. The lengthy journeys to and from Carstairs, together with his waning reputation, meant communication between the two was now infrequent. Freddie had almost no contact with the outside world.

Over the years his health had greatly deteriorated and the once-fit, intimidating villain had recently been diagnosed with pancreatic cancer. The prognosis was poor, his condition was inoperable and according to the medics he had six months at most.

Determined not to spend his last days in prison, Freddie had a plan. Allegedly there was no escaping from Carstairs. Many had tried over the years, but few had succeeded. So who would suspect that a dying man would attempt such a feat, especially one undergoing such debilitating therapy? Freddie Williams knew he was not out of the game yet.

If he agreed to undergo the harsh and invasive treatment suggested by the quacks, he would be transferred to the Western General Hospital and might just stand a chance. He'd rather die trying, than lie in wait for the grim reaper.

Freddie fully intended to leave this world a legend. He was, after all these years, still an angry, bitter man with more than a few scores, real or imaginary, to settle before he popped his clogs. What had he to lose? he asked himself. But, he was going to need help and there was no point in enlisting Ronnie's assistance. His brother would be the first on the rozzers' hit list. Who else could he trust? He had to admit his choice was limited.

Freddie's plan was genius in its simplicity. All he had to do was convince Mags. He knew how to appeal to his old flame's vanity, but it was the offer of a decent wedge that swung the deal.

The prisoner would be under armed guard during his stay in hospital for safety of the staff and patients, excluding the time he was receiving treatment. This would give them at least a three-hour window to carry out the escape.

His plan was for Mags, dressed as an orderly, to collect him in a laundry trolley and sneak him out into a waiting van.

Mags had been surprised, to say the least, to receive a scribbled note from her ex, professing his undying love and his deathbed wish for one last visit before departing this world.

What had she to lose? The 'bragging rights' after such

a visit would more than restore her somewhat diminishing notoriety.

"It seems too easy, we'll never get away with it," Mags deliberated.

"That's the beauty of the plan," Freddie said, trying hard to convince her. "We do it right beneath their noses. No-one will suspect a thing."

What the hell was she letting herself in for, Mags questioned? Why on earth had she responded to his visiting order? She really didn't need this shit.

"Okay, but if it looks like I'm going to get stopped or questioned, you're on your own. I mean it, Freddie."

Unbelievably Freddie's plan went exactly to order. No-one, absolutely no-one questioned their movements. In fact, there was one scary moment when a hospital orderly actually assisted their departure by holding open the door.

Freddie Williams' return from captivity took precisely eight minutes. Eight minutes that would change the lives of many.

He didn't spend his first night of freedom celebrating, as one would expect. There was no night of boozing and shagging as he had anticipated. As a result of his chemotherapy he had spent the night spewing over the sink in one of Mags' superior rooms. Thank fuck he was having no more treatment, he thought, it was worse than the fucking illness.

"Are you alright, mister?" Hope had heard Freddie being sick during the night. "Can I get you a drink?"

"Tell Mags to come up." The little girl must be her daughter, Freddie thought, although he had no recollection of one.

"You're on the early morning news," Mags informed him. "Fame at last. It says you're armed and shouldn't be approached."

"Good, I hate crowds. Right, I want you to phone Ronnie and get him here."

"Are you sure that's a good idea? The cops could be watching him."

"My brother's no mug, he'll not lead anyone here. Who's the kid by the way? She's a cute wee thing."

"I didn't think you were into kids," Mags snapped at him.

"Of course not, fuckwit. I just meant she was a pleasant wee thing. She brought me some water. Sorry I mentioned it. Now fuck off and get Ronnie on the phone."

Edinburgh Evening News

An escaped prisoner, receiving treatment at the Western General Hospital, has been named as Frederick Williams. Police are warning the public not to approach him as he is thought to be armed and dangerous…

CHAPTER SIXTY- FIVE

Brothers in Arms

Ronnie had been expecting a call. As soon as he heard Freddie was on the run, he knew his brother would be in contact. Taking great care to ensure he wasn't being followed, Ronnie arrived at the bed and breakfast within the hour.

"Jesus, Freddie, what the fuck are you playing at?"

"What does it look like? According to the doctors I've maybe got six months, a bit longer if I have treatment, but after yesterday's dose I'll take my chances. And I'm not spending my last days on this earth in fucking Carstairs. I've a few debts to collect then I'll spend the rest of my time somewhere nice and warm, okay?"

Ronnie sympathised with his brother, but ill or not, he was a devious bastard and couldn't be trusted.

"So who do you have to sort out?"

"It's best you don't know that for now."

Ronnie shuddered at the thought of his psychotic brother running amok in the city, collecting on long forgotten, possibly imaginary debts or slights. And if he had known who was at the top of his crazy brother's hit list, he would have turned Freddie in himself.

"I need supplies, Ronnie, some threads for a start. I can't go about in hospital gear. That would definitely draw attention. I also need wheels, a shooter and of course, some folding money."

"Do you really think you're fit to be running about the city shooting punters? Why don't I get you a nice little villa in Spain with a couple of dolly nurses, where you can live the life of Reilly for the foreseeable?"

"Fuck off, Ronnie no one gets the best of us. I'll collect

from the grave if I have to."

At that moment Big Mags arrived with a tray of tea and, sloshing a decent drop of whisky into each cup, she asked. "Right, boys, what's the plan? Sorry to say this, Ronnie, but he can't stay here indefinitely. At some point the cops are going to land on my doorstep. They'll be checking all known associates as we speak."

"So?" asked Freddie.

"Well, everyone knows we were an item before you got banged up, so it stands to reason they'll pitch up here eventually."

"We were?" Freddie looked blankly at the woman.

"Of course you were. Mags, everyone knows that, he's a bit confused, that's all."

Mags, although appeased at Ronnie's words, was wishing she'd stayed well away from this game. She really didn't need it. "So when are you moving him?" she asked.

"In a couple of days. Let him recover a bit, Mags, then I'll move him to a safe house."

"Okay, two days' maximum. There are too many folk in and out of here to keep him much longer."

"No problem, Mags. We'll see you alright for your trouble."

True to his word, two days later Ronnie arrived in a small, black, nondescript family car and drove his brother to a flat in the Gorgie area of the city. This was bedsit land, populated by students, single men and women. Freddie could move about with complete anonymity, even though the police hunt for him had increased.

Edinburgh Evening News

A spokesman for Lothian and Borders Police Force told the evening news that the hunt for the escaped prisoner had intensified. There have been reports of sightings in the Leith area and the public are asked to look out for the man, but advised not to approach as he is thought to be armed and dangerous...

A smug Mags was finally appeased when she received a visit from the police, as she was a known associate of the escapee. The visit served as a double blessing, it increased her standing amongst the low-lives she associated with and she had Hope firmly believing the officers were looking for her.

The child was convinced she was the subject of a manhunt and only Auntie's benevolence had kept her from being taken straight to jail. Hope believed every lying word the woman spewed.

Things were more tolerable for Hope now, at least she was being regularly fed and clothed, in reward for her regular afternoon party participation.

Most days she was sponged down, clothed in her party dress, still wearing no underpants, not that it mattered now, she couldn't care less what she looked like. Why should she bother what her mum thought? She didn't care what happened to her precious daughter and sending a policeman to look for her was the last straw. She hated her mum almost as much as she hated her dad. She was never going home.

Now that Auntie was being nice to her and she could have anything she liked to eat, she was able to cope with what the men did at the parties. Sometimes there was more than one man, so she just shut her eyes and thought of nice things, like going to the fair. After all, it was no different to what her dad had been doing.

Sometimes at night, if the medicine wore off, she would lie, tears running down her cheeks, wondering if her mum really knew what was going on. All that rubbish her parents had spouted about being chosen made her more special was pure nonsense. It hurt though, she really did love her mum and she still wanted to go home, but she wasn't going where she wasn't wanted.

There had been no parties while the sick man was staying. Hope had heard him throwing up during the night. He was so thin and his face was such a funny colour. The little girl had never seen anyone so ill. She prayed he didn't want a party, he looked like he was about to die. The parties were horrible enough without him sticking a dead thing into her.

For the first time since arriving at Auntie's house, Hope was being allowed out with Kylie and Chelsea. Mags issued threats of dire consequences should she do anything she shouldn't, with strict instructions that she must stay with the two girls and do exactly what they told her. Within minutes of landing on Princes Street the girls had robbed two tourists and were already lining up the third. It was a profitable morning and Hope had no idea that she was the patsy; all their proceeds were stashed in the hood of her parka.

In need of a fix, the girls returned to the squat they shared with Kevin, a good-looking young black guy of about fifteen. Edinburgh, known as the drugs capital of Europe, was home to thousands of dealers and users.

"Who's this little peach?" Kevin asked.

"She's one of Mags' party girls," answered Chelsea.

"Really? She's a cutie." He flashed a smile at Hope. Kevin knew exactly what services the girl performed for Mags' clients.

Never having had a boyfriend, or even a crush until now, Hope felt her knees wobble. He was like a pop star, he was so good-looking.

Kylie and Chelsea giggled and teased, "Hope's got a boyfriend, Hope's got a boyfriend."

The youngster's face was on fire; she couldn't look Kevin in the eye.

"You stay away from him, he's a bad boy," Chelsea warned

Hope, but it was too late. Hope was smitten.

The two friends soon gave up teasing her, they had much more serious business to attend to as they got ready to shoot up.

"Hey kid, there's a party on downstairs, want to crash it?"

At the mention of the word party, Hope froze. "I have to stay with them. I'm not allowed to go anywhere without them."

Kevin understood immediately that the girl thought he was asking her to a different kind of party. "You'll be okay with me. I won't let anyone hassle you."

"I better stay here."

"Well, if you want to sit in this shithole waiting for those two coming round, you're welcome but I'm off. See ya," the boy headed for the door.

"Wait, maybe I could go for a little while?"

"Come on then, what are we waiting for?" The young dealer led her towards the music.

The flat was packed with youngsters hanging out on the balconies and stairwell too. Hope was entranced, she'd never experienced anything like this ever. As she clung like a limpet to Kevin, she didn't want the party to end.

She almost choked on her first puff, but by the time the toke came back round, she was floating six feet off the ground. Kevin was kissing her, slowly, gently; he wasn't going to scare this little beauty off. She was worth a lot of money but he didn't want Big Mags on his case. Kevin was going to have to box clever.

Mags was in a furious temper when the three eventually returned home. Fearing she'd lost a good earner she viciously lashed out at them. The older girls, having been on the receiving end of Mags' beatings many times before, dodged most of the blows, leaving Hope to bear the brunt of the attack.

"It wasn't my fault, I had to wait for them," yelled Hope. "I had no idea where I was and I had no money."

Had the worm turned, much to the surprise of her captors?

"Don't you answer me back, you cheeky bitch," Mags screamed, thrashing her all the harder. "That's your last time. No more swanning off with that pair," she threatened Hope as she threw her into her room, locking the door.

Hope cried herself to sleep again, but this time with no thoughts of home.

CHAPTER SIXTY-SIX

Never-never Land

"My God," Ronnie Williams gasped.

She looked sensational. The foyer of the Usher Hall was teeming with fans. But none came close to the vision that was Rosie Royce. The press were snapping away, frantically delighted to have such an infamous pair out on the town together.

"Wow, you scrub up well." Ronnie led his partner over to the bar.

"You're not so bad yourself, for an old guy."

"What's with the 'old'? I'm hardly in my dotage."

"I suppose not, it's just, you seem to have been around forever," Rosie replied.

"Started young," was Ronnie's answer.

"Me too," laughed his date.

"Have you heard these guys before? Everyone is raving about them but I'm not sure if it's really my sort of thing."

"Actually, I knew one of them years ago. I'm hoping to have a word."

"There goes my promise," Ronnie laughed.

He had to admit, he was a bit disappointed, she was excellent company. Rosie Royce had an air about her, just as Stella had had all those years ago. She drew men like a magnet, but was completely unaware of her attraction. Ronnie Williams decided he wanted to know her better.

They took their seats, the best in the auditorium of course, the lights dimmed and there he was even more handsome than she remembered. Rosie could hardly breathe. No-one else existed, she was transfixed. Ignoring her companion for the next two glorious hours Rosie Royce gave herself up to sound and sight of the only man she'd ever loved.

The performance over, Rosie battled through the throng of people with backstage passes undeterred. She was confident Toni would see her. Edging her way to the front, just like the first time back at the base, she called his name. Toni Francitti cocked his head to one side, memories stirring. He gestured silence to the crowd of twittering females surrounding him. And there she was, right in front of him.

The world stopped for Rosie Royce; the crowds and her date for the evening melted away.

Staring at him as he slept, she couldn't believe this was real. She would wake up any moment to find it was all a dream. But no, she really was with this perfect specimen of manhood. If it were possible he was even better looking than before. She had long given up on ever seeing him again but here he was, large as life. Rosie had never found anyone to match this man, her first love, her only love. Unfortunately there was a downside, the small matter of a wife and several children. Rosie had no illusions of a 'happy ever after'. Since she had found him again everything in Rosie's life took second place. She had not returned to Danube Street and for the first time ever she'd neglected the business. What was even more unbelievable was that she'd kept the knowledge of Hope from him.

It was not until their last day together that she finally broached the subject of their daughter. She knew she was being selfish but their time together was precious and it would be his reaction to this news that would seal their affair, one way or another.

She had been right to have her doubts. Disappointingly, he appeared totally uninterested.

"It's for the best, Rosie, she would have a far better life with parents who want and cherish her."

"I wanted her. I would have cherished her but that chance was stolen from me," Rosie begged him to understand.

Toni had no words of comfort for her. What was done was done and there was no room in his life for any other complications. It was then Rosie realised being with him was nothing but a flight of fancy. He was not the man she had imagined him to be. Sadly, she admitted to herself he was a star whose world revolved around him, a self-centred, egotistical performer, interested only in himself. She could have been anyone; a plaything to pass the time, just as she had been all those years before. What a fool, she thought. It had been fun, but it was over.

He'd been dumped. He couldn't believe it, the cheeky mare had simply walked off with that American ponce without even a backward glance. What the fuck did she see in him? Okay, he could carry a bit of a tune, but he looked like a nancy-boy in that get up. Imagine swanning off and leaving him high and dry. Although Ronnie was peeved at the outcome of his evening, he had to laugh. Only Rosie Royce would have the gall to kick him to the kerb without a thought. Well, she'd had her chance, good luck to her. He had more to worry about than a cancelled dinner; he dreaded to think what Freddie had been up to.

But Ronnie needn't have worried about his brother, he was laid up in bed, too ill to collect any debts.

"Freddie, you can't stay here on your own. The cops are on my tail constantly now, so I can't just come and go as I please. Give it up, man. Let me get you somewhere decent to live and proper medical treatment."

"Fuck off, I'll be fine in a couple of days," the invalid replied.

CHAPTER SIXTY-SEVEN

Two down…

Freddie Williams had spent the last 3,650 days plotting revenge on all those bastards who thought they'd got away with mugging him off, just because he'd been out of circulation for a bit. Well, he was back and soon they'd all know it. No-one would get away with taking liberties, causing him or Ronnie grief or generally pissing him off. Freddie had a long memory but unfortunately, not a particularly accurate one. Being off his meds was not helping. It seemed even Ronnie was trying to persuade him to leave well alone. What was he all about? Letting cunts get away with murder. He'd show them all, brother included.

He waited outside Bannerman's bar in the Grassmarket, a favourite haunt of his old cronies. It was closing time and the ponce he was waiting for was just leaving.

"Hello, Davie, long time no see," Freddie addressed the lone customer.

"Christ, Freddie, you nearly gave me a fucking heart attack," the man smiled at his old friend. "I'd heard you were back in circulation, how's things?"

"Fine, Davie, just fine, but surely you're not surprised to see me? You must have known I'd come looking for you, ya treacherous bastard. To collect what you owe me."

"What I owe you?" the man asked in astonishment. "Somebody's been messing with your head, pal. It's the other way round, you owe me, you stupid arse, so if anyone's doing the collecting it'll be me."

This wasn't right, Freddie thought. Davie should be pleading for mercy, not arguing back. His head was thumping, he was confused and he wasn't about to debate the point.

Davie Scott had disrespected him and that was good enough.

"Fuck you. Davie." His old mate fell to the ground. "One down, two to go," chanted Freddie, as he walked off into the dark night.

What had the idiot been talking about? How could he, Freddie Williams, be in debt to the likes of him? But something was niggling at the back of his brain. So what? It would make the others sit up and take notice. One down, two to go, Freddie repeated to himself, but who? For the life of him he couldn't remember. There were times when he could barely remember his own name, never mind some fucker's he hadn't seen for over a decade. It was the lawyer, he suddenly remembered, Kramer and his sidekick, Stella Gold.

He would take great pleasure in disposing of that pair, but he had a bad feeling about her and his brother. Ronnie had insisted she was dead, but Freddie knew that wasn't true, it was a lie to stop him catching up with her. Why? he pondered. Was it something to do with the boy? Didn't Ronnie want him to harm the mother of his son? No matter how much he denied it, Freddie knew the score and mother or no mother, she was going to pay.

Freddie had staked Marcus out years ago, when he was acting for Stella and that other slag, Mary. If only Ronnie hadn't been so stubborn back then, having no reason to believe his quarry would have changed the habits of a lifetime. Sure enough, at precisely 8.30am the black Mercedes pulled into the underground parking lot. A creature of habit, Marcus removed his briefcase from the back seat and locked the car before turning to come face to face with a nightmare from the past.

"Well, well, if it isn't my old adversary," Marcus sneered, in his best courtroom drawl. "To what do I owe the pleasure, Mr Williams? I'd heard you were AWOL. Surely you don't want to engage my services? Good though I am, even I would struggle to defend you. Not that I would consider doing so."

This was not going to plan, Freddie puzzled. He should be asking the questions, not the lawyer. He was confused, he knew this fucker was taking the piss. Let's see who has the last laugh, he thought, and another victim hit the floor.

Edinburgh Evening News

The bodies of two men have been found, one late last night in the Grassmarket area of the city and another early this morning in a private car park in the New Town. Police are treating these deaths as suspicious. The victims have yet to be named...

CHAPTER SIXTY-EIGHT

Bending the Rules

The city was in the grip of gun fever. It would appear the escapee from Carstairs had shot two men in cold blood. Davie Scott, a known associate of Williams was hit whilst walking in the Grassmarket area of the city. Marcus Kramer, an eminent Edinburgh barrister, was found in the basement parking lot of his offices, and yesterday shots had been fired at Rosie Royce, owner of the popular Gentlemen's Club in Danube Street. Reports of sightings were coming in thick and fast and all police leave had been cancelled for the immediate future. The pressure was mounting for Ross to capture Freddie Williams. He pulled in Ronnie, along with other members of his family, for questioning. All of them maintained they knew nothing of Freddie's whereabouts; Ross drew a blank on each one. He ordered a significant increase in the number of officers on the beat to calm the public's fear.

With all this going on, it was almost a month before Superintendent Ross came across the folder given to him by Jeannie's son. He flicked through report after report from various private investigation agencies, noting all had drawn a blank.

"Cummins, I've got a job for you," he called through to the outer office.

"Sir?"

"Take a look at this. I want you to gather all the information you can on this case."

"What case, sir?"

"It's all in here, sergeant. I've got reason to believe this child, may be in danger." He could hardly tell the sergeant he was looking for the illegitimate child of Rosie Royce.

"What kind of danger, sir?"

"It's enough you know it's top priority. She was adopted when she was a year old, so you'll have to contact the welfare department."

"They won't give us anything without a warrant, sir."

"Tell them it's a paedophile ring, that should make them co-operate. If not, I'll apply for one, but get started on it now."

Sergeant Cummins had applied for the post of Ross's assistant almost three years previously. The incident with Raymond Smith had put paid to his promising career. Never before had the goodnatured Cummins hated and despised a fellow officer as he did Ross. Sergeant Cummins was determined to vindicate himself, no matter how long it took. Most of his spare time was spent piecing together his boss's movements, no matter how inconsequential. He would seek out past colleagues and quiz them about Ross. No one liked the man, however, they all agreed he was an excellent police officer, if somewhat unorthodox.

It was well known that anyone who stood in Ross's way had a habit of disappearing. The only problem was, Cummins had not one shred of evidence. Everything he had was circumstantial and he would be drummed out of the force for even suggesting the 'blue-eyed boy' could be responsible in any way. Superintendent Ross was held in great esteem by the hierarchy. He got results; it was a shame no-one asked how.

And what the hell was this new case all about? There was nothing the sergeant was aware of, under current investigation, that involved a child. Christ, he hoped this wasn't another cover-up. But Cummins was an excellent detective, his talents wasted on a desk job. First on his list was a call to the welfare department.

*

"Yes, I remember the case," Miss Susan Bridges, senior welfare officer conceded, offering the sergeant a cup of tea. "I'd only been in the department for three or four months. It was a strange one, and you know I've often thought how differently I would have dealt with the case now. What you have to remember, sergeant, is that I was new to the job and terrified of making the wrong decision. Her father signed away his parental rights and she was under the guardianship of Stella Gold, living in a brothel. Not exactly the ideal family environment."

"True," agreed the policeman. "I'm sure you did the right thing at the time. We're all clever with hindsight, Miss Bridges. I need some information on the child, we have reason to believe she could be in danger."

"I'm sorry, but I can't tell you any more. You will need a court order to see the files."

"Couldn't you maybe bend the rules this once? You've just said you would do things differently, maybe this is your chance to make up for the past?"

"Sorry, I can't give you anything further. Now, if you'll excuse me for a moment, finish your tea and I'll be right back." The welfare officer left the room, leaving the file open on her desk.

Cummins extracted the information he required just as Susan Bridges appeared back.

"Thank you, you may have just saved her life," he said.

"How are you coming along with that case, sergeant?" Ross asked, stopping on his way to the morning's briefing.

"Nothing yet, sir. I'm hopeful I'll get something from the welfare department later this week but I might need a warrant," Cummins replied, buying himself a bit of time.

"Keep on top of it. I want the case on my desk before the end of the week, understood?"

"Understood, sir." Swearing under his breath, Cummins followed his boss into the squad room.

"Any news on the Williams case?" The superintendent questioned the assembled squad. "I won't have a crazed gunman running amok on my patch. Get out there and pull anyone who ever stood beside him at a bus stop. Somebody is sheltering him. Make sure it's known that whoever it is, they will be going down for harbouring a fugitive, accomplice after the fact, and anything else I can think of. I'll throw the book at them."

CHAPTER SIXTY-NINE

The Best Laid Plans

What the fuck was he going to do about Freddie? He had just come back from Danube Street, after a frantic call from Rosie. It was the first time he'd seen her since the night at the concert, only to be told his brother had tried to kill her.

"What the fuck have I done to him, Ronnie?" Rosie challenged. "I've only met him once, the night of his accident, so what the fuck has he got against me? Don't tell me it's random, he came here 'specially."

"I honestly don't know, and I don't have a clue how to stop him. I haven't seen him since last week. He's also off his meds which makes him even worse. Christ, he shot my best mate for no reason, a guy who's been with us since we came on the scene. He's lost the plot completely, so, until I find him, you should stay here."

"I've got a business to run, Ronnie. I can't hide away in the hope you eventually catch up with your lunatic brother."

"Shame your fancy man's gone."

"Don't be smart. Anyway, he's not my fancy man, he's not my anything," she replied. "Just someone I knew a long time ago."

"Look I have to go, Rosie. Please do as I ask. He's dangerous and believe me, he'll try again. I'll keep you posted."

"Don't bother, just find the maniac."

The man in question had just parked his car in the street behind Mags' bed and breakfast. As he made his way round to the front he spotted the landlady showing two beat cops out. Great, they weren't likely to call back for a while, meaning he would be safe for the moment.

"What the fuck are you doing here, Freddie? I've just had

a visit from the cops."

"I know, I passed them on the way in," he laughed.

"You can't stay. The girls are upstairs cleaning and believe me, the older two would turn their granny in for a pound. It's not safe."

"Get rid of them, Mags, I'm knackered. I need a couple of hours' kip then I'll be on my way."

"Dear God, man, you'll get me banged up. I vowed after the last time, never again."

"For old times' sake, Mags, I just need to rest."

"You three finished up there?" Mags bawled upstairs.

"Yep, all done," replied Chelsea.

"Get yourselves down here now."

She closed the parlour door and ushered the girls into the kitchen. "I've just had a request for a cashmere coat, size twelve and fawn in colour, from Jenner's."

Kylie and Chelsea looked at each other, there was something up.

"We don't shoplift to order, Mags, and not in Jenner's, we're too well known."

"Send her in." The big woman pointed to Hope.

"Her? You must be joking. She wouldn't get past the doorman, she's like a tramp."

"Are you telling me you won't deliver?" Mags was threateningly close.

"No, of course not, but don't be surprised if we come back empty-handed," said Chelsea, facing up to her.

"Get going and don't come back without it, or else." Mags was determined to get rid of the nosey twosome.

Hope couldn't believe her luck. She would see Kevin; she'd make the girls take her to see him.

"Forget Jenner's, we've no chance. Like I said, we'd never get past the doorman, never mind all the way up to the third floor." Chelsea repeated

"What will Mags say if we come back without it?"

"Fuck Mags. She knows this isn't our bag. Let's have a dash through Woolies instead."

The girls headed out on a shoplifting spree. Princes Street was a magnet for seasoned shoplifters, unlike Hope who had only managed a lipstick, some marshmallows and a can of hairspray.

"Not quite at the cashmere coat stage yet, are you?" the two pals chuckled.

The two older girls emptied their bags on the ground, they had quite a haul, but knew they'd easily get rid of the lot.

Sure enough they punted all of it, including Hope's meagre contribution, to eager punters looking for a bargain in the back streets of the city.

"Why don't we go back to your place?" Hope asked.

"Aye, so you can see your boyfriend? Do you think we're daft?" Chelsea sneered. "Just you go back to Mags and tell her we couldn't get the coat."

"She wasn't interested in a coat, that was just an excuse," Hope argued back.

"What are you talking about?" Kylie pushed her against the wall.

"She just wanted us out. Think about it, I'm supposed to be grounded, not getting out ever again. That was only two days ago and now I'm out here with you two. The sick man was there, I caught sight of him through the door. He looks even worse than he did before."

"That's the geezer the cops are hunting for, he shot loads of folk," said Kylie.

"You know there's a big reward out for him?" Chelsea informed the other two.

"How big?"

"I'm not sure, but it's thousands."

"Are you sure it's him?" they both asked Hope.

"Who else would it be, and how often have the cops been around?"

"I vote we shop them and claim the money."

"I'm not going near any cop shop," Chelsea insisted. "As soon as they clap eyes on me, I'll be straight back inside."

Kylie looked across the road at the imposing Scotsman building and said, "Why don't we go to the papers? It's probably them who are putting up the reward anyway."

They looked at each other and made their way into the foyer of The Scotsman building where they headed straight for the receptionist.

"We've got information on the guy the cops are looking for."

"Aye, you and two hundred others," replied the bored receptionist.

"I'm telling you, we know where he is right now."

"I'm sure you do," she wrinkled her nose at the offensive smell emanating from the other side of her shiny desk. "Here, fill this in, if you can write." She slid a sheet of official-looking paper across to Kylie.

Seeing the reward money slipping through their fingers, Chelsea grabbed the female's long, bleached hair and pulled her face level with her own. "Listen, fuckwit, don't make me hurt you, because I will. Get us someone who knows about this geezer before it's too late."

"Security, security!" the receptionist squealed at the top of her voice.

"What the devil is going on here?" Rupert Breslin, the Editor-in-Chief asked, returning from a very productive lunch to find a bunch of vagabonds cluttering up his reception area.

"We've got information on the murderer and she doesn't believe us."

"She doesn't, does she? I'll speak to you later." he informed the receptionist. "Right you three, come with me."

*

"Gayfield police station? Put me through to Chief

Superintendent Ross, please."

"Sorry, sir, he's out until late this afternoon. Can Sergeant Cummins be of help?"

"This is Rupert Breslin. I need to speak to someone about Freddie Williams. I have information about his present whereabouts."

Mags poured her unwanted visitor a large mug of tea with a liberal dash of whisky, just as Freddie liked it, "Okay, what was your beef with Davie Scott? I always thought you two were tight? I liked Davie, he never got above himself."

"He owed me."

"Davie? That wasn't like him."

"You're having a laugh. If I say he owed me then he did."

"Okay, keep your hair on. Kramer, I can understand."

"I got him nice and square, but I fucked up on his other half. I fucking hate that bitch."

"What bitch?" Mags was completely confused.

"Gold, Stella Gold."

"Well fuck me, you missed her alright, by about twelve years." Mags tried not to laugh.

"What do you mean twelve years?" Surely Mags wasn't in on the deception too, Freddie thought.

"I don't know who you think you shot at, but it wasn't Stella Gold. I for one can testify to that."

"Why are you all protecting her?" Freddie was getting agitated. "I saw her in Danube Street, what does she have over everybody?"

"Freddie, you couldn't have seen her. You want to know why? I took her out. I was paid to do it. How do you think I got the cash for this place? Certainly not by lying on my back. Marcus Kramer paid me to do her."

"Why?"

"I'm fucked if I know, or care. He paid me ten big ones.

That's how I know you didn't shoot Stella."

Before Freddie could reply, the sound of a megaphone drowned out any further conversation.

"What the fuck is that?" Mags rushed to the window.

"Come out with your hands."

"Jesus Christ, Freddie the street's full of cops. Armed response by the look of it."

"Oh Mags, you were the one person apart from Ronnie I thought I could trust."

The police recovered only one body from the house. There was no sign of the escaped prisoner.

CHAPTER SEVENTY

Payment Withheld

"This certainly looks kosher," Jack nodded to Ross. "Here," he handed over a brown envelope.

"I take it I don't need to count it?"

The two men had arranged to meet at the Old Chain Pier, a popular watering hole down near the harbour at Granton.

"Piss off. Is this definitely the right one? Not that I doubt you, but Rosie has had so many disappointments over the years."

"I'm not interested in Rosie Royce's disappointments, but this came direct from the welfare department so you can depend on it being accurate. I also checked the voters' role to verify the address and the family still stay there. Tell me, how are you going to approach this? Remember, you shouldn't have access to this information and questions could be asked."

"I'm hardly likely to broadcast the fact I paid a senior police officer to procure it for me. Don't worry, your name won't come up in conversation, well, not unless it has to," said Jack, picking up the folder and making ready to leave. "Is there any word on that lunatic, Williams? I still can't believe he shot at Rosie. Jesus, a bit to the side and she could have copped it like those other two."

"The man's psychotic, no-one is safe."

"But why Rosie? He doesn't know her. It's time you lot were getting your finger out. It's a bad job when a whole police force can't catch one mad bugger running around shooting folks," Jack tormented the officer.

*

Mags had been so sure she was high up on the list of known associates that she had shown Freddie her hidey hole, just in case the cops arrived unannounced. The safe place where she kept her contraband was ingenious. This was where she hid the merchandise she bought from shoplifters, cases of alcohol and tobacco from the docks, but more importantly, where she stashed drug deliveries.

The previous owner had blocked off the recesses at each side of the chimney breast in the sitting room, creating two decorative alcoves with a large, empty space behind. Big enough for a fugitive to quite easily squeeze into and remain undetected for days.

The cops had turned the place upside down, but despite being within inches of the wanted man, had left without success.

The girls hung about the newspapers offices for what seemed like hours.

"Sorry girls, he wasn't there by the time we got to the address." Rupert informed them.

Turning to the receptionist, Chelsea made a dive for her. "This was your fault, you stupid bitch, all your fault."

The receptionist wasn't looking too clever now.

"Girls, behave. Here," the editor handed each of them a twenty-pound note. "You're right, it was her fault, and because of that she's fired."

"You can't do that," the girl blustered.

"I just have. Now move or I'll let this lot loose on you again. If this maniac murders anyone else, I'll have you done as an accomplice."

"Do we still get the reward?" Kylie asked hopefully.

"I'm sorry girls, you definitely deserve it, but at the end of the day we didn't get him. The reward is given on the basis he is captured and he wasn't. Keep your eyes open. If you can think of anywhere else he might be, call me on this number. You'll get straight through."

CHAPTER SEVENTY-ONE

Hiding Place

"Can I stay with you tonight? I can't go back to that house on my own," Hope begged her two friends. "I've nowhere else to go."

"Sure, but I thought you'd catch the first bus home," Chelsea said.

"What's the point? They don't want me and I don't want to see my dad."

"Fuck! I forgot, we left our gear at Mag's. I can't go without it," blurted Kylie. "We have to go back."

"There's bound to be a cop on duty, how the fuck will we get past him?"

"You two could distract him while I go in through the back window, it doesn't lock," offered Hope. "I'm smaller than either of you."

"The way you've been piling the weight on, I wouldn't be so sure."

"Cheeky mare, are you calling me fat?" Hope challenged Kylie. Her clothes certainly seemed tighter than before, but she was eating mostly rubbish, as her mother called it.

Kylie was right. PC Plod was on duty at the front gate when the two gallous young hussies tipped up.

"Got the time?" Chelsea asked. "You know the old saying," laughing at her own joke.

"I've only heard that a hundred times since I joined," the young recruit answered her.

"Isn't this where the murder took place?" Kylie asked. "Surely you don't think he's coming back?"

"No, but we have to protect the scene of the crime."

"They say he's a psycho, murdering anyone who looks at

him the wrong way," exaggerated Chelsea. "You wouldn't get me standing out here on my own."

Hope climbed in the window with some difficulty; she certainly had piled on the weight. She didn't want to be fat like Brenda, her old classmate; she would definitely have to cut back on the sweets.

As she walked through the dark house Hope didn't feel so brave and seeing the outline on the floor, where Mags had lain, completely spooked her. She almost gave up, but she continued on because she desperately wanted the girls to let her stay with them. It was creepy and she had a horrible feeling someone was watching her. There was a funny smell in the sitting room too, one she'd smelled before. Turning quickly, she was positive she saw something watching her from the cupboard.

She grabbed Kylie's gear and got out out as quickly as she could. This place gave her the heebie-jeebies.

Back outside, she turned the corner and signalled to the two girls she was ready to go.

"Fuck, how did you have the nerve?" Chelsea marvelled. "I'm not sure I would."

"It was scary," Hope admitted. "Still, I got your stuff."

"Ta. You're a pal." Kylie put her arm round Hope's shoulder.

Back at the squat the girls recalled their adventurous day to Kevin.

"My God, you could all have been murdered."

"I could have murdered that fucking woman at the front desk, it was her fault they missed him."

"That was it!" Hope called out. "He was still there."

"What are you talking about?" Kylie slurred, having just taken a huge hit.

"I'm telling you, he was still there when I went back."

"Don't talk rubbish, there was a cop on duty, he would have known."

"He was still there, I smelled him."

"Fuck," laughed the two girls. "You're one to talk."

"Listen to me," pleaded Hope but the two were already chasing the dragon and way gone.

"Go on, I'm listening," said Kevin.

"I saw the reflection of the moon in his eyes, but I was too scared to check it out. I'm sure he was hiding behind the alcove in the sitting room."

"Sounds a bit barmy," Kevin brought her down to earth.

"Maybe so, but don't forget, it was me who worked out it was him in the first place. I know they're your pals, but they're both as thick as each other."

"Okay, brain of Britain, what do you want to do?"

"Kylie's got the man's number, he said to ring any time."

"Why don't we go look for ourselves and then ring him? We don't want to look like a couple of turkeys now, do we?"

Hope would have agreed to anything to be with Kevin. She would come to regret that, but she was young, infatuated and free.

Why were they all in league to protect Stella Gold? What was the attraction? What was it about the bitch that made grown men putty in her hands? Kramer, for instance. The man was a top brief, smart, a few bob in his tail and yet he had let that woman use him. Conned him into bringing up another man's kid, his brother's. It was obvious Ronnie didn't want any harm to come to her, but why would his brother betray him? What spell had the bitch cast on him? And as for Mags admitting to having murdered her on Kramer's behalf, what a load of shit. None of it made any sense. Well, whatever the reason, he would finish the job and that would just leave Ronnie for him to deal with.

CHAPTER SEVENTY-TWO

Missing

"Jack, how can I ever thank you?" Rosie hugged him tightly. "I can't believe it, after all this time."

"Save your thanks till later. We have to be very careful, you can't just turn up on the doorstep and announce you're her biological mother. They might not even have told her she's adopted." Jack warned her.

"I know, but I have to see her for myself. I want to know who she resembles, what colour her hair and eyes are."

"Why don't we take a drive round the area, see what we can find out?" Jack suggested.

Rosie jumped at the chance, saying "Let's go now." She hurried off to collect her coat and bag.

"Calm down, there's no point going just now, she'll still be in school," Jack pointed out.

"She certainly landed on her feet," murmured Jack, sitting outside the smart bungalow with the proverbial roses around the door. "Definitely a million miles away from Danube Street, wouldn't you say?"

"Okay, okay, I get it she's not living in squalor." Rosie bit back at him.

"Whoa!" challenged Jack. "Surely you must be glad she lives in a nice house in a nice area?"

"Of course I am," answered a forlorn Rosie, "but it doesn't stop me from feeling a bit cheated."

"Look, let's grab a coffee from that café," Jack suggested. "We can keep a watch on the bungalow from there."

"Two white coffees, please," Rosie ordered from the cheery waitress.

"Certainly. Can I tempt you with some chocolate cake or our special lemon drizzle?"

"No thanks, coffee's fine," replied Rosie.

"You're not from around here," the woman commented. "We don't get many strangers in nowadays. Well, not since the case wound down."

"Case, what case?" Rosie asked.

"A local child went missing. A nice little thing she was, lived right over there." The waitress pointed to the bungalow.

Rosie was dumbstruck. Here they were, so close to finding her after all this time and this woman was telling them Hope was missing.

"It must be about nine months since she was last seen," the waitress volunteered. "We had the newspapers and television crews here daily when she first disappeared, but it's as if they've all given up. Where did you say you were from?"

The tinkle of the shop bell was the only reply.

"Let me do the talking," Jack insisted as they walked up the path to the Roberts' house.

A small blonde woman answered the door.

"Are you Donna Roberts?" snarled Rosie before Jack could get a word in.

"Yes, and who are you?" Donna asked warily.

"I'll tell you who I am. I'm Hope's mother, that's who I am." she barged into the house with Jack trailing behind. "You better have a bloody good reason why my kid has run away from home."

"Don't you think I haven't asked myself that question a hundred times a day since she left?"

"Are you sure she left willingly?"

"She packed a case and left a note."

"Saying what?"

"Here," Donna handed Rosie the crumpled piece of paper she took from the mantelpiece.

In childlike writing the note read:

Dear Mummy, I'm sorry I was naughty, but I don't want to go into a home, love Hope.

"Why did she think she was going to be put in a home?"

"She'd been naughty. She was always naughty and we used it as a threat, every mother does. I wasn't planning to carry it out."

"When did you report her missing?" Jack asked.

"She'd been sent to her room, I checked on her about an hour later and that's when I found the note."

"What about the police?"

"They were okay to begin with, but because she hadn't been abducted, there wasn't much for them to go on. They said most kids eventually return home."

By now the woman was in floods of tears. "I'm sorry," she said, wiping her eyes. "She was such a loving little girl, well-behaved and a joy to be around. She changed the moment I told her I was pregnant, that there was going to be a new baby. You can imagine, I was delighted after all these years of trying and that's when she turned into a monster."

"Jesus, woman, she was only a kid."

"You try living with her. It's easy for you to come here and criticise me, but where were you? You couldn't wait to get rid of her."

"Believe me, nothing could be further from the truth," Rosie answered. "Did she know she was adopted?"

"Yes, we told her from the beginning. Made out she was special, that we had picked her. It couldn't have been anything to do with that."

"What has your husband to say on the matter?"

"Same as me, we're both at a complete loss as to why it happened. Mike's been out most nights searching for her. She'd been a real daddy's girl until her brother was born."

"Do you have a recent photograph you could let me have?" Rosie could see that the woman was genuinely distraught, but that didn't excuse the fact her daughter had been so unhappy she'd run away Something had happened and Rosie was determined to find out what.

The picture was a recent one and had been taken two days before she'd run off. What had made her take that drastic step? Rosie wondered, and more to the point, what was making her stay away?

CHAPTER SEVENTY-THREE

Hide and Seek

The same cop was on duty when Kevin and Hope arrived back at the crime scene.

"What if the gunman is still there? He'll shoot us."

"No he won't," Kevin assured her. "He's probably miles away," he said as they entered the house by the same window Hope had used before.

"I'm scared," Hope whispered.

"Don't be, there's no-one in here. C'mon let's see what old Mags has got stashed away."

"I think he was behind the alcove. Look there," Hope pointed.

Kevin, with some effort, managed to pull back a false panel, revealing a well-stocked hiding place.

"Shit, take a look at this lot. It must be worth a fortune."

The void was filled with alcohol, tobacco, and a variety of high end merchandise.

"What have we here?" Kevin picked up a package and an old biscuit tin stuffed with money. "Keep your mouth shut about this," he warned Hope.

Making sure the alcove looked exactly as it had been, the two climbed back out the window.

Back in the squat, Kevin emptied the biscuit tin and counted the money; there was over three hundred pounds. The package was just what he had suspected: approximately a kilo of heroin. This was better than any reward. The heroin was worth a king's ransom and Kevin was just the one to punt it. This was his big break. Unlike his contemporaries, Kevin had never shoved his merchandise either up his nose or into a vein. He was smarter than that, drugs were for mugs.

The young lad had been dealing since he was thirteen but this find, well, this could catapult him into the big time. There was only one problem, he thought, the kid. Would she keep her mouth shut? He had no intention of staying in this rat-infested, shithole but first he had to find a buyer, so until then he had to call it home. In order to keep his good fortune to himself, he had to get Hope on his side, make her totally dependent on him. There was only one way to ensure that – he had to get her hooked.

"Hey, we've netted fifty quid each," Kevin blithely lied to his accomplice.

"Really?" Hope hadn't a clue what her boyfriend was talking about, she was just grateful he seemed pleased with their adventure.

"I'll keep it safe for you, so those two don't get their hands on it. Christ, they'd go through it in a day."

Of course he could keep it for her, she trusted him, didn't she? He said he was going to take care of her. She just wished she felt better. Her stomach was killing her and getting worse, she must have eaten something really bad.

"You okay?" Kevin asked, watching her intently. She didn't look too clever.

"Just feeling a bit sick, must be something I ate."

"Do you need a doctor?"

"I'm not going near any doctor, he'd send me back home."

"I've got just the thing to sort you out." In more ways than one, the crafty beggar thought.

Hope couldn't describe how his medicine made her feel. It was nothing like the stuff Auntie had fed her. This was unbelievable. She had no pain, no worries, everything was fantastic and the colours were out of this world. Wow!

Shifting Mag's stash was proving more difficult than Kevin had bargained for. Three days later he was still trying to punt the gear whilst playing nursemaid to the kid. It was one thing getting her hooked and keeping her under control but she was suffering from some kind of stomach bug. Despite the gear he was feeding her she was getting worse, much worse. She was rolling about the filthy floor in agony, begging him for help.

"Please, Kevin," she screamed. "I need something. I can't stand this. I think I'm going to die." Hope writhed in excruciating pain.

Where the fuck were those two? Kevin raged. Unaware of his windfall, Chelsea and Kylie had gone out early that morning to score and still hadn't come back. A multitude of thoughts ran through his mind. He couldn't cope with this on his own, he needed someone to help. Christ, maybe she was right, maybe she was going to die. There was nothing he could do, he wasn't a fucking doctor. Maybe another hit would help?

Hope had no idea what was wrong with her. The pain was excruciating; it had been going on for nearly two days now, but this was absolutely the worst. It had been so bad yesterday that she had wet herself. How embarrassing, a girl of her age having an accident and now, she was rolling about the floor in front of her boyfriend, but fuck, she was past caring. She couldn't handle this anymore. If she was going to die, let it be now. She kept having the greatest urge to push, like she needed a number two.

"Kevin! What's happening?" the girl called out in terror.

Fucking hell! It looked like her fucking insides were coming out. He was in a panic. He had no idea what to do or where to go.

"Help me!" she screamed at the top of her lungs. "Help me!"

Hope gave birth to a 6lb baby girl and Kevin took off like a bat out of hell.

He'd done his bit, he told himself. He was decent enough to sort her out with some gear from the package. That would see her through the next few days. He also left her twenty quid.

She wasn't his responsibility. The other pair had brought her to the squat, they could deal with her. He had places to go and people to see. Hope would have to get on with things just like the rest of them.

CHAPTER SEVENTY-FOUR

Memories

It was a pity the raid had gone wrong. Rupert Breslin was convinced those three young minxes had been right. Freddie had indeed been holed up in the bed and breakfast. It was the fault of that bloody receptionist they'd missed him. What an exclusive that would have been. He always maintained that all good reporters went on their gut instincts and he was doing so now. He had a niggling feeling about one of the girls, the youngest. Hope Roberts, where had he heard that name?

He flicked through recent back editions of his newspaper and there she was. Front page eight months ago. A runaway. Parents distraught, terrified something dreadful had happened to her.

Well, the least he could do would be to pass on the news that she was alive and well.

"Sergeant Cummins, hello, it's Rupert Breslin."

"Hello, sir, what can I do for you?"

"Shame about yesterday, thought we had our man."

"That's policing for you, sir."

"Well a little bit of good came out of it. The name of one of the three girls involved seemed very familiar. I checked through our back copies and found it had been a big story a few months ago. Hope Roberts – missing child – West Lothian. I thought maybe you could let the family know she's alive and well." There was no response from Cummins. "Are you there, sergeant?"

"Sorry, sir, something wrong with the line. Yes, I'll contact them, thanks."

The sergeant had been so taken aback at the news he hadn't known how to respond. What the hell was his super up to now? Whatever it was, Cummins knew he couldn't sit on his findings any longer.

CHAPTER SEVENTY-FIVE

Games Up

Mike Robert's arrived home from work just as the phone rang.

"Hello, Mr Roberts?"

"Yes, whose calling?"

"It's Sergeant Cummins sir, Gayfield Square Station."

"Hello, sergeant. I hope you've got some good news for us," Mike's stomach hit the floor.

"I think so, sir. I'm pleased to report that we had a positive sighting of your daughter yesterday. She was with two other girls."

"Can you tell me where?"

"She was in the Scotsman offices. Unfortunately the person who contacted us didn't know it was her until she'd left."

"It was definitely her?"

"It was."

"Thanks for calling, sergeant, my wife will be so relieved."

"Who was that?" Donna Roberts asked.

"Gayfield police station, a sergeant. He was phoning to tell us someone spotted Hope."

"Thank God! Where was she? Who was she with? Is she alright?" The woman was overcome with relief.

"That's all I know."

"That's incredible, not a word about her for months and then twice in one day we get news."

"Twice?"

"Yes, twice. You won't believe who turned up looking for her today."

"Who?"

"A woman called Rosie Royce, claiming to be her birth

mother. She says Hope was taken from her against her wishes and that she has been searching for her ever since."

"Rosie Royce, the club owner?"

"Yes, the very one. Telling me I hadn't taken care of her child and God help us if anything's happened to her."

"Why the fuck did you let her in?"

"I couldn't stop her, she barged in, her and her partner."

"You should never have spoken to them, she's got no legal right to come here and frighten you."

"I've got nothing to hide and if it helps to find Hope, I don't care what she threatens. They also want to talk to you."

"I can't tell them anything, I know just as little as you. That bloody child's been more trouble than she's worth."

"Mike, don't say that."

"Well it's true and I'll tell Miss bloody Royce the same." Mike Roberts was one scared man.

No way could he have the brat turning up now and spilling her guts.

"I don't care how upset she was. She didn't take care of my child. Hope's out there, possibly on her own." Rosie fumed.

"We'll find her, Rosie, I promise."

"You can't promise me that, we don't even know if she's alive."

"If she's her mother's daughter, she'll survive."

"I want to speak to the father. If he's been out every night looking for her, all well and good, but we need to pay them another visit. I can't get over the feeling that something bad stopped her from going back. If they've harmed her, I'll swing for the bastards."

Kylie and Chelsea were not having the best of days. They had to find a new dealer but first they needed some cash. The easiest and quickest way was to stake out a Post Office. Some old biddy collecting their pension would do fine. They waited a good fifteen minutes before a likely candidate emerged. A frail old soul, struggling with the zip on her shopper, looked easy meat. Kylie approached from behind while Chelsea walked up, offering to help. They had performed this double act successfully countless times in the past, but they had never encountered Mrs May Campbell. Elderly? Yes. Frail? Yes. Frightened? No. Mrs Campbell had worked hard for her money all her days and was still working hard at seventy-nine. She had no intention of letting this pair of scallywags get away with her money and let fly with her umbrella. Raining blow after blow on both girls and shouting for assistance, May Campbell was not giving up without a fight.

The two culprits were far too fragile to take on this mighty atom. They took off, abandoning their prize and ran smack bang into two beat cops who had heard the rumpus. Mrs May Campbell was hailed a heroine.

Edinburgh Evening News

A seventy-nine-year-old Edinburgh woman warded off two would-be attackers this morning. May Campbell was leaving the Post Office in Queen Street when the muggers struck. Mrs Campbell, armed only with her umbrella fought the pair single-handed. "No way were they having my pension," the brave old soul declared. "I'd do the same again to anyone else who tried." The culprits cannot be named for legal reasons…

Rupert Breslin was proofreading the evening edition when he came across the piece on the 'have a go hero'. The old lady certainly had gumption, but it was the two assailants who drew his attention. Mug shots of the two girls leaving the court sparked the editor's interest. There, in black and white, were the two who'd been after the reward for Freddie Williams. Unfortunately, there was no sign of the runaway. But Rupert was sure they were his best lead to finding the missing girl.

"Sergeant Cummins, Rupert Breslin here. How are things? Any news on our man?"

"No sir, I'm sorry to say it looks like he's gone to ground."

"What about the missing girl, Hope Roberts? I know the trail went cold, but I think you'll be interested in what I've got to tell you."

"Go on."

"I take it you heard about the pensioner who got mugged the other day?"

"Yes, game old bird."

"Well, the girls responsible were the two in my office with Hope Roberts."

"Was it just the two of them?"

"I'm afraid so, but they might know where she's hanging out. It's worth a shot."

"It certainly is," Sergeant Cummins replied. "I'll look into this right away. Hopefully we'll get a break."

"Thanks, sergeant, keep me posted."

It took Sergeant Cummins just under an hour to trace the whereabouts of Hope's partners in crime. The two girls were being held on remand in a juvenile facility on the other side of Edinburgh.

Residential care was nothing new to the pair, but being summoned to the governor's office this soon was a record, even for them.

"Sit down, girls," the governor offered. "You're not in trouble but I'm hoping you can help with an ongoing investigation."

"Nothing to do with us, we don't know nothing." Chelsea answered for both of them.

"As I said, you're not in trouble. I just need some information concerning a friend of yours."

"What friend?" Kylie asked suspiciously.

"The girl, Hope Roberts, what do you know about her?"

"Nothing except she was one of Big Mags' party girls," Kylie replied, omitting to inform the governor that they had introduced Hope to Big Mags.

"Have you any idea where she is?"

"Is she in trouble?" Chelsea asked.

"No, not at all, her parents are desperate for information and we know from the editor of the Evening News that she was with you."

"No, sorry, we don't know anything about her."

"Okay, girls. If you remember anything please let me know. Take them back to their rooms," the governor dismissed them.

"Do you think we should have told her?" Kylie was feeling the tiniest bit of remorse.

"I'm not a grass and what about Kevin? We say where she is and the cops are all over the place. He could get done for possession."

"She was alright, the kid. She went back for my gear, remember. And she wasn't well when we left. She looked like she was ready to pop any minute. What if something goes wrong?" Kylie's imagination was running wild. "I think we should say something. She was nice enough and there's no way Kevin will look after her."

"Hi Ronnie, it's Rosie, how are things?"

"Oh, just fine and dandy. I've got a maniac brother still on the loose, but other than that everything's okay."

"I take it there's no sign of him?"

"No, so to what do I owe the pleasure? Want some tickets to the ballet or a rock concert? Mind you, it would only be for one, I'm not running the risk of being dumped in public again."

"Smart-ass," she countered. "Ronnie, I need your help."

"That's flattering," the laird of Edinburgh's underworld replied.

"I'm serious."

"What's the problem?"

"It's a long story, can we meet up?"

"Of course, but I've a feeling Freddie will get in touch soon and I want to be here when he does."

"That's fine, I can come to you. I'll be there within the hour."

He was intrigued as to why Rosie Royce would need his assistance, but he would help if he could.

CHAPTER SEVENTY-SIX

Mistaken Identity

Freddie had remained in the bed and breakfast while CID had conducted their investigation. Even when the police had searched the gaff, he'd been safe. What a result. Mags had been so sure she was a major player in his life she had shown him the space behind the alcove where he could hide out if they got raided. Shame he'd had to take her out, but she'd betrayed him, just like the rest.

He'd been sleeping in the car for the past two nights, in full view of his old gaff in Danube Street. He knew it was time to finish things off. His health was deteriorating, he was exhausted and he knew that all this time without his meds was beginning to affect him. He had missed the bitch on his first attempt, but he wouldn't this time. She had to come out some time and he'd be ready and waiting.

Just as Freddie had predicted, Rosie came running down the front steps, jumped into the smart little sports car and sped off through the city, out to the suburbs. He kept her in sight, but far enough back that she wouldn't suspect she was being followed. Too busy concentrating on his quarry, it was a while before Freddie recognised the neighbourhood she'd led him to.

Well, well, what was she doing out here? Why would she be visiting his brother if they weren't in cahoots? It was hard to believe his brother, his best mate, would sell him down the river for a bird. He'd always had Ronnie's back and took it for granted that Ronnie had his. It was all the fault of that devious cow, she had snared him. Well, it stopped today.

The sports car pulled into the drive and he watched as Rosie entered the house.

Chief Superintendent Ross had ordered that Ronnie Williams' home was to be under twenty-four-hour surveillance. It was a long shot but he was convinced the fugitive would turn up at his brother's house at some point. And he was right, the two constables were on the radio to HQ before Freddie had even parked up.

"Nice place," Rosie complimented Ronnie.

"What were you expecting, something out of Playboy?"

"I'm not sure, but certainly nothing as smart as this. I'm impressed."

"I like my comfort. Now what's your problem?" he asked, as they settled down in his opulent living room.

"When I was young, I got involved with an American GI."

"The ponce you dumped me for?"

"The very same. Well, he was shipped out to Vietnam and I was left pregnant."

"You and a hundred others like you."

"When my father found out he threw me out on my neck."

"Doting family, eh?"

"Because of him my child was taken from me, put into care and adopted. I've spent the last twelve years searching for her. There's more to it, but you get the gist."

"I do, but what do you need me for?"

"A few weeks ago Jack managed to get details of her whereabouts. I was desperate to get a glimpse of her but discovered she'd run away and has been on the run for nearly nine months. There's something not right, Ronnie, and I aim to find out what..." She was interrupted by a familiar voice.

"This is very cosy," the bedraggled figure at the door sneered. "I haven't interrupted anything, have I?"

Ronnie spun round to see his brother standing in the doorway holding a gun.

"Christ, Freddie, I've been worried sick. Where the hell

have you been?"

"Oh, I've been around." Freddie turned to Rosie, "I've been staking your place for the past two days and no bugger paid any attention."

"What's your beef with me?" Rosie snapped. "What the hell have I ever done to you? You don't even know me."

"Don't know you? Of course I know you, Stella. You and that fucker, Kramer, did my brother and me out of millions."

"Stella? I'm not Stella, you stupid fool. Jesus, look at me. Stella Gold would be at least twenty years older and she's been dead for years. I'm Rosie, Rosie Royce."

"Sit down, Freddie and put that bloody thing away." Ronnie approached Freddie warily.

"Don't think you can kid me. I've found out you're in league with them, keeping everything I worked for to yourself. It's because of you I got banged up."

"I had nothing to do with you being sectioned. You threw some poor bugger off a roof. You attacked hospital staff and patients. So you managed to get locked up all by yourself," Ronnie squared up to his brother.

"Don't talk shit, it was your fault. She turned you against me and she's going to pay."

Any further conversation was drowned out by the sound of a police loudspeaker.

"Come out with your hands up." the voice boomed. "The property is surrounded by armed officers."

"Jesus, they must have followed you." Ronnie exclaimed.

"Come out with your hands up," the voice boomed once more.

"Please, Freddie, don't do this. You're my brother and I love you. Let Rosie go, she's nothing to do with Stella. We'll go out together."

"How fucking stupid do you think I am?" Freddie asked, raising the gun.

Ronnie dived at his brother as a single shot rang out.

Freddie Williams got his wish. He did not spend his last days in Carstairs Mental Hospital. Nobody, including his brother, mourned his passing.

Nothing would stop her from finding out what had happened in this house, the house Hope had grown up in. Rosie squeezed Ronnie's hand. She couldn't have faced this on her own.

Having rung the doorbell, Ronnie didn't wait for the door to open, but smashed his way into the Roberts' living room, pinning the whimpering coward up against the wall.

"Did I frighten you?" Ronnie sneered. "Would that make you run away? No? So what would?" he roared, throwing the man across the room.

"You can't come in here," yelled the wife. "I'll call the police."

"You do that. Tell them you've got Ronnie Williams in your living room and see how long they take to arrive. Now you," he turned back to the husband. "Tell me what happened to make the child run away. The truth or I'll beat it out of you."

Mike Roberts watched as the big man slipped on a brass knuckleduster. A dark stain was already spreading across the front of his trousers. Half an hour later he lay snivelling on the floor, having spilled his guts, literally.

"She wasn't mine, she wasn't my kid," he cried. "I didn't hurt her, honest. I was just fooling around. She enjoyed it."

That was the comment that broke Rosie's heart. The mother seemed to have done alright by Hope but she must have known; nothing would convince Rosie otherwise. She had let that evil bastard hurt her child, the child they said Rosie couldn't look after. They hadn't done so well by her, had they?

"Make sure nothing happens to your son, because your husband won't be able to give you another," she spat at the cowering woman and delivered a killer kick to his testicles.

When there was nothing left to smash, the two took their leave. However, they were no nearer to finding Hope.

Edinburgh Evening News

Police are seeking witnesses to an attack on a West Lothian couple. Donna & Michael Roberts were admitted to hospital after a vicious attack at their home. Mr & Mrs Roberts' daughter went missing nine months ago. A spokesman for Lothian and Borders police stated that they do not believe the incidents are connected...

CHAPTER SEVENTY-SEVEN

Open Book

Sergeant Cummins stepped out of the lift on the floor below the Commissioner's office. What the hell was he doing here? Was he really prepared to throw away his career, his pension, everything he'd worked for, to take a chance that his superiors might believe him? He must be mad to even contemplate that Ross, the blue-eyed boy, one of the most senior detectives in the station, the one with the best record, who got results, was a serial killer. He, not Ross, would be taken from the station in a straitjacket. Even if he was believed, they would bury him along with every scrap of evidence or conjecture against Ross. No way could a scandal like this ever surface. The public would never be allowed to know that a high-ranking police officer could be a mass murderer. Cummins realised he would be committing professional suicide.

Ross wasn't hiding the fact he wanted information on the girl. If he intended to harm her, he would not have farmed the job out to him, thought Cummins. So who was this information for? Not the adoptive parents, they already knew everything. Who else could be looking for the child? It had to be the birth mother. It was the only thing that made sense and who was the birth mother? Suddenly he made the connection and made his way to the nearest unattended phone.

"Hello, can I speak to Miss Royce?"

"This is Miss Royce."

"This is Sergeant Cummins, Gayfield Square police station."

"Yes sergeant?"

"I have information concerning your daughter. I'd like to come and speak with you."

"When?" Rosie asked, gripping the handset.

"I can be with you in ten minutes."

"Well, sergeant, what news do you have for me?" Rosie demanded.

"I'm pretty sure I know where your daughter is, but before I go barging in, there are a few unpleasant facts you need to know."

"Look around, sergeant, there's not much that can shock me."

"Hope has been living in a squat for the past while and I'm sorry to tell you, we think she's been forced into child prostitution. She is also pregnant and due to deliver any time soon."

"Are you sure?"

"Unfortunately I have it on good authority."

"I've paid a fortune over the years to investigators who've assured me they know exactly where Hope is and I'm still waiting."

"I believe my boss told you something similar?"

Rosie, taken aback at the sergeant's statement asked. "What makes you say that?"

"I'm his assistant, so nothing much gets past me," Cummins lied quite glibly.

"Is this some kind of ruse to get more money? Trust me, if the two of you think you can put one over on me, think again."

"He has no idea I'm here and quite frankly, if he finds out I'll be in serious trouble. My life could possibly be in danger. That man is evil and will stop at nothing to get what he wants."

"Look, sergeant, I'm not interested in station politics, my only concern is to get Hope back, nothing else matters. This is strictly between you and me, and you'll only get paid if there is no involvement from the welfare, doctors or police, no matter the circumstances."

*

On his way to the squat, Cummins stopped to make the first of two of the most important calls of his career.

"Afternoon, Mr Breslin, Sergeant Cummins here."

"Hello, sergeant, any luck with our runaway?"

"I'm on my way there now, sir, but that's not the reason for my call."

This was it. Cummins knew that there was no going back for either him or Ross. Once he spoke with Rupert Breslin the die would be cast.

"As soon as I finish dealing with the girl I'll need to speak with you immediately. I have evidence concerning a high-ranking officer that will blow the lid off policing in the capital."

"Good God, man, why do you want to speak with me? Why not your superiors? Surely that's the way to go?"

"It's too hot, they would never let this information get into the public domain. Trust me, they'd bury me along with my findings. This is sensational. The man is a serial killer."

As soon as Cummins kicked the door open the smell was overpowering. The rank stench of decaying flesh and bodily fluids, coupled with the sweet, cloying reek of poverty hit him like a truck.

The flat was almost derelict. The only furnishings were an ancient, stained sofa and a coffee table littered with evidence of the tenants' activities. He was having great difficulty retaining the contents of his stomach. God knows how long the poor kid had lain there, decomposing, with the needle still in her arm.

Christ, it was true. He could hear the feint mewling of a child, giving credence to the rumour that Hope had been pregnant. Although the young girl had been dying, she had done her best to look after her baby. The tiny infant lay beside her dead mother, covered by a dirty blanket. It was a miracle that something so tiny and neglected could still be alive, but only just. Its pulse was so faint it seemed unlikely the wee mite would survive much longer. Time really was of the essence. Cummins wrapped the baby in the foul-smelling blanket and dashed for the door. There was nothing more he could do here and the smell was unbearable.

His instructions had been to find the mother and return immediately to Danube Street. Rosie had decreed there was to be no involvement from any authority, no matter what the circumstances. He presumed the same dictum applied to the child, but looking at this tiny scrap of humanity could he afford take the risk? It was almost the same distance from this shithole to either destination: Danube Street or the Western General Hospital. Cummins was no medic, but even he knew this child wouldn't survive without immediate treatment. However, he wouldn't survive if he failed to carry out her instructions. So there was no contest.

Cummins turned out of Caledonia Street just as the first police car screeched to a halt outside the door of the squat, followed by several others. He heaved a sigh of relief, he had made it just in time. God only knew what the baby's future would be, if it even had one. What fate lay in store for the wee soul? The product of a junkie mother, father unknown and just delivered to the richest, most notorious Madame in the city. However, that was not his concern. He had one more urgent call to make.

CHAPTER SEVENTY-EIGHT

Money, Money, Money.

"Hello, it's Cummins."

"Where the blazes are you, sergeant? It's like a three-ring circus here."

"I'm sure it is, especially with another dead body on your hands, and a young one at that."

"Dead body? How do you know?" Ross questioned.

"I know because I reported the incident."

"What? What the devil are you on about? Get back here immediately."

"I don't think so. We need to have a chat away from the station."

"I don't know what you're on, son, but whatever it is, you're in serious danger of ending your career."

"You made sure of that a long time ago."

"Cummins, stop this nonsense and get back here now." Ross was becoming more exasperated by the minute.

"I need to speak with you away from the station," Cummins insisted.

"Away from the station? Were you not listening, man? It's bedlam here!"

"I was listening, but this is far more important. Meet me on the top floor of the St James car park in an hour."

"Sergeant Cummins, I don't know what's got into you and quite frankly I couldn't care less. I'm far too busy to play silly games. Whatever it is, it'll have to wait."

"You'll want to know what I've got to say. It concerns the suicide of Cadet Peterson and your father for starters."

"Who? Christ, man, Peterson died twenty years ago and as for my father! Interesting though a trip down memory lane might be, I don't have the time."

"By the way, that's not just any dead junkie in Caledonia Street. It's Hope Roberts, the kid you were so anxious to find a few months ago. The daughter of your good friend, Rosie Royce."

Ross was taken completely by surprise. "Don't talk rubbish, man! How do you know who she is?"

"I was first on the scene. It was me who broke the door down and it was me who reported the incident. Warrender House, young girl aged about twelve, deceased. Evidence of drug abuse, found with hypodermic syringe in right arm?"

"My, you've been a busy boy," his senior officer scorned.

"Be at St James' car park, top floor, in one hour. No later, or I start making calls."

From his position, he had a bird's-eye view of the surrounding area and had seen nothing. Cummins had waited almost an hour longer than the time he'd designated and it looked like Ross was calling his bluff. He'd blown it, the devious bastard was most likely closeted with the top brass right now, stitching him up, he agonised. Just as he was on the point of leaving, a knock on his car window startled him. He hadn't expected his man to arrive on foot.

"So what's this all about, sergeant?" Ross mocked the nervous man.

"It's about you getting away with murder."

"Goodness, I never realised what an active imagination you possessed."

"There's quite a list." Cummins got out of the car and squared up to his boss.

"Do enlighten me, sergeant, but make it quick. As I said, I've got a dead body to deal with."

"From what I gather, you've been responsible for a number of dead bodies in your time."

Sergeant Cummins could see he had finally got the man's attention. "I know about Peterson, and your father, but Ray Smith was the one who triggered my interest. Everyone in the station knew the man was a serial confessor. He couldn't have been involved in any of the cases he took the rap for because he was a patient in the Royal Edinburgh Psychiatric Hospital at the time. It was my first day on the job as acting sergeant and I did everything, and I mean everything, by the book. I checked and double-checked. I went through the correct procedures meticulously. There was no way I could have overlooked his belt. Not only because it was so distinctive but because I remember checking it in with his possessions. You set me up. You knew because I was a rookie that no-one would believe me. You were responsible for his death."

"Dear God, man, you've brought me here to go over a case that was closed ears ago?"

"That man never committed suicide and he had nothing to do with the rent boy murders. His confession let you conveniently close down those cases. Having tampered with evidence and several witness statements, you got away with it once again. You committed those murders on one of your damned Christian crusades and no-one higher up ever questioned it."

"Good detective-work, sergeant, but do you really think the powers that be will listen to the ravings of a bitter, disappointed officer, who screwed up years ago but hasn't got over it? Do you imagine these cases will be reopened? I don't think so."

"You're right, they won't want the scandal. The public could never be allowed to find out that the great and good Chief Superintendent Ross, defender of the people, was in fact a serial killer."

"Prove it."

"I don't need to prove it. The facts speak for themselves."

"So, Cummins, where do we go from here?"

"I want you to resign."

"Or you'll do what?"

"I go public with my findings, and there's no going back when that happens."

"You think you can sell your story? There's no way an editor will publish these allegations without making sure they can't be sued."

"They wouldn't, not unless the informant is a reputable officer of the law, of several years standing. Someone will listen and whatever the outcome, you'd be finished."

"And if I refuse to tender my resignation?"

"You don't have a choice."

Taking a thick brown envelope from his inside jacket pocket, Cummins taunted Ross. "This, by the way, should have been yours," he waved a bunch of notes in his face.

"What do you mean, mine?"

"This is payment for rescuing Rosie Royce's grandchild."

"Grandchild?" Ross was puzzled.

"Yes, the baby I found at the scene and delivered to Danube Street. If you'd acted on the case immediately, the mother might still be alive and Rosie Royce knows that."

Ross made a grab for the money, but he wasn't quick enough.

"I've never taken a bribe in my life and I'm not starting now. Here, catch," Cummins grinned as he backed towards the wall overlooking Leith Street and tossed the bundle of notes high into the air.

The notes fluttered down towards incredulous pedestrians below.

"Idiot! Why did you do that?" Ross screamed, furiously grabbing hold of Cummins. "You stupid fool." And with one mighty push, he sent the sergeant hurtling to his death.

CHAPTER SEVENTY-NINE

Cover Up

Back in the commisioner's office, Ross asked, "How else can you explain thousands of pounds falling from the sky? He must have been on the take. No straight cop would ever have that kind of money." Facing his inquisitors with supreme confidence, Ross had no fear of these men. The Lord had proved once more that he was invincible.

"He was your righthand man, Ross. How did you miss what he was up to?" the Commissioner asked him directly.

"Forgive me, sir, but have you seen this month's stats? Our clear up rate is the highest on record. So you might forgive me for being occupied elsewhere. I've been chasing criminals. I didn't expect to find them sitting across the desk from me."

"What are we going to do?" the chief addressed Ross and the other officers present. "What are the chances we'll ever find out what he was up to?"

"Little or none," replied the chief superintendent. "I hardly think anyone's going to own up to pushing him over the parapet and claim their money back."

"The Evening News has already run a piece on the incident," commented the commissioner. "Money from Heaven was the headline. Cummins has already been portrayed as a dedicated cop, killed in the line of duty."

"Why don't we give him Full Honours? Get the funeral out of the way and take it from there," Ross suggested.

"I'll agree," spat the commisioner. "On two conditions. This stays firmly behind closed doors and you, Ross, undertake the investigation."

Chief Superintendent Hamish Ross breathed a sigh of relief. Case closed.

Edinburgh Evening News
Obituary

The Full Honours funeral of Sergeant David Cummins, aged forty-two, took place on July 20th. Sergeant Cummins, a long serving officer with Lothian and Borders Police Force, was killed in the line of duty. David Cummins joined the force at the age of seventeen as a cadet and was regarded by his superiors and colleagues as a dedicated, competent, professional officer. He is survived by his wife Hilary and their two children, Ewan, aged ten and Ailsa, aged eight.

The service took place in St Ninian's Church, Edinburgh, and was conducted by the Rev. Sidney Adams. The eulogy was given by Chief Superintendent Hamish Ross. Also in attendance was Sir Hugh McPherson, Police Commissioner.

Rupert Breslin had attended the sergeant's funeral as much out of curiosity as respect. He had been intrigued by the phone call from the officer on the day of his death. What information did he believe he had that would blow things in the force wide open? Who could Cummins have been going to name? All his enquiries concerning the incident had been met with brick wall after brick wall, the force had closed ranks. Even his usual contacts were conspicuous by their silence. This only made Breslin more determined and he figured the wake would be a great opportunity to ferret out any secrets. For there were secrets, of that he was convinced.

"Shame about Cummins, he was a good man," Breslin addressed Ross.

"He was. It's a risk every officer faces out in the street and unfortunately, this time it was his name on the bullet."

"He phoned me the morning he was killed, you know."

"He did? Was it anything I should know about?"

Watching Ross's reaction closely, Breslin dropped his bombshell. "He wanted to come and see me concerning information which, in his words, 'could blow the lid off policing in the city'."

"What did he mean by that?" Ross had paled somewhat.

"I've no idea. I thought maybe you could help?"

"Me? Sorry, no idea. He was a good man but could be a bit fanciful."

"That's an odd description for a police officer."

"He took offense at the slightest thing, always imagining his colleagues had it in for him."

"Strange. Judging by the turnout, I would have guessed he was extremely popular."

"Don't be fooled, most of these are professional mourners. Anything for a day off and a free drink."

"Just shows how wrong you can be," said the editor. "It's a shame about the runaway. I can't understand how you lot got there first. I spoke to Cummins just after ten that morning and he was on his way then. But the girl wasn't found until much later, and it was later still before he met up with his killer. Very strange. I might give you a call later to check out some of the facts."

"Sure, any time. Now, if you'll excuse me," Ross shook Breslin's hand and the two parted company.

Well, well, Breslin said to himself, I smell a story here. And like most good journalists, he always followed his nose. Hamish Ross needed more than God on his side if he was going to out run this man.

Rosie and Ronnie almost missed Sergeant Cummins' funeral, so concerned were they with the health of the baby. All else had gone by the board.

Rosie would never forget what the man had done for her. Were it not for him, she would most likely have lost not only

Hope but her granddaughter also. His actions had saved the baby but possibly cost him his life.

For days the child's life had hung in the balance. She was badly dehydrated and suffering acute withdrawal symptoms from the drugs fed to her mother. It seemed impossible that she would survive and if she did, poor little mite, what permanent damage had she suffered?

To avoid questioning from the authorities, Rosie had taken the decision that together with her old friend, Dr Anderson, she, Kitty and Dora would nurse the child themselves at home in Danube Street. She couldn't risk involving any outside agency.

"What difference would it make?" Rosie had asked. "Would she receive better care if she were in hospital?"

"She'll be fed and cared for here just as well," Kitty replied, as mistrustful of the authorities as Rosie. "And someone will be watching over her every minute of the day."

"That's all well and good, ladies, but my concern is that if an emergency arises you won't be able to cope," the doctor warned. "Things happen so quickly in these cases, especially with babies. However, barring emergencies, there's not a lot more that can be done. She'll either survive or not, and that, my dear, is in God's hands. I'll call back this evening after surgery to check on her."

So here they were, a little over a week since they'd had the conversation with the doctor, the baby much improved and in the care of Kitty and Dora.

The sergeant's funeral had been an emotional affair. The man was honoured by his colleagues for his bravery, and the sight of his distraught wife and his two young children tore at even the hardest heart.

As they left the graveside Rosie spotted Rupert Breslin. "Mr Breslin?" Rosie called him aside. "Let me introduce myself, my name is..."

"As if I wouldn't recognise the most well-kent face in Edinburgh, Miss Royce," interrupted the editor.

"Mr Breslin, I have something for you, a package. Sergeant Cummins left it with me on the morning he died. He made me promise I would give it to you personally, should anything happen to him."

"What is it?" Rupert asked quizzically.

"I don't know, I didn't open it. I figured, if he'd wanted me to know, he would have shown me."

"A woman without curiosity, there's something new!"

CHAPTER EIGHTY

Goodbyes

"I've been to see Donna Roberts," Ronnie announced as Rosie attended to the baby.

It had been a few weeks since Cummins had delivered the precious bundle to Danube Street and then lost his life.

"Would you mind telling me why you went to visit that scum?" Rosie was taken aback at Ronnie's news.

"Hope's body has been released for burial. I went to make sure neither of them thought they had any right to make funeral arrangements. I can assure you, you'll get no interference from that corner."

"I couldn't give a toss about them, but they were her legal guardians," she answered, with tears in her eyes. "We have no say in the matter."

"We have now," Ronnie answered with a sad smile.

Despite her best efforts, her search was finally at an end and Rosie had to come to terms with the fact that she would never see her daughter alive again. Ten days at the beginning of her short life, that was all the time Rosie had spent with Hope. She'd missed so much – never seen her first steps or heard her first words. But there was one thing Rosie could still do. She could ensure her daughter left this cruel, ugly world with dignity and as a beloved child.

Thanks to Ronnie, Rosie had somehow got through the worst period of her life. Rosie's feeling of utter desolation was gently nursed by this big, rugged, hard man. He'd barely left her side and now, thanks to him, it was time to put Hope to rest.

Despite the dozens of mourners, Rosie stood alone in the small village churchyard. At last she'd brought her daughter home. She now lay beside her grandparents, they'd watch over her. Hope was at peace and among friends. Here in this tiny churchyard, she would never be alone. Curiously, Rosie no longer felt anger towards her father: James Royce, a stubborn, self-righteous man, who, rightly or wrongly, had stood by his principles. As for Francitti, he hadn't even bothered to reply to Rosie's telegram informing him of Hope's sad demise.

As for the miracle baby, Rosie vowed, as she stood listening to the swell of voices in the small country church, no-one would ever take this child from her. She would fight tooth and nail to keep her safe and free. Whatever the curse of Danube Street was, she would break it. Both of the women associated with that house had paid a huge personal price. Each had lost a child to bricks and mortar, but never again.

Epilogue

"Are you sure you won't miss the place?" Ronnie asked.

"I'm sure I will, but I have enough with this little one on my hands. I'm quite happy to hand Danube Street over to this young man." She looked at Oliver swinging the squealing toddler high in the air.

"I still think he's a bit young," Ronnie remarked.

"For God's sake, he's twenty-three. I was fifteen when I took over and you were probably only twelve when you began fighting your way up through the thugs in Edinburgh. Don't be such a wally. Some tough guy you are," Rosie laughed at her husband.

Ronnie Williams had never, in his forty-odd years, felt for any woman what he felt for his wife. The hardest man in town was captivated.

"Nanny, Nanny, tell Oliver, swing!" squealed Miracle, her two-year-old granddaughter.

The greatest miracle of all, though, was yet to happen. Despite being told, all those years ago, that she would never have another child, here she was, ready to deliver.

The End